THE HONEYMOONER

A Paradise Bay Romantic Comedy, Book 1

MELANIE SUMMERS

Indigo Group

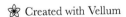 Created with Vellum

PRAISE & AWARDS

- Two-time bronze medal winner at the Reader's Favorite Awards, Chick-lit category for *The Royal Treatment* and *Whisked Away*.
- Silver medalist at the Reader's Favorite Awards, Women's Fiction category for *The After Wife*.

"A fun, often humorous, escapist tale that will have readers blushing, laughing and rooting for its characters."

~ Kirkus Reviews

"A gorgeously funny, romantic and seductive modern fairy tale…"

~ MammieBabbie Book Club

"…perfect for someone that needs a break from this world and wants to delve into a modern-day fairy tale that will keep them laughing and rooting for the main characters throughout the story.

~ ChickLit Café

"I was totally gripped to this story. For the first time ever the Kindle came into the bath with me. This book is unputdownable. I absolutely loved it."

~ Philomena (Two Friends, Read Along with Us)

"Very rarely does a book make me literally hold my breath or has me feeling that actual ache in my heart for a character, but I did both."

~ Three Chicks Review for Net galley

Books by Melanie Summers

ROMANTIC COMEDIES
The Crown Jewels Series

The Royal Treatment

The Royal Wedding

The Royal Delivery

Paradise Bay Series

The Honeymooner

Whisked Away

The Suite Life

Resting Beach Face (Coming Soon)

Crazy Royal Love Series

Royally Crushed

Royally Wild

Royally Tied (Coming Soon)

WOMEN'S FICTION

The After Wife

The Deep End (Coming Soon)

Dedication

For you.

Because if you've opened this book, it means you need a laugh, which likely means that:

a) you've been either working far too hard,
b) you're not having a good go of things right now,
c) you're stuck on a long train ride with no Wi-Fi and someone has left this book on a seat, so you figured what the hell? Might as well read until I'm sleepy enough to have a nap,
Or d) all of the above.

If you fit into any of those categories, it means you are my muse. And since every writer needs a muse, I thank you for being mine.

Melanie

Author's Note

Dear Reader,

Three years ago, I wrote a short story called *Honeymoon with a Billionaire* for a rather steamy, multi-author boxed set about...you guessed it, really friggin' rich guys. I always loved bits of the story, especially the hilarious way the uptight heroine met the hero. Because the original had to be under seventy pages, I had to leave a lot of the good stuff out and always meant to go back and make it a full book.

This spring, I decided to do just that, only as a comedy. The funny thing is, when I went back and reread the story, I realized I didn't really like the hero (he was a little on the controlling side – eww!), so I needed to scrap him and start over. There are still a few bits and pieces of the original (so if you've read it, you'll recognize a couple of scenes), but what it has turned into is so much more.

Our hero, Harrison Banks, is not a billionaire at all, but a guy trying to keep his family's resort open in the face of tough times. Our heroine, Libby Dewitt, is no longer an uptight librarian but is now an ultra-uptight business analyst.

The story begins in an unusual way — with some maps, a wedding invitation, a resort brochure, and then you'll get a chance to read some of our hero's mail before we jump into the action. I hope you'll give these a look/read because they really are fun and they are *definitely* important to help set the stage.

So, without further blabbing, I'll let you get to it because there's a whole lot of ridiculously romantic moments and laughs to be had in this book. (Plus, there are maps! How crazy fun is that?)

Thank you for being part of my writing life! Without you, I'd have to go back to being an adult again (and that was *not* my thing).

Happy escaping!
Melanie

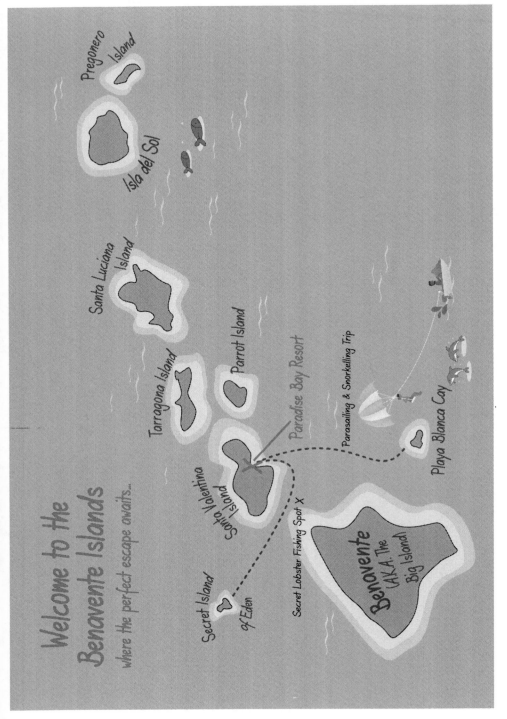

Welcome to the
Benavente Islands
where the perfect escape awaits...

Pregonero Island

Isla del Sol

Santa Luciana Island

Tarragona Island

Parrot Island

Paradise Bay Resort

Parasailing & Snorkelling Trip

Playa Blanca Cay

Santa Valentina Island

Secret Lobster Fishing Spot X

Secret Island of Eden

Benavente (A.K.A. The Big Island)

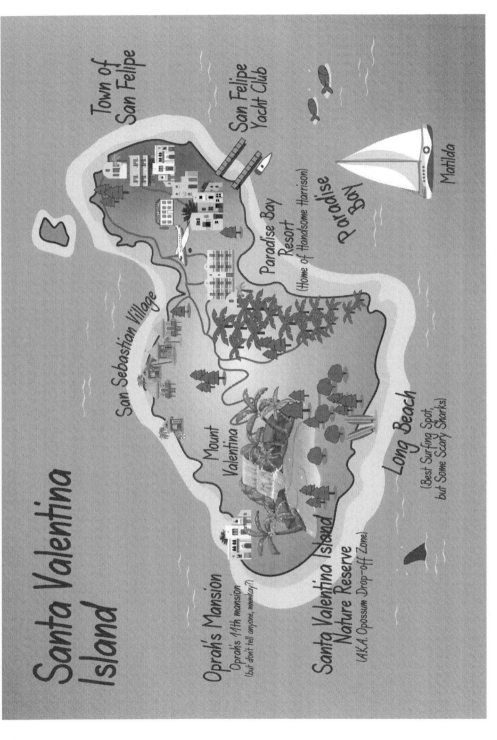

Paradise Bay
All-Inclusive Resort

Enjoy our pristine, white–sand beaches caressed by crystal-clear waters. Relax in our newly renovated luxurious rooms decorated in soft, muted tones for an elegant design. Enjoy a whole array of fun activities and excursions or just lay by one of our five pools and soak up the sun.

Paradise Bay Resort sits on a 12-acre property nestled along the calm, protected south shore of Santa Valentina so the water is always warm and inviting. Surrounded on three sides by jungle, the resort enjoys the ultimate in privacy, including our 500 ft of exclusive beach—yours to explore uninterrupted.

Our 274 rooms have spectacular views of the ocean, our lush tropical gardens, or the stunning emerald green jungle so you'll wake each morning with a smile. Immerse yourself in the relaxed pace of the Benavente Islands as you stroll through the beautiful gardens on your way to one of our seven à la carte restaurants. Treat yourself to a soothing, rejuvenating spa treatment customized to your personal needs. Spend a day snorkeling along the bay or take one of our signature catamaran trips to our private island, Playa Blanca Cay.

Dive into the culture of the Benavente Islands with salsa classes, a pottery workshop with one of our local artisans, or try the Caribbean-inspired dishes at one of our exclusive restaurants. Live the magic of the Caribbean nights with a delicious cocktail in one of our bars or enjoy an evening show, then let yourself go to the local rhythm and dance the night away at our open-air night club.

Your Authentic Caribbean Escape is Waiting for you at Paradise Bay...

Book today and get 15% off or enjoy three free spa services.

Happily Ever After

Mr. and Mrs. Edward Dewitt
along with
Lord and Lady Phillip Tomy
request the honour of your
presence
at the marriage of

Liberty Dawn
to
Richard Phillip

Saturday, the twenty-second of
September
two thousand and eighteen
at one o'clock in the afternoon
St. Stephen's Church
5 Church Street
Valcourt, Avonia

Reception to follow
at three o'clock in the afternoon
125 Fairmont Court

The favour of a reply is requested by the twentieth of August.

The One Time It's Okay to Read Other People's Mail

August 2nd, 2018

From: Libby Dewitt
Business Analyst
Mergers and Acquisitions
GlobalLux Inc.
510 Windsor Road
Valcourt, Avonia
A8V 4G7
Office Number: 23-334-4545 ext. 201

To: Harrison Banks
Owner/Proprietor of Paradise Bay All-Inclusive Resort
1 Seaview Lane
Paradise Bay, Benavente Island

B3Y T3H

Dear Mr. Banks,

I am writing to follow up on the telephone messages I've left with your front desk staff over the past few weeks. I am a member of the mergers and acquisitions team at GlobalLux Inc., one of the world's premier luxury hotel groups. GlobalLux is currently expanding our brand to include several high-end all-inclusive resorts. In an effort to expedite this expansion, we are seeking to purchase properties that are well-run and well-reviewed, such as Paradise Bay. Your property is of particular interest to our team, as it is the largest ocean-front property on the Benavente Islands.

GlobalLux is willing to consider either a straight purchase of Paradise Bay, or —what may be a more attractive option to you, depending on your goals—a partnership, where GlobalLux would underwrite your current operation, leaving you in place as the owner/operator but with the capital and purchasing power of an international organization required to stay competitive. As your property is currently carrying a substantial loan, it's in your best interest (and that of your staff) to consider this opportunity.

The days of privately owned, one-off resorts such as yours are coming to an end. Conglomerates like GlobalLux have the advantage of bulk purchasing from all vendors, which greatly reduces operating costs. We also enjoy robust promotional budgets, thereby attracting a much larger clientele for whom we are able to provide a comparable guest experience at a much lower cost.

The next steps would be to arrange a call so that I can better explain our intentions and see if we can come to an agreement in principle, which would allow us to move forward with what will certainly be a lucrative opportunity for you.

Please email me at ldewitt@globallux.com or phone me at your earliest convenience to discuss this further.

Best Regards,
   Libby Dewitt

———

Email from Libby Dewitt to Harrison Banks
  Date: August 10th, 2018

Dear Mr. Banks,

I sent you a letter a week ago on behalf of my employer, GlobalLux. As I have yet to hear from you, I wanted to make sure that you received my correspondence.

I have gone ahead and booked a stay at your resort for my honeymoon (September 23rd - October 14th) so we can meet in person to discuss the offer. If you have any questions, please email or phone.

Warmest Regards,
  Libby Dewitt

———

Email from Libby Dewitt to Harrison Banks
  Date: September 5th, 2018

Dear Mr. Banks,

Hopefully my previous email didn't end up in your spam folder. As I will be travelling to Santa Valentina Island in a little over two weeks' time, I am hoping we can connect straight away to set up a time to meet between September 23rd and October 14th.

Regards,

Libby

———

September 17th, 2018

From: Mary M. McNally
Benavente Credit Union
62 Main Street
San Felipe, Santa Valentina Island
B3A P2N
Phone: 248-355-2535

To: Harrison Banks
Owner/Proprietor of Paradise Bay All-Inclusive Resort
1 Seaview Lane
Paradise Bay, Santa Valentina Island
B3Y T3H

RE: Loan Number 5493-07842-012

Dear Mr. Banks,

According to our records, payment on the above referenced loan account is now 60 days in arrears. Recent attempts to reach you by mail and phone have been unsuccessful.

This is the final notice for the entire past due amount, including accrued late charges. The payment is to be received in our office within 7 days. If you are unable to meet these payment terms, you are required to call me to discuss other collection options.

Failure to make payment or respond to this letter within the aforementioned timeframe will force Benavente Credit Union to begin bankruptcy proceedings.

Regards,
  Mary McNally

Get Me to the Church on Time...

...

Libby Dewitt
Valcourt, Avonia, United Kingdom

THE SECRET to the perfect life is to always have a plan. That and really great hair. The hair will cost you (in my case, a lot, due to the many products needed to tame my bright red curls), but the plan is free of charge and will *definitely* change your life. In my opinion, the old adage 'if you fail to plan, you plan to fail' is 100% true. And if there's anything I refuse to be, it's a failure.

That sounded harsh, didn't it? Failure is such a bleak word. It sounds so...final and loser-ish. But in my case, I've had to outrun the possibility of turning into a total failure my entire life because it's the very word that describes the woman who gave birth to me.

For the bulk of my formative years, I was keenly aware of the fact that everyone who knew me was watching and waiting to see how far the apple would land from the tree. My mother, Penny Dewitt, could best be described as someone who never finishes what she starts, whether it's a pottery class, washing up the pasta pot after supper, or raising a child.

Penny was twenty-one when I was born, and she never seemed to feel shy about telling people she had no idea who my father was. Instead, she seemed to find it hilarious that I was the end result of a three-day folk festival in Edinburgh.

As a little girl, I didn't know any better than to think the world of her. I was certain she was the most beautiful, most fun person on the planet. One of my earliest memories is of her grinning down at me with a gleam in her eye, saying, "I'm bored. Let's do something incredible."

We didn't have what you would call a conventional lifestyle, but rather drifted from place to place, overstaying our welcome at her friends' houses before we'd leave and land on someone else's doorstep. In my first five years of life, I lived in over twelve different countries as far as Bali, Australia, and even Brazil for a while. Somehow, Penny managed to scrape up money for flights. (I now suspect it was given to her by people who were happy to see us go. There's only so long even the most patient person will put up with a hippie and her daughter who rarely bathe, sleep on your couch, and eat your food but don't bother to help with the cooking or the dishes).

Sometimes I wonder how long we would have gone on living like nomads if my great-grandmother hadn't passed away just before my sixth birthday. My grandparents paid for us to fly home, all the way from Rio to Valcourt, so their daughter could make an appearance, and I imagine so they could see their granddaughter for the second time. I remember not liking them at all. For some reason, they wouldn't call me by my real name, Breeze, and instead called me Libby (which is the short form of my middle name, Liberty). I couldn't understand why they were so angry with my wonderfully perfect mom. We were there for weeks, and the tension was so thick, I ached to get out of their house.

Clearly so did Penny, because that's exactly what she did. Except this time, she left without me. They must've convinced her that I would be better off with them. Either that, or she grew tired of me just like she grew tired of everything else. I suppose I should have felt lucky that she kept me around as long as she did. Instead, I was utterly paralyzed with grief to discover that my mum, my best friend, who I'd slept with every night since I was born, could just abandon me. I remember her smiling back at me as she got in a yellow cab. She gave me a little wave and said, "Have fun, Mini-Me!"

Have fun? How the hell was I supposed to have fun without her?

Those first few weeks, I was *so sure* my mum would show up and whisk me away from this strange life of regular bedtimes, eating peas, and going to school. I'd sit at the front room window, watching for a cab to pull up. (Not constantly — that would be ridiculous. Just each night after supper, when I missed her the most.) But when a month went by, and she hadn't come back for me, I decided to give her a secret deadline. Ten more days, then I'd give up on her.

Ten days came and went. Then it was fifty, which turned into one hundred, which turned into a full year. Then, when I was seven, I promised myself to give up forever after five hundred days. The disappointment on day five hundred was so overwhelming, I was sure I'd never recover from the pain of it. I sobbed every bit as hard that night as I had the first night she left.

But the next morning, I resolved to grow up to be her complete opposite. For every irresponsible thing she'd ever done, I'd do double the responsible things. I'd never rely on others for money or a home but would make my own way. I'd accomplish big things in my life and settle down with the right man, not go from fling to fling.

When I was ten, my grandparents asked if I wanted to legally change my name to Liberty Dawn from Breeze Liberty. I said yes, without hesitation.

Penny finally did show up, long after she was no longer wanted. I see her every few years when she pops back into Avonia, usually looking for an infusion of cash from anyone willing and able to provide it. Each time, she's with a new boyfriend, and as she gets older, they seem to be getting younger. I'm pretty sure by the time she's seventy, she'll be dating a sperm sample. I can just imagine it now: *"This is sample 15428Q, from a Norwegian pediatric surgeon. He's a champion swimmer, and he just loves to ram his head against things..."*

When she shows up, it serves as a reminder of how far I've come and how lucky I am that she let me go before I turned into someone like her. Instead, I'm a highly successful, highly organized person. Each year on New Year's Day, I sketch out my next twelve months, including a breakdown of goals and projected timelines. Sunday mornings are spent developing my schedule for the week so each day when I wake, I know exactly what the day holds. Some may find that boring, but to me, there's nothing dull about life going off without a hitch.

Take today, for example. I'm about to have the perfect wedding, and I could not be more thrilled. I have just gotten into the back of the limo with my cousin and best friend, Alice, who is my one and only bridesmaid. In an effort to avoid drama, I've elected to go with one attendant for myself and one for my husband-to-be, Richard (his useless brother, Tom). This eliminated potential conflicts surrounding dress styles, shower planning, and any cattiness caused by jostling for top position as the bride's BFF. On the groom's side, it avoids the 'let's get wasted' pack mentality that crops up when a group of horny young men get together in a place where everyone's looking their best.

My mum won't be at the wedding, by the way. I didn't invite her because having her appear would create more drama than nine bridesmaids in a limo. Her presence would be an utter disaster, especially around Richard's very posh, ultra-conservative, and slightly disapproving family.

Anyway, Alice and I are finally on our way from the salon to the church where I will become Mrs. Libby Tomy. Oh, did that sound really old-fashioned? I hope not. I'm just a little excited. Taking Richard's last name will make things so much easier when we have children. I briefly considered hyphenating our names but quickly realized it wasn't a good idea. If you say Dewitt-Tomy out loud, you'll hear the problem. Tomy is pronounced "to me," which means my name would be Libby Do It To Me. Since I'd rather not have people snickering every time I introduce myself, I'm just going with Tomy.

Richard and I are perfect for each other — we're both professionals with busy work lives. I'm a business analyst in mergers and acquisitions at the world's largest luxury hotel chain, GlobalLux Inc., and Richard is a corporate tax lawyer at Avonia's largest law firm,

McDougall, Grammit, and Fitzpatrick. We've been together since university. After surviving the chaos of campus life, we then spent the next five years climbing our respective corporate ladders. We're both go-getters who thrive on routine and a healthy lifestyle, although on Saturday mornings, we do have a bit of a lie-in while we catch up on the news via the weekend edition of the *Financial Times*. Don't tell anyone, but Richard loves to read the comics (which I find adorable).

While I'm sharing secrets, I have my own guilty pleasure, too. It's a shame to have to keep this one, because it smacks of kowtowing to elitist literary snobs, but I absolutely *love* all things romance. Romantic movies, television shows, and books are what I secretly devour when no one is looking. I know it's a total juxtaposition to be a very organized, logical, professional woman and to also turn to mush over a predictable-yet-heartwarming tale, but I just can't seem to help myself. I've loved a good hero ever since Mr. Darcy admitted to Elizabeth Bennet how ardently he admired and loved her. Sigh…

But that's fiction. This is the real world where romance is just a phase at the beginning of a relationship. Richard and I had our time like that, but after several years together, we've now settled into a comfortable routine we both find quite pleasing. Hmm, when I really think about it, I'm not sure we ever had a wildly passionate phase in which we had spectacular rows, only to make up all night. Not that that matters.

What really counts is building a relationship on the solid foundation of shared values and goals. We both want the same things — a four-bedroom house in Hanover (considered by most to be the best neighbourhood in Valcourt), a small but roomy yacht, and two to three children (depending on how it goes once we have the second child). In addition to yachting, each of us will develop two hobbies to be enjoyed individually and one together during our retirement, which will happen at age fifty-five based on our annual income, investment savings, and projected inflation rates.

So, I guess you could say we've already charted our course and the waters are calm. Yes, it'll be smooth sailing for Mr. and Mrs. Richard and Libby Tomy.

Then why do I have that nagging feeling like something is wrong?

I stare out the window as the limo smoothly makes its way through traffic. We're five minutes ahead of schedule, every detail has been taken care of, and it's a beautiful, sunny autumn day. There's really no reason for me to feel worried at all.

I glance at Alice, who is on the phone with her husband, Jack. Alice's father and my mother are siblings. After being dumped at my grandparents', Alice and I were together so much, we might as well have been sisters, except to look at us, you'd never guess we're even related. She's a tall, willowy woman whose skin turns a lovely bronze in the summer, whereas I'm curvy, short, and can get a sunburn if I even *think* of going out without a hat. Alice also got lucky when it comes to hair. I inherited our gran's wildly curly red hair, while Alice has beautiful, straight raven-black hair she got from her mother.

I've always envied Alice, and not just because of her supermodel looks — she's also utterly confident and commands respect wherever she goes. She has a loving, normal family, including two parents who dote on her and a brother who drives her nuts but would do anything for her. Alice was a surgical nurse before she had children. Now she's what I call a Pinterest Mum. You know the type — she could whip up a festive table centerpiece fit for the royal family out of some tooth-picks, a handful of cotton balls, and some homemade beet dye, all the while breastfeeding a newborn and making a Béarnaise sauce. Please don't hold that against her, though, because she's also ridiculously nice.

But I don't have to wish I were Alice anymore because now I'm one step closer to having a perfect life like hers.

Six years ago, she married Jack McTavish (her boss at the time), who, although a very competent oral surgeon, seems to have no clue how to look after their three-year-old son, Colby, and their six-month-old baby, Maisie. Every time Alice leaves the house, she can expect a barrage of texts and phone calls from her bewildered husband. But you can hardly blame him — she leaves a large void of perfection when she glides out the door.

Alice nods while she listens, then says, "The frilly part goes in the back." Pause. "I don't know why, maybe it's for extra padding." Pause. "I promise her nappy will fit under the tights."

Knowing she'll be a while, I sneak my mobile out of my white pearl-encrusted clutch and decide to answer a few work emails. Alice glances over at me, rolls her eyes, then notices what I'm doing and swats my arm, giving me a rather irritated look. She made me promise I wouldn't do any work today, and yes, I agreed to it, but I mean, seriously, she's busy on the phone and it just *makes sense* to turn this downtime into something productive.

She hangs up the phone and sighs. "Honestly, I love Jack dearly, but when it comes to the children, he's absolutely useless. And you…" she says, fixing a steely gaze in my direction, "…promised not to work today. It's bad enough you've turned your honeymoon into a business trip. Don't do the same with your wedding day."

She's referring to the fact that Richard and I will be spending three weeks at a resort my company is looking at taking over. But really, *why not* have your boss pay for your honeymoon? It's rather brilliant, if you ask me, because it allows us to have a holiday *and* get one month closer to the down payment on our dream house. And honestly, how much lounging around beside a pool can a person do? "If it doesn't bother Richard, I don't see why you're so offended by it. Besides, I'm not going to work *that* much while we're there."

"Well, be glad you're marrying Richard and not me. I would've killed Jack if he suggested turning our honeymoon into a business trip." Alice glances at the window and gasps. "Is that a cloud? On the great Libby Dewitt's wedding day?"

I crouch down a little so I can look out her window. "Oh, I told the weatherman I would allow the white, fluffy ones." I give her a wry smile, then notice the limo is no longer moving. Glancing around, I realize that the traffic has come to a standstill. "What the hell? Why aren't we moving?"

"Ooh, slide the glass thingy down and ask Xavier what's going on." Alice looks suddenly gleeful, which I'm sure has *nothing* to do with the fact that our driver is stupidly handsome. She chatted him up while she was waiting for me to pay the salon bill. It turns out he used to be in the military and has recently moved to Avonia in hopes of getting a high-end security job. For now, he's driving limos.

I find the privacy screen button and press it. "Excuse me, Xavier, do you know why the traffic is backed up?"

"They opened that Krispy Kreme Doughnuts this week." He shakes his head. "I have a bad feeling it's going to negatively affect both traffic and people's waistlines over the next several months."

Damn. Why didn't I think of that? I vaguely remember hearing about it and realizing it would be right before the wedding, but I didn't anticipate the extra traffic. My gut tightens at the thought of being late. "How much of a delay do you think this will be?"

"According to the GPS, we're looking at about a fourteen-minute wait."

"Crap. That's going to put us behind for the pre-wedding photo shoot. I should text the photographer."

"Better yet, let's open the champagne!" Alice says.

"Oh, you won't want to do that," Xavier says over his shoulder. "If you start drinking now, you're going to end up with a headache in about two and a half hours, so it's probably best to wait until dinner."

I'm just about to murmur to Alice that Xavier is a bit of a know-it-all, but the look of adoration she's wearing says don't bother. She asks him if he has an interest in health and fitness while I text Roland, the photographer, to let him know we're delayed. As soon as I send it, my mind wanders back to feeling like I've forgotten something.

"Alice," I say suddenly. "Did you have a sense of foreboding the morning you married Jack?"

"Foreboding? That sounds ominous," Alice says jokingly.

My expression must tell her I'm not kidding because her face falls.

She looks at Xavier and says, "Sorry, Xavier, I think the bride needs a little girl talk."

"Say no more," Xavier replies. A second later the screen slides up.

Alice turns her body to face me. "I guess I felt nervous, like I needed to pee even though I knew I didn't really have to. Do you know what I mean?"

"I think so."

"But I definitely didn't have a sense of doom or something. When did this start?"

"Just this morning."

"Oh, hon, don't worry about that." Alice puts her hand on my forearm and gives it a slight squeeze. "It's just nerves. Totally normal."

I let out a long, slow breath, trying to steady my racing heartbeat. "And you and Jack, you're happy, right? Like, you know for sure he's it for you for the rest of your life?"

"Well, nobody can be sure every minute of every day. I mean, there are times when I wouldn't mind pushing him off his parents' yacht and watching him disappear into the sea," she says casually. "But that's usually when I'm short on sleep and haven't had my Kombucha. The rest of the time, I'm totally sure."

I chew on my bottom lip for a second while I digest what she's just said, then I nod confidently. "I'm sure it's just nerves."

"Definitely. You and Richard are perfect for each other. Nothing's going to break you two up."

"Yes, you're right." I do a quick mental body scan, noting that I still feel rather tense.

"You know what? I'm pretty sure it's this traffic. We're off schedule, which is bound to make you feel tense. You need to find a way to relax." With that, Alice grabs the bottle of champagne out of the cooler, opens the window, and holds it outside while she pops the cork off. It dings off the side of the van stopped next to us. Pulling it quickly back inside, Alice giggles as she does up the window.

"You're such a badass," I say as she hands me a flute. She pours me a drink that comes dangerously close to the brim, then does the same for herself. "A little Zen compliments of Dom Pérignon." Clinking her glass to mine, Alice says, "To happily ever after."

"Amen, sister." I tip the glass up, feeling the cool bubbles bounce across my tongue. Taking three big gulps, I smile, deciding to fully give in to Dom.

There really is nothing to worry about. Everything will be just fine as long as we can get to the bloody church on time…

3

The Laid-Back Guy's Guide to Handling Everything...

Harrison Banks

Long Beach, Santa Valentina Island, The Benavente Islands, Caribbean

"Don't fight the current next time, okay buddy?" I smile and ruffle the young boy's drenched hair. "If you get caught in a riptide again, try to relax and let it carry you — eventually you'll get to the shore. Otherwise you'll tire yourself out and end up being a shark's lunch."

That's actually not bad advice when it comes to life. Sometimes, you get hit hard and fast by a crushing wave, and your first instinct is to fight it, even when you know nothing can be done. You'll save yourself a whole lot of trouble by just going with the flow.

After the boy's mum gives me a teary-eyed thank-you, I dislodge my surfboard from the sand and start the long trek back to my favourite entry point on Long Beach. I was paddling out for my first run when I heard screams coming from the shore and took a hard right to play lifeguard.

Glancing at my watch, I see that detour didn't leave me with much time to catch a few waves before I need to head back to the resort to sign off on the pay-stubs. Not that I'm complaining — I know I've got it good. Inheriting a resort in the Caribbean isn't exactly a burden. It just doesn't leave me with all that much free time, and today I really need some time on my own to think. I'm pretty sure I'm about to get slammed by one of life's shit waves, and I need to figure out how to avoid it if at all possible.

I've been shit-slammed more than once. The first time was the night my parents went out for a dinner date and never came back. Up to that point, I was a pretty typical eleven-year-old, dawdling on the walk to school each morning, yanking at the irritating tie that went with my St. Mary's uniform, and occasionally teasing my little sister, Emma, and my baby brother, Will (but only when I was bored). I played football on the weekends with my mum cheering from the sidelines and my dad coaching. I complained about bedtime and begged to watch movies I was too young to see but 'everyone else in my class had already seen.'

The oldest child of a school teacher and Valcourt's best podiatrist (according to the Podiatry Association of Avonia), I was doted on and fussed over. Everything was safe and cozy and perfect. Right up until it was yanked from me in the time it takes to run a red light.

At the funeral, we were introduced to Uncle Oscar — my dad's older brother and a man I'd only heard stories about. I knew he lived a bit of a 'wild life on some tropical island in the middle of nowhere' and was not my parents' 'sort of person' based on the hushed tone they used whenever his name came up. It was for that very reason I was absolutely riveted by any mention of him. What did they mean by wild? Did he swing from jungle vines, eat with his hands, and beat his chest? I expected him to show up at the funeral with long, shaggy hair, an out-of-control beard, and be dressed in only a loin cloth, but he looked disappointingly normal. Black suit, white shirt, clean shaven. He looked a lot like my dad, actually, only with grey hair around his temples and a dark tan.

I spent most of the service glancing at the pew behind mine, trying to catch a glimpse of him. He was one of the pallbearers for my dad's casket, so he left the church ahead of me and stood on the opposite side of the grave site as I held Will and Emma's mitten-clad hands and tried to wrap my head around the fact that my parents were in those boxes being lowered into the ground. After that, I completely forgot about my wild Uncle Oscar until the luncheon at my great-aunt's house.

I was eating the corner piece of a chocolate cake (for maximum icing-to-cake ratio) when I felt a tap on the shoulder. I looked up, and for the briefest moment, I thought I was looking at my dad. An incredible wave of relief washed over me until reality bashed me over the head again.

Uncle Oscar shook my hand, told me he was sorry about my folks, then dropped the next bombshell on me. "Well, I guess you're coming to live with me now. Do you like boats?"

Two weeks later, Emma, Will, and I were living halfway around the world on Santa Valentina Island. Instead of St. Mary's, I went to San Felipe Secondary School (where at least the uniform had short pants instead of thick, wool, long ones). I still played football, but this time, my mum wasn't there to feed me orange slices and my dad wasn't there to get on me about my inability to hook the ball. Instead, when I went to the field, I had to bring Emma and Will along for the walk from our new house — an ocean-front cottage badly in need of a feminine touch (or at the very least, some curtains). At the park, there were no uniforms, no coaches, and no regulation nets. We'd meet whichever kids happened to show up that day, split into teams, and play until the sun started to go down. It didn't take me long to realize that football, like most things, was a good deal more fun without all those adults around, not that I wouldn't have traded every second of fun for another day with my parents.

But I'm not telling you this so you'll feel sorry for me. Being pitied is almost as bad as being stuck behind a desk. I only told you about that so you'll understand the importance of going with the flow in life and the wisdom of not getting too attached to anything with an expiration date — pets and humans included. A laid-back, island-life approach makes everything so much sweeter — especially relationships, because like the tides, relationships come and go, and you'll be much better off if you know that going in.

Anyway, over time, the resort became our home, and the staff our surrogate family, as cliché as that may sound. Oscar did a pretty decent job raising us — he taught us the three s's of Caribbean life: surfing, sailing, and scuba diving. Other than that, he let me take over as *de facto* parent for Emma, who is four years younger than me, and Will, who is five years my junior. I made them finish their homework and eat all their peas, and for some reason, they actually listened to me. I have to say, they've both turned out to be pretty decent human beings (but don't tell them I said that).

Emma is finishing up her chef's training at the Culinary Institute of America in New York, which is costing me an absolute fortune, so she better be one hell of a magical chef when she comes back to work at the resort. Will is off exploring the world and eking out a living as a professional adventurer (yeah, that's a thing. I didn't believe it either when Will told me that's what he wanted to do). Turns out he's pretty good at it, because he recently landed a six-part TV docu-series on the Avonian Broadcast Network called *The Wild World*, which has him filming him all over the globe in the harshest of climates. Right now, he's in Antarctica for three weeks, which kind of makes me laugh a little, because as brave as he is, he's a total wimp when it comes to the cold.

And here I am on a sunny beach in the Caribbean. *Aaah.*

I'm finally back to my favourite entry spot along the shore when I hear my name being called. I turn and see my best friend, Nelson Clarke. He's the youngest bank manager in history at a Benavente Credit Union. He runs the San Felipe branch in the nearest town (San Felipe, obviously) to Paradise Bay, and the fact that he's out here on a Wednesday afternoon, dressed in a suit, means he's not here to catch a few waves with me (also obviously).

"Hey, Reef," he says as I near the road where he's parked his Jeep. I got saddled with the nickname Reef when I was a teenager, thanks to my affinity for getting reef rash when I was first learning to surf. As much as I don't love the origin of my nickname, it's a hell of a lot better than if they'd started calling me Rash.

"What's up?" I ask, even though I already know what's up and who sent him. I'm about to default on the loan the bank approved for a major renovation on the resort, and Rosy Browne (the general manager/woman at Paradise Bay who took over as a sort-of mum for us) is the one who called Nelson. She opened the latest overdue notice from the bank yesterday and completely lost it. I told her I have a plan, but clearly, she doesn't trust that I can handle it without her help. Unfortunately, she still thinks of me as the eleven-year-old kid she met two decades ago.

Nelson loosens his tie, looking worried. "Just wanted to check in with you about your loan status."

"I take it you heard from Wikileaks?"

He grins at the use of my nickname for Rosy, then his face falls. "This is serious, man."

"It *was* serious, but I've got it all figured out," I say with a confident smile. "I'll be caught up by Monday."

Nelson gives me a skeptical look. "You're really going to come up with sixty-seven thousand dollars by Monday?"

"What? You don't think I can do it?" I ask with a mock hurt expression.

"It's not that, man. I know you can pull a rabbit out of your hat when you need to, but this is one hell of a huge rabbit," he says. "And the last thing I want to see is for you to lose the resort."

"For a lesser man, not an easy feat, but for me…" I shrug nonchalantly. I'm being deliberately vague because my plan involves something that makes my stomach churn, and if anyone tries to talk me out of it, I'll definitely cave. And since caving isn't an option, I'm keeping my plan to myself until I've seen it through. Time to change the subject. "You didn't happen to bring your board and some trunks, did you?"

Nelson shakes his head at me and lets out an exasperated sigh. "Jesus, you're in real trouble here, and you're acting like we're talking about a hundred-dollar loan for a pair of sneakers."

Ever since I've known Nelson, he's been completely uptight, but he comes by it honestly — his mum is a forensic accountant and his dad is one of only three air traffic controllers on the island. Nelson was their only child so they put *a lot* of pressure on him. I've always been his laid-back friend — the Ferris Bueller to his Cameron (a much better gig if you can get it). "You know, buddy, all this stress isn't good for you. If you don't learn to relax, you're going to have a heart attack before you're forty."

He ignores my deliberate attempt at trying to side-step this conversation. "Rosy said you don't have the money. And if you don't have it today, how's it supposed to be there in five days, especially when you're out here surfing instead of working on it?"

"Have you even looked at those waves, Nelson? How could I *not* be out here?" I point to the shore and grin at him, then I let my smile fade when I see the look on his face. "Don't worry about it. I swear on your life, I'll be completely caught up by Monday."

"By Monday?"

"At the very latest."

That is if I can force myself to follow through with the very last thing I want to do.

4

Something Old, Something New, Something Bloody, Something Blue

Libby

"HERE'S THE BRIDE! Come give us a kiss." Granddad, who is dressed in a very smart dark grey morning suit, takes his pipe out of his mouth and smiles at me.

He, along with my entire family and the photographer, are waiting in the garden behind the old stone church that has played host to all the biggest weddings in Valcourt for the past four hundred years. The late morning sun shines down, softly warming me, and I start to relax a little, letting go of my sense of doom. It is a perfect autumn day, and even though we're only six minutes behind schedule, we can easily make it up if we skip two of the poses I was going to do under the rose trestle.

I cross the grass to Grandad, my eyes filling with tears as they've been doing since I woke at four a.m. in a panic that my alarm wasn't going to go off. I'm working on only three hours of sleep, but I hope I have enough makeup caked on that no one will notice.

He gives me a careful hug, clearly having had enough experience with brides to know you don't want to mess with their hair or makeup.

"Libby, you look tired," Gran says, looking down her nose at me from under her pink fascinator. "But your dress really is lovely, and I'm glad you decided to wear your hair up properly instead of hanging down like a bohemian."

Alice, who has just finished hugging Grandad, rolls her eyes in my direction at our Gran's comment. Then she glances toward the side door of the church and gasps.

When I turn, I see my mother and a young man who must be her new beau hurrying over to us. My mum's long hair is down (like a bohemian) and she's in an off-the-shoulder mini-dress that belongs on a much younger woman. "Mini-Me!" she shouts, sweeping across the lawn as though she belongs here.

Her boyfriend trails behind her, wearing white slacks and a pink button-down shirt he should probably finish buttoning up. He's got one of those horrid man buns perched on top of his head like a nest belonging to a bird whose eggs should be taken away by child services — and he has a very ironic beard. His earlobes bear holes big enough to poke your index finger through and he's beaming at me like a proud father.

My entire body tenses as they come near, and I touch the space under my nose to make sure it's not bleeding. I'm a stress-bleeder, and the sight of my mum at this moment has put all my nerves on high alert that something is very wrong.

"Nosebleed, Libby?" Alice asks, digging around in her purse for some tissues.

"Not yet, but I think I feel one walking toward me right now," I say as Penny floats in my direction. Alice hands me a wad of just-in-case tissues, and suddenly I'm overwhelmed by the smell of pot as my mum gives me a long, deep hug.

"My baby! How'd you grow up so fast?" she asks, obviously unaware of the fact that it happened during the twenty-two years she's been M.I.A. Pulling back, she says, "You're gorgeous. Jorge, isn't she gorgeous?"

"*Sí*, Penny, you two could be sisters." Jorge gives me a kiss on both cheeks while my mind races, trying to come up with a way to get them out of here before my nose starts gushing.

"I can't believe you're here," I say, trying to look happily shocked instead of shockingly horrified.

"I wouldn't miss this for the world." My mum tilts her head to the side and sighs happily. "I just had to be here for my little girl's big day."

"Why start now?" Gran scoffs.

My mum stares Gran down for an uncomfortably long moment. "How about we set aside our differences and really just *be here* for our little Breeze Liberty today, okay?"

Gran stiffens at the sound of my full name and snorts. "Be here for her? Unlike the rest of her life, you mean?"

Grandad puts a hand on Gran's arm. "Now, Clara, let's not get into this. It's not going to get us anywhere, and it'll only spoil Libby's wedding."

My mum, having already grown tired of her parents and only child, turns to Alice, who's been joined by Jack and their kids. Penny squeals with delight and starts gushing over the great-niece and nephew she's never met while Roland, our wedding photographer, hurries over with his equipment at the ready, snapping candids of this 'happy' reunion.

My alarm on my mobile phone goes off, and I open my silk clutch to silence it. I'm using my phone to set alarms for the entire day so as not to forget anything. "That's my reminder to give you your gratuity, Roland."

Roland breaks into a wide smile and holds out his hand. "Thank you, Libby. Most people leave it until the end of the day, and by that point they're either too knackered or too drunk to remember."

Roland pockets the envelope, then quickly moves on to lining up Alice, Jack, and their children for a photo. I wanted to give them a photo of just their family as a thank you to Alice for being my maid of honour.

Standing next to Roland, I make goofy faces so Maisie and Colby will grin in the general direction of the camera. Maisie smiles, displaying her entire set of three teeth, while Colby sticks his hand up in front of his face to block the camera. I'm not sure, but I'm guessing that this behaviour is a direct result of being the first grandchild and the subject of at least ten thousand photos in his three-year lifespan.

"Colby, put your hand down," Jack says, a tight smile plastered to his face.

Colby makes no move to obey, which leads both Alice and Jack to alternate between pleading and barking orders at their son through clenched teeth.

"Oh, he's got a mind of his own, that one. Just like his Great Aunt Penny!" my mum says with a big laugh.

Alice, looking distraught at the idea that her son will end up an irresponsible freeloader, has a pinched voice when she says, "Put your hand down *now*, love."

Grandad chimes in with, "Colby, listen to your mum or you're not getting any of the jelly beans I brought."

Jorge joins in, waving his hands in front of Colby, as if he's been part of the family for thirty years instead of thirty seconds. "Come on, buddy. Shows us what a good boy you are. Do it for your Auntie Breeze. For her special day."

As I watch the mayhem unfold, I suddenly become aware of the fact that Richard's entire staff at the law firm, as well as all of his relatives (some of whom have royal titles), are going to meet Penny and Jorge, who will most likely make out like a couple of horny teenagers on the dance floor in a few hours. I check my nose, amazed to find it's not bleeding. However, my gut is churning and my palms are starting to sweat. It's going to be utterly humiliating to have to introduce her and Jorge, who I'm pretty sure is younger than me, based on the very classy neck tattoo of what I assume is his birthday: 01-10-96. Let's see, if he was born in 1996, that makes him six years younger than me. So…twenty-two. Nothing gross about that, right?

Suddenly, I realize I must have had some type of premonition about my mum showing up. *That's* why I've been so anxious! It's nothing to do with Richard and me at all. I smile and let myself relax for a second.

My phone distracts me, reading aloud my latest text message (I've left it on driving mode so I can keep up with any new developments during the day without slowing things down unnecessarily).

"Incoming text message from Aunt Bea: *Uncle Geoffrey and I are running a few minutes late getting to town. We should be there by 12:05. Should we come around the back of the church so as not to interrupt the ceremony?*"

I quickly text her back while the struggle for a perfect family photo continues. *That's fine, Auntie. We might be a few minutes behind ourselves. Just come in the front doors, which actually lead to the back of the church.*

"Oh, forget it then. He's just not going to cooperate," Jack says, shaking his head in disgust.

Roland lets the camera hang from his neck and gestures for the rest of us to line up for the next set of photos. "What if we try for a group shot? Maybe Granny here can hold one of the little guy's hands and Dad holds the other one."

We all get in—including Jorge, of course, because, why wouldn't he? Roland arranges us, then leans down at Colby and smiles. "Listen, mate, I have a little secret for you. There is a tiny elf living inside my camera, but he only comes out when kids smile nicely. Do you want to meet him?"

Colby gives him a long, skeptical look. "Does he bite kids' cheeks off?"

All the grown-ups wear matching horrified expressions, except my super-high mum, who seems to be wondering the same thing as she squints at the lens.

Roland shakes his head and says, "No, of course not. He's quite a funny little bloke. He might stick his tongue out at you if you're really quiet."

Quickly picking up his camera and glancing at the rest of us, Roland says, "Be ready. I think this might be the one."

We all stand perfectly still and wait while he snaps away.

"Oh, little buddy, you need to smile bigger than that if he's going to come out. I think I hear him."

I stand, my cheeks already sore from smiling, as I silently pray that Colby will just cooperate for the twentieth of a second it will take to get a good shot. Of course, chances of that happening at the exact moment Gran will actually have her eyes open are pretty much nil, so Roland is likely going to earn every dollar of that gratuity trying to mix-and-match faces to create the perfect portrait.

My phone beeps loudly, then reads out: "Incoming text message from Richard: *If your phone's on driving mode, you better shut it off now, okay? Otherwise this will be awfully embarrassing. Is it off? Okay. I'm really sorry, Libby. I'm not going to make it today. I can't marry you. I know I should have told you sooner, but I've been trying to convince myself to go ahead with it.*"

I slowly process what I've just heard while my stupid face remains frozen in place in a wide grin. Around me, chaos ensues.

"What the hell did he just say?"

"He said he's not coming. What kind of a man texts that he's not coming to his own wedding?"

"There's no elf in that camera! You lied to me!"

"Oh Libby, I'm so sorry."

"Ouch! That little brat just stomped on my foot!"

"He's not a brat. He just doesn't like being lied to."

I blink and realize Jorge is standing in front of me with his hands on both my upper arms. "Are you okay, Breeze? As basically your step-father, I would be proud to beat him to a pulp if that will make you feel better."

My mum's faces crumples in concern. "Are you all right, love?"

I hear her talking, but her voice sounds very far away, like it's coming through a long tube.

"Mini-Me." She shakes me a little. "Breeze. Answer me. Oh, Sweet Jesus, she's catatonic! Jorge, get her a joint!"

"What...what just happened?" I suddenly feel my entire body going limp, and I just want to sit down. I'm not sure what I'm doing at the moment because I'm completely disconnected from my physical self, but I'm vaguely aware of the fact that Granddad and Jorge have now taken me by either arm and are guiding me to a park bench. The feeling of the cold stone through the thin chiffon and silk layers of my dress brings me back to reality. "Did he just say he's not coming?" I whisper.

When no one answers me, I blink at my mum. "Richard's not coming."

"I know, Mini-Me. I heard the message. We all did. Oh, God, honey, your nose still bleeds when you get upset?"

I place my hand under my nose and feel the familiar wet sensa-

26

tion. Alice grabs the tissue from my other hand and shoves it under my nose, but it's too late. It's already dripped down the front of my dress.

"It's okay, we can get that out with some club soda," Alice says.

Roland, who is suddenly standing next to me, pats me awkwardly on the shoulder. "Probably for the best. Better to find out now than when you're three children into the whole thing like I did."

I nod as though I understand any of what is currently happening.

He sucks in a deep breath, then says, "Listen, Libby, I know this isn't the right moment, but the contract *does* state there are no refunds within seven days prior to the wedding."

"Not now, you ninny!" Gran shouts at him, sending him scurrying off in the direction of his camera bag.

"Do you need a moment of privacy?" Mum says, handing me my phone. "Perhaps you should call him."

I nod slowly. "Yes, I suppose I should."

Alice, who has Maisie in her arms, barks, "Do not phone him, whatever you do! If he's going to call this whole thing off via text, he doesn't *deserve* to hear from you ever again."

"I always knew he had no balls!" Granddad hollers suddenly, shocking us all by both shouting and using the word 'balls.'

"Language, Edward!" Gran says in a shrill tone. Turning to me, she says, "I think we should take a moment to pray for wisdom during this difficult time."

I stare at her for a second before saying, "Umm...maybe in a bit. I...I think I will phone him. Not God, *Richard*. I'm sure there's been some sort of mistake, and we can work this out in time for the ceremony." I smile weakly at the members of my family, then realize smiling is completely pointless due to the wad of tissue hiding the lower half of my face. "Why don't you all head inside and give me a minute to sort this out."

Shoulders drop in relief around me, and I watch as my family disappears through the side door to join over three hundred people who are waiting for me to walk down the aisle so Richard and I can become Mr. and Mrs. Happily Ever After.

My pulse thumps in my ears and my hands shake as I dial his

number. Holding the phone slightly away from my ear, it occurs to me that I'm filled with dread at what he might say. I gaze down at my diamond ring as I wait for him to answer.

When he finally picks up, his voice is quiet. "You had your phone on driving mode, didn't you?"

"Yes," I whisper.

Why am I not screaming at him? I should be screaming into the phone right now. If ever there was a time for anyone to really let someone have it, it would be me at this moment, speaking to this man. And yet, I feel so utterly confused, there's no room for anger.

"Are you having car trouble? Because I can send the limo for you. Or maybe you're trapped under the refrigerator and need to be rescued. Is that it? Because I can't think of a reasonable explanation for you not to show up."

"I'm so sorry, Libby. I should have told you weeks ago, but I thought it was just cold feet."

I gulp down some air. So this is really happening. My hands go all tingly. I hear him talking, but none of it makes much sense. Cutting him off mid-apology, I say, "Is there someone else?"

"No. Of course not."

This revelation hurts almost worse than if he *had* fallen for another woman because this means it's simply about me not being good enough, not because he's found someone better.

He lets out a long sigh. "It's just that…over the past few weeks, I've realized I'm not in love with you anymore. To be really honest, I'm not sure I ever was. I think I was more in love with the *idea* of us than us as a real couple."

"The idea of us? That's a little cliché, don't you think? I thought you hated clichés, Richard." I find my voice, and it turns out it's an extremely bitter one.

"You're right. I'm sorry. This is why I thought it best to text you. I knew I was going to say the wrong thing."

"This is not about you saying the wrong thing. It's that you didn't say *anything*!" I stand and pace the lawn while I rant, completely forgetting my nose. "I can't believe you didn't tell me this *before* I spent months of my life planning this and thousands of dollars paying for it.

Before I got up at 4 o'clock this morning to get my hair and makeup done so I could look beautiful for you! *Before* all of our relatives travelled from all over the bloody kingdom to be here! *Before* we had a church full of people waiting for us! Who's going to tell them the wedding's off, Richard? WHO? Clearly not you, since you've decided not to come today!"

"Perhaps Alice could do it?" he says weakly. "Or, if you'd like, you could leave now and I can show up just to tell everyone the bad news. It's my responsibility after all."

"Forget it. I'll take care of it, just like I took care of every other detail of the wedding you no longer want to have." A rush of anger flows through me as I stare at the door to the church.

"Are you sure? I don't want you to face that type of humiliation alone."

I let out a forced laugh. "If you didn't want to humiliate me, you should've done this much, much, much, much, much, *much* sooner!"

"I know. I'm so sorry for putting you through this, Libby."

Instantly, I go from furious to horribly hurt. Tears prick my eyes, but I will them back inside with everything in me. "I just have to know, what is it about me that makes you not...?" My voice cracks.

There's a long pause, then Richard says, "I don't think it's such a good idea to get into this right now. Not when things are still so raw."

"Is it because I don't want to do the butt stuff? Because if it is, that is really unfair. You know I had that hemorrhoid and it will flare up if we—"

I stop talking, suddenly aware that my Aunt Bea and Uncle Geoffrey are standing to my left with their mouths open. My face flames with embarrassment while my aunt whispers, "We'll just go inside and wait."

"Yes, thanks," I say, nodding.

"You're going to want to wash up, love," Uncle Geoffrey says. "You've got blood all over you."

Shit.

As they walk inside, I catch a few bars of the string quartet playing *The Best is Yet to Come.*

"Oh, Libs, did someone just hear all that?" Richard asks.

"My Aunt Bea and Uncle Geoffrey." I swallow, trying to hold it together long enough to ask my fiancé why he's decided not to come today. "I need to know why you don't love me anymore, Richard. It's the least you can do."

He sighs as though this is such a chore for him. "I promise it's not the butt thing. That might matter to some guys, but for me it's no big deal." I can picture him, rubbing his temple and giving me an apologetic look. "It's just...don't you sometimes think our life together is... well, sort of...boring?"

Boring? "I love our life together. If I didn't, I wouldn't be standing here in this stupid dress." The tears are coming out now, and I pat at them, hoping to salvage my makeup.

"How can you love it? We've been having the same day every day for the past six years. We go to the same restaurants, watch the same TV shows, eat the same meals. Saturday mornings we read the paper in bed, then go to the farmer's market, then cook an early dinner... It's like we're in our seventies instead of our twenties. I'm not ready to be old yet, Libby. I'm young. I want to be spontaneous, you know? Have some adventures in life, like...I don't know...skydiving or bungee-jumping or booking a trip at the last minute without checking TripAdvisor for any mention of bed bugs."

"Bed bugs are *a lot* more serious than most people realize. It costs thousands to—"

"Libby," he says, raising his voice so I'll stop. "We're just not a good match anymore. I want different things. I know it hurts right now, but someday you'll meet the right guy for you, someone who will be thrilled to live by Libby's routine. I'm just not that guy. I'm going to hang up now, okay? This is just too hard for me."

"Too hard for *you?* Oh, I didn't realize I was making you feel awkward. In that case, maybe I should be apologizing to you."

"No, it's okay. You don't have to."

"I was being sarcastic."

"Right. Of course. Sorry," he says.

"Well, I should go tell everyone you aren't coming today."

"I guess so."

I hang up without saying goodbye, which quite frankly feels like a total power move because I've never done it before, and certainly not to Richard, not even the time he forgot my birthday and went for drinks with his workmates.

I stop at the steps to the back of the church and grasp the handle, my mind racing with what's just happened. I'm gripped by fear because the entire future that was so perfectly laid out before me has now gone up in smoke.

No, this isn't how my fairy-tale is going to end. No way. Not if I have anything to say about it. It's not only up to Richard. It's also *my* decision, and I say we *are* getting married. Not today, mind you, but I am *definitely* going to be Mrs. Libby Tomy someday very soon and we *are* going to live happily ever after.

Shaking my head, I say, "No. This is not happening. I will not let this happen."

I can fix this. I just need a plan. I'll deal with the people in the church, then go back to our flat and make Richard see the light. We're perfect for each other, and deep down he knows it. He's just having some quarter-life crisis. No, that's wrong. A third-life crisis? What's it called when a guy is twenty-eight? *Oh, Libby, it doesn't matter, you idiot. Just get in there and fix this.*

Taking a deep breath, I walk into the church and straight up the aisle as quickly as possible. By the time I reach the front of the church, the string quartet has stopped playing *Pachelbel's Canon*, and the only sound is coming from my heels on the stone floor.

Lifting the hem of my dress, I hurry up the steps to the altar and nudge the Minister out of the way of the microphone. When I look up, I see the horrified faces of everyone I know, and it's clear to me they've already heard rumblings of what's going on. Christ, I hope Aunt Bea hasn't told anyone about the butt stuff.

Clearing my throat, I say, "Well you've probably heard the groom is not going to make it today. Please don't be alarmed, however. He's very sorry, but he's had a…work emergency…so we'll have to postpone to a later date. In the meantime, we'd love it if you'd stay and partake in the luncheon and enjoy the photo booth and the dance. It's all paid for and it's too late to get a refund, so…"

I lift my chin and smile serenely. "Oh, and don't forget to take your presents and your cards with you when you leave. Thank you for coming to support us. Have a wonderful weekend."

An audience of stunned faces stares up at me. I find my mum in the front pew, and the very sight of her strengthens my resolve. I won't end up like her, flitting from man to man. I already have a man. I just have to convince him to change his mind.

5

I Never Liked That Song Anyway...

Harrison

EASY COME, easy go. That's what I've been telling myself all day about selling Waltzing Matilda, my yacht — well, Stew Milner's yacht now, I guess. He's been wanting to get his hands on her longer than Harvey Weinstein has been wanting to get his hands on young actresses. Matilda, who used to reside in Australia, is a 90-foot classic schooner that they never should've stopped making. Reliable, sleek, with clean lines and polished wood, it's the type of yacht people take photos of when it's sitting at the harbour.

I don't even want to think about how pissed Will and Emma are going to be when they find out. We spent half our childhood on Matilda. Uncle Oscar would be rolling over in his grave if he knew she was about to be boarded by Stogie Stew. On the other hand, I'm pretty sure Oscar would much rather I sell the boat than sell out Paradise Bay's staff to some evil corporation. There was an article in *The Post* a while back about some study that showed how one in five corporate CEOs fit the clinical definition of a psychopath. So if me letting go of Matilda is the one thing stopping my friends from ending up in the clutches of Tony Soprano, it's kind of a no-brainer.

I stand on pier 15 at the San Filipe Yacht Club, waiting for Stew to bring me the cheque that's going to solve my current financial crisis. I let out a long, slow breath, wishing there were some other way than sacrificing Matilda. I stare at her and strongly consider getting back on and sailing away where nobody needs anything from me ever again.

I shouldn't have let my mind go there. That thought is far too tempting.

My mobile buzzes. It's an email from that irritating Libby Dewitt person from Avonia. I sigh and open it.

Dear Mr. Harrison,

I'm on my way to my wedding and had a slight traffic delay so I thought I'd touch base. I'll be arriving tomorrow in the early part of the afternoon and plan to spend the first two days of my trip honeymooning. As I haven't heard from you, I've booked a time for us to meet Tuesday morning through a woman in your office. I look forward to seeing you then to discuss how we can be of help to each other.

All the best,

Libby Dewitt

What kind of nut is sending work emails a few minutes before her wedding? A future CEO who'll gain easy entry into the 1-in-5 Psychopath Club, that's who. When she shows up at my office next week, I'm going to give her a hard no on the takeover, ask her to pass along my apologies to her new husband, then show her the door.

That settles it. No sailing off into the sunset with Matilda. I really do have to hand her over to Stew.

My mobile phone buzzes again, and I swipe to ignore another call from Rosy. She's been trying to find me all day about the loan, but I'm purposely avoiding her until the sale is final.

I force my feet to remain planted on the wide slab of concrete. I smell Stew before I hear him walking up behind me — the stench of the Kristoff Maduro cigars that precedes him everywhere he goes. I turn, trying not to think about the fact that Matilda will soon smell like a manure-filled barnyard.

Stew holds a cheque in one hand and a handkerchief in the other. He's walking much faster than he usually does, probably to get the deal finalized before I can think better of it. A transplant from northern Scotland, Stew loves the heat more than the heat loves him. He runs the handkerchief over the top of his grey hair and pats at his forehead and ruddy cheeks while he beams at Matilda. Shoving the handkerchief in the back pocket of his Bermuda shorts, he takes the cigar out of his mouth and flicks some ash into the water next to the pier. Arse. "Glad you finally came around, Banks. A beauty like that needs a real man to handle her."

Gross, isn't he?

Stew hands me the cheque, and I take a moment to look it over, making sure it's dated and signed — I wouldn't put it past him to 'accidentally forget' so he'll have a few more days with his money. I fold it in half and tuck it into the pocket of my shorts. "Enjoy, Stew. May you captain her in good health."

"I will, I will. Do you need a ride back to the resort?" Pinching the cigar back in between his lips, Stew chews on it, allowing a little bit of yellow juice to dribble down his chin.

"Thanks, but I haven't had a chance to get a run in yet today, so I figure I'll make my way back along the beach."

"You're going to run all that way? In this heat?" He shakes his head at me, looking bewildered.

"I have to find some way to stay in shape for the ladies. It's either run or give up fried food and beer."

"Well, I suppose at your age, you might as well enjoy the women. I'll just settle for enjoying my money and my new boat." He laughs, which turns into a wheezy cough that makes me wonder how many months he'll have to defile Matilda. "Oh, and when you're ready to sell that little hotel of yours, let me know. I'll be waiting."

"I'll keep that in mind." No, I won't. No fucking way is he getting his hands on the resort.

I slide my mobile phone in my arm band, put my earbuds in and set off, walking to the end of the dock. With one quick look back at Matilda, I pick up my pace, telling myself I've done the right thing.

Go with the flow, even when it hurts.

———

Forty-five minutes later, the resort is coming into view along the beach. The late day sun is making the ocean look awfully inviting. I consider diving in for a long swim when I hear my name being called.

Squinting, I'm just able to make out Rosy standing on the steps that lead to the beach from the resort. She's dressed in her usual uniform — a bright button-up shirt (today's is lime green) and a long colourful skirt with one pair of reading glasses on a chain around her neck and her other pair sitting on top of her head. Her black hair is pulled back into what she calls her 'facelift bun.'

"Shit," I mutter under my breath. I should have answered that last call from her. I knew I was pushing it.

If Rosy's outside, it means I'm in trouble. She hates the sun, the sand, and pretty much anything else that has to do with nature, which is exactly what makes her the perfect manager. There's nothing she likes more than being in the air-conditioned office bossing people around.

Even though Rosy's just about to turn sixty, she's not going to retire anytime soon. It would be the end of her forty-year marriage to Darnell, who retired from the fire department a couple of years ago, because as calm as Darnell is, there's no way he'll put up with being ordered around twenty-four seven. He says doing what Rosy wants is more of a weekends and evenings pastime.

When I get closer, I can hear her foot angrily tapping away. "Where the hell have you been? I've been trying to phone you all day."

Giving her an easy smile, I come to a stop. "Good afternoon, Rosy. Nice to see you outside getting some sun for a change." Oh, I should not have said that. She's literally snorting mad now.

"Don't screw with me, Harrison Theodore Banks. I swear to God, I will leave you."

"All right, sorry. I'll straighten up." I'm not and I won't, by the way. It's far too fun for both of us, even though she'd never admit it. "I don't know where I'd find another tiny dictator to keep me in line."

She purses her lips together and rolls her eyes before letting out a long sigh of irritation. This means I've got room for maybe one more joke before she really loses it. As much as I like to wind her up, Rosy can be a little scary when you push her too far. But I'm an adrenaline junkie, so... "You look stressed, Rosy. Maybe you and Darnell should take a vacation. I know a nice resort with some empty rooms. I know the owner, so I could probably get you a deal."

"I've had it! You're off doing God-knows-what all day while I'm trying to figure out how the damn loan is going to get paid." She spins on her heel and starts up the steps, miming washing her hands of me. "I'm going home. I don't need this shit."

"Wait!" I jog up the steps, following her as she heads down the path toward the main building. "Don't you even want to know where I've been?"

She turns and glares at me. "This better be good."

"It is." I glance to my right and see that we've stopped right next to the beach bar. "I just need to grab a water first. I'm really parched from my run." I go around to the back of the bar, ducking under the counter and making a beeline for the refrigerator. Calling over my shoulder, I ask, "You want anything? A mojito or a margarita, maybe?"

"No, I do not want a damn drink! I want to get back inside."

I grab a bottle of water, then jog over to her. "Yeah, I suppose you don't have time for a drink anyway. Not when you need to take this over to the bank." I pull the cheque out of my pocket and hand it to her.

She wrinkles up her nose as she unfolds the now slightly damp piece of paper. Her eyes light up when she sees all the zeros. "How did you—"

"The how is top secret. All you need to know is that it'll buy us a few more months while we turn things around."

Out of the corner of my eye, I spot a middle-aged couple on the path. One of them is feeding a wild opossum an ice cream cone while the other one videos. Bloody brilliant.

At the same time, Rosy and I say, "Sir, please don't feed the opossums." I add, "They're wild animals," while Rosy says, "They carry rabies and definitely bite."

The man drops the ice cream cone, straightens up and backs away slowly. The opossum grabs the cone and scurries into the brush along the path.

Instead of saying 'seriously, moron?!' like I want to do, I smile and say, "Thank you for your cooperation in keeping the wildlife wild." God, I hate myself sometimes.

Rosy and I continue toward the offices, Rosy moving very quickly for someone of her short stature. She holds up the cheque again, then something in her demeanour changes and she slows down a little. When she looks up at me, her eyes are soft. "You sold Matilda, didn't you?"

I take a long swig of the cold water, then shrug. "She was getting old anyway."

Rosy stops and turns to me. "Harrison, first the cottage, now the boat? Why would you do this? If you'd at least have kept one of them, you would've had somewhere to live when this place goes into receivership."

I grin and waggle my eyebrows a little. "Actually, I was hoping to move in with you and Darnell. Finally give you a chance to mother me properly."

"I don't know why I put up with you." She shakes her head and starts walking again.

I match her pace, not wanting to let her leave angry.

Looking up at me, she says, "This isn't a permanent solution, you know. You're still going to have to look at the overspending — particularly when it comes to the staff bonuses. Unless you make some major changes, all of this" —she gestures around in the air— "is going to belong to the bank very soon. You've got nothing left to sell."

"Oh, I don't know about that…" I gesture up and down my body.

A loud growling sound comes from deep within Rosy's chest, and I know I've hit the limit with her.

"Look, I'll find a way to get things back on track. As long as we don't have another hurricane for a while, we'll be back in the black very soon."

"Reef!" one of the bartenders, Fidel, calls from across the court-yard. Rosy and I both turn and watch as he jogs toward us, looking very excited. "Winnie just went into labour."

I slap Fidel on the shoulder. "Congratulations, man. You better get out of here then."

A look of relief crosses his face and he grins at me. "Thanks, boss."

He hurries off in the direction of the parking lot and I call after him, "Good luck! And don't worry about your shift tomorrow. I'll make sure you're covered."

He turns, now jogging backwards. "Thanks, but I can't afford to take another night off. I'm going to be a father!"

"Don't worry about it. You'll still get paid." I smile as I watch him make a fist pump in the air and let out a little whooping noise.

He disappears around the side of the main lobby, shouting, "I'm going to be a father!"

When I look back at Rosy, she's glaring up at me from under her drawn-on eyebrows.

"What?" I ask.

"That," she barks, pointing to where Fidel was standing a few seconds ago. "*That* is why this resort is in trouble."

"*That* is the whole point of having a resort. To give people a great place to work so they can have a good life."

"No, Harrison, that's not what having a resort is about. It's a busi-ness. *To make money.*" She pokes me on the chest to emphasize her point. "You run around this damn island like you have a cape and a big "S" on your chest, but you can't be everybody's hero, not if you're going to survive."

"Hey, I thought we agreed not to talk about my secret identity?" I lower my voice and gesture with both hands in a downward direction. "Speaking of which, if you tell anyone why I sold Matilda, I'll tell Darnell you have a thing for the FedEx guy."

"You don't scare me. Darnell and I have an agreement. I can look as long as I don't touch." A flicker of a smile crosses her lips, and I know she's thinking about the delivery guy's tight shorts. Then her smile fades, allowing her scowl to return. "Don't think you can distract me, young man. We're still talking about your money problems."

"Damn. That usually works," I mutter.

"Well, not today. This is serious, Harrison," she says. "You know what you should do is—"

"—Tell my lazy, good-for-nothing brother to come home and help out at the resort so I can stop financing his reckless lifestyle." I quote her word-for-word.

Her mouth snaps shut, then she says, "Yes. That."

"No can do, Rosy," I say. "He's living his dream. Besides, now that he's got the show, he's not going to need to borrow from me anymore."

"Just you wait. He'll spend it all on women and be back begging in a few months."

"Or...it'll turn into a regular gig and he can start paying me back."

"Doubt it." Patting me on the cheek a little too hard, she says, "You're not Superman, Harrison. At best, you're Clark Kent."

"But a guy can try, can't he?" I give her a wink.

She purses her lips together. "I don't know what I'm going to do with you."

"For now, if you could get that cheque to the bank, I'd really appreciate it." Cupping one hand next to my mouth, I lower my voice conspiratorially. "I'm not sure if you're aware, but money's a little tight right now."

She tries to smack me, but I'm too quick and step out of her reach.

I take a couple more steps backward while I gesture with my thumb over my shoulder. "Okay, I better run. I need to shower and go work a bar shift. Some idiot gave Fidel the night off."

6

Long Ass Flights and Complimentary Whine

Libby

As soon as I step outside of the church, I stand at the top of the steps, blinking into the bright sun and trying to figure out what to do next. A sense of urgency propels my feet forward because any second now, these doors will open and everyone I know will come spilling out of them. I hurry down the sidewalk to the limo, only to find the driver doing push-ups next to the car with one arm behind his back. *Hmm. Weird.*

"Excuse me, Xavier," I say as calmly as possible. "Bit of a change in plans. Turns out there won't be a wedding today after all. I'm going to need you to get me over to my flat as quickly as possible." *Well done, Libby. You definitely do not sound like a distraught, jilted, barely hanging on by a thin thread bride.*

Xavier looks up at me and gasps, "Jesus! What happened to your face?" He pops up and quickly opens the front passenger door to the limo, retrieving a box of tissues.

I glance down, see that the front of my dress is covered in blood, and know the bottom half of my face must be as well. That is probably why my boss's wife, Gina, was hiding her son's face in her bosom during my announcement.

Xavier's just handing me a wad of tissues when I hear Alice's voice behind me. "Get in! We have to get the hell out of here!"

Xavier glances back and forth between us for a second, then says, "You two didn't do anything illegal in there, did you?"

"What?" Alice's face scrunches up in confusion until she looks at me. "Oh, that," she says. "She's a stress bleeder. Now get behind the wheel so we can track down her arsehole fiancé! Take us to her flat as fast as you can drive!"

The three of us pile into the limo just as the front doors of the church swing open. As we pull away, I glance back in time to see my mum comforting Jorge, who looks like he's close to tears. Yeah, that makes sense. My mum should totally be there for him right now…

Alice grabs the bottle of champagne from the ice bucket and takes a swig, then wipes the back of her hand across her mouth. "Richard is *so dead*. Like, roadkill dead. There won't even be anything left for his parents to identify. Except maybe his balls. I might put those in a jar of formaldehyde and keep them on my mantle." She tips the bottle back again, then says, "What am I talking about? *You* should keep his balls. They belong to you. Plus, I have kids, so that would lead to a lot of awkward questions. Drink?" she asks, holding the bottle out to me.

"No, thanks. I'd like to keep a clear head right now."

"Good. Good thinking. Somebody needs to keep a clear head. Otherwise, we'll get caught and I can't afford to do prison time. Jack can't even handle if I go out for the evening. Imagine if I were put away for ten to twenty. He'd completely fall apart." She pops the bottle back into the bucket, then gets out a water and wets some napkins. "Let's get you cleaned up a bit. It kind of looks like it's Halloween and you're dressed as a zombie bride."

"Listen, Alice, I appreciate your support and all, but I'm honestly not mad at Richard, so I don't want you to say anything you'll regret when he and I sort this all out."

She stops wiping my neck. "Sort it…not mad…*Libby?!* HE LEFT YOU AT THE ALTAR! How can you not be angry?"

"I mean, I'm hurt and humiliated, yes, and I know it'll take a long time for me to feel better, but I also know I'll get over it. Richard and I are perfect for each other, and I'm not about to throw away a six-year really terrific relationship over one bad morning," I say confidently. "I mean, that would be a little short-sighted, don't you think?"

Alice just stares at me blankly while grabbing the champagne and sucking down a long swig.

"I'll just go home, he and I will have a long talk, and we'll fix things. There's no need to overreact."

"I am *not* overreacting. If anything, you're under-reacting!"

Xavier chimes in with, "I don't know. You'll never regret taking the high road. A calm and logical approach is always the right one."

"Thanks, Xavier. I really appreciate your support." I give Alice a pointed look, only to have her reach across me and press the button for the privacy screen without saying a word.

Fifteen blocks and several protests later, Alice gets out of the limo with me in front of my building. I turn to her and smile. "I think it's better if you go back to the church. Maybe Jack and the kids are still there?"

"There is no freaking way I am letting you go up there alone. You're obviously in some sort of delusional state with your emotions completely shut off, and when this all finally hits you, you're going to need me."

"I'm fine, really, but if it makes you feel better, you can come upstairs with me and hand me off to Richard," I say. "But, you have to promise not to say a word to him or go in search of sharp objects."

"Fine," she says, folding her arms across her chest.

"Now I see where Colby learned that world-class pout of his." I wink at her, then turn to Xavier, who is still holding the door open. "Will you please wait here until my friend comes back down, then take her wherever she needs to go?"

"Yes, of course," he says. "And may I say, it's very impressive how calmly you're handling everything?"

"You may." I give him a satisfied smile, then start for the building.

Two minutes later, I open the door to our tenth-floor loft-style flat with Alice hovering next to me as though we're conjoined twins.

Silence greets us and my heart sinks because whenever Richard is here, you can hear the low hum of the telly.

On the kitchen table, a note is waiting for me.

Dear Libby,

I wish I could find the words to express how sorry I am about all of this. Had I been a braver man, I would have told you months ago how I was feeling and spared you the humiliation you must be feeling now.

I've gone out to give you some space while you get ready to go to the Benavente Islands. I know you're not about to let your boss down just because I've done the same to you. Plus, I know how much comfort you take in following through with a plan.

I hope three weeks away will allow you to heal, and that when you return, we can discuss the division of our assets.

You deserve to find a man who is good enough for you, and as much as I wish I could be that man, I am not.

Apologetically yours,

Richard

"What a bunch of crap," Alice, who has obviously been reading over my shoulder, scoffs. "Go on your honeymoon anyway?! That is maybe the worst idea he's ever come up with. Well, second only to not showing up for his wedding, the bloody arse."

I carefully fold the letter in half and place it back on the table. "Actually, I think it's a perfect idea." Turning my back to her, I gesture over my shoulder at the buttons down the back of my dress. "Can you help me? I should really soak the blood out of my dress before it sets."

Alice sets to work on my dress, her fingers moving much more quickly than they did this morning when she fastened them up. "How can you be so damn calm right now?"

"Because this is just a blip in the road. Everything is going to be just fine. I'll go on the trip, do my job, and the best part is, it'll give Richard twenty-one long days to realize the mistake he's made. By the time I get back here, he'll be so desperate to make it up to me that I'll

44

have him wrapped around my little finger." Smiling at her, I add, "Actually, now that I think about it, this whole thing could turn out better than if we'd gotten married today. After all, nothing makes a man fall for a woman like thinking he's lost her forever."

―――――

Text from Mum: *Oh, Mini-Me! I can't believe Richard's stood you up. This just solidifies my beliefs about the shackles of marriage. Jorge is devastated, of course, because he was hoping I would marry him. I'll be rushing him back to Argentina as quickly as possible so that he may heal. Let me know where you end up. We should do a girl's trip, maybe to Bali or Thailand!*

Voicemail from Quentin Atlas, Manager of Mergers and Acquisitions, Caribbean Team: *Libby, not gonna lie, that looked pretty rough today. I hope everything is okay with you and Richard…and your nose. Jesus, that was a lot of blood.*

Listen, I need to know ASAP if you are unable to go on your trip to Paradise Bay. I'm pretty sure I could get Alan to take your place since he's about to close on the Atlantis Cove deal. The guy's a shark. I'm certainly hoping I've got two sharks on my team but completely understand if you're unable to do your job right now. Just call, text, or email back as fast as you can.

―――――

"I know I sounded really confident when I said all that to Alice, but between you and me, now that I've been sitting on this plane for the past six hours, I'm suddenly not so sure. I mean, I would've felt *a lot* better if I could've at least seen Richard in person before I left town. What if he really is serious that he doesn't want to marry me?" I say, offering my last tiny pretzel to the woman sitting next to me.

Her name is Greta. She got on the plane at our stopover in Frankfurt and is going to Benavente for her fiftieth birthday. She's renting a villa overlooking the ocean where several of her friends who live in various places around the world are going to meet her. How fun is that? Anyway, she's a really great listener. We got to talking about, oh, four hours ago, and I've pretty much unloaded my whole life story on her.

She shakes her head at my pretzel offer, then says in her thick German accent, "That is a real possibility, since he didn't show up for the wedding."

I pluck the pretzel out of the bag and take a tiny nibble while I consider her words. "Oh God, Greta, what if he really doesn't love me? What if no one will ever love me?"

"I suppose that could happen. Lots of people in the world never find someone to spend their life with. But there are worse tragedies—terminal illness, homelessness. Those are both much worse."

"Good point. Thanks, Greta. It *is* important to keep this whole thing in perspective, isn't it?" I take a long swig of the white wine the flight attendant brought by a few minutes ago. "But if you had to guess, what would you say the chances are that Richard and I will end up together, you know, percentage-wise?"

"Well, based on our four-hour conversation, I'd say you clearly love him, but I don't think the feeling is mutual, you know, because he decided not to marry you. So, unless you can suddenly become a completely different person, I'd say…maybe five percent." She pats me on the hand and then closes her eyes. "You should get some sleep now. I should too."

"Right. You're probably right," I say with a sigh. I close my eyes for a second, then sit up with a start. "Oh my God, who am I kidding? Richard doesn't love me! I'm boring and predictable and…and quite possibly unlovable."

She jerks awake and blinks a few times. "No, no. This is not true. Well, some of it. Boring, yes. A little crazy? Most likely. But I promise, you are lovable."

"How can you be so sure?"

"Because there's something to love about each person. Except Richard. He sounds like a complete jackass," she says with a firm nod. "I'm sorry to be the one to tell you, but I'm afraid it's true."

I sit with my shoulders slumped.

"Now, you go on your honeymoon. Try to meet a handsome man

and have some wild sex — only not the butt stuff, I agree with you about that. Just have a fling. Find someone who can help you feel good about yourself again."

"Like Angela Bassett in that movie about the woman who needed to get her groove back?"

"Sure, like that."

"I can't," I say, shaking my head. "What if Richard wants me back and then changes his mind when he finds out I've slept with some strange man?"

"He's not going to want you back, dear. So, do whatever makes *you* happy. Then go home with your head held high and a little secret in your heart. And if by some miracle he wants you back, you make him beg."

7

Sometimes Cute Things Come in Drunk Packages

Harrison

"Did I miss anything good?" I ask Lolita, the other bartender on shift this evening.

The snorkelling trip I was captaining got back late so I ended up missing the first half hour of the shift, leaving Lolita alone to handle things.

Without looking at me, Lolita says, "We've got about twelve customers down on the beach in addition to the ones you see here. There's a drunk blabbermouth redhead sucking back piña coladas over at the far corner, otherwise everyone seems to be behaving themselves." She continues pouring the ingredients for margaritas into the blender while she talks. A second later, she turns it on and the loud motor overtakes the reggae music we play before supper. When she shuts it off, she says, ""You're covering for Fidel again? You didn't cover any shifts for me when I got a puppy," she says.

"Did you give birth to the puppy?" I ask with a grin.

Narrowing her eyes, Lolita says, "Did Fidel?"

"Touché," I answer, grabbing a beer from the fridge for myself and surveying my surroundings.

The bar, which is a large open-air square structure with a grass peaked roof, sits at the top of the resort's private beach. There's a large wooden platform that extends out to one side, where thirty tables are spread out under as many umbrellas. The three other sides of the bar have sand leading right up to the counter, and instead of stools, there are wooden swings, which make for some interesting moments depending on how much people have to drink. Rosy's been after me for years to get rid of them, but I love them — the comic relief they provide is amazing.

I glance over at the redhead, pleasantly surprised to see she's kind of adorable in that girl-next-door, natural sort of way. Her long, curly hair looks like it's just barely under control, and at any moment, it might spring up and out to the sides. She's humming and patting her hand on the bar top to the reggae beat. Hmm…looks single too. The single ones always have a paperback with them.

Lolita must be watching me watch the redhead because she sidles up next to me and says, "Stay away from that one. She'll tell you her entire life story if she thinks you're willing to listen. Apparently, her groom didn't show up to their wedding so she decided to go on the honeymoon alone."

"Huh. That takes a lot of guts when you really think about it."

"Trust me. She's crazy. You do not want a piece of that." Lolita finishes popping tiny paper umbrellas into the drinks she just made and picks up the tray, disappearing down to the beach where guests wait on loungers.

Grabbing a rag out of the drawer, I wet it, then spray down the shiny wooden bar top with some cleaner and get to work on today's watermarks. The sun is starting to set, which means the crowd on the beach will soon be heading back to their rooms to get ready for dinner and things will get a lot quieter for the next couple of hours.

As I wipe down the area closest to the redhead, she smiles at me, her eyes growing wide with what looks like pleasant surprise. Holding her empty glass up, she says, "Hey, Big Pants, this drink is not going to drink itself. Refill itself. Did I just call you Big Pants?"

"Yes, I'm pretty sure you did."

She bursts out laughing and slaps her forehead with her palm.

"Sorry. That sounded better in my brain. I was aiming for feisty but missed. I meant to call you Handsome, then I thought I'd call you Big Guy…"

"Well, Big Pants could be taken as a compliment, depending on how you mean it," I say, not bothering to suppress a laugh.

She shuts her eyes for a moment and scrunches up her face. "But that would make me extremely flirty, and I'm not that kind of girl." Her accent is very familiar, and I know immediately she's from Avonia by the way she pronounces flirty.

"Right, you're just feisty. Not flirty." I stare at her for a moment, taking in her bright blue eyes and the sprinkling of freckles across her nose. She is cute. Too bad she's been drinking. "It was a piña colada, right?"

"That's the one." She nods with her entire upper body. "Wait. How did you know that?"

"I'm a mind-reader."

"No, you're not!" she slurs, giving me a skeptical look.

It's tempting to mess with her a bit, but I decide to let her off the hook. "You got me. I'm not a mind-reader. My co-worker over there told me," I say, pointing to Lolita as she walks back up the steps from the beach with a tray full of empties.

I pour some pineapple juice into the blender while the cute redhead sways back and forth, singing along to Bob Marley's *Stir It Up*. For someone so hammered, she's not a bad singer, and I find myself joining in. Lolita passes by behind the cute redhead, twirling her finger by the side of her head and mouthing "crazy."

I slide the drink over to her, and she catches it, but barely, even though I aimed it right into her hand. Wow, she is *really* tipsy.

"I love this song. Who sings it again?"

I open my mouth to tell her, but she holds up her hand. "Wait! Now I rememer, rebember…ha! Rebember. I made up a new word, Handsome."

"Is that so? What does it mean?"

"I don't have the first clue, but it sounds like it should be a real word, doesn't it?" She stares at me while she sticks her tongue out in search of the straw. When she finally gets it, she clamps on with her full pink lips and takes a long drink. "What should we say rebember means?"

Lolita gives her a hard look. "How about regretting something you did because you had too much to drink?"

Freckles stares at her for a second, then whispers loudly to me, "I don't think she likes me very much."

Grinning, I say, "Don't worry. She doesn't like me much either."

Lolita rolls her eyes and walks over to one of the tables to take their order.

"Heh! You're funny. My mouth is numb." She mashes her fingers against her lips, poking and prodding until her eyes widen in triumph. "Ahhh, I'm finally numb! I've been waiting to feel nothing since... well, when was the last time I felt unhumiliated? Hmm...must have been in the garden outside the church. *Before* the text message. Hey, but you know what? I didn't die from embarrassment like I thought I would. Good for me. I should celebrate with another drink."

"Do you want to maybe get something to eat first? I'd hate to see you overdo it."

Shaking her head, she says, "Don't worry about me. I've never taken anything too far in my entire life. I'm just going to sit here and drink until I forget my own name."

Hmmm, maybe Lolita was right about staying away from this one. A couple sits down kitty-corner to Freckles, and after I take their order, I notice Freckles is staring at them. She slurps more of her drink, then asks, "Are you on your honeymoon?"

They cuddle up to each other and say yes, then start nuzzling each other's noses.

"Me too," she says loudly, interrupting them.

Uh-oh. She's gotten to the obnoxiously drunk stage. I cut in, hoping to draw her attention from the happy couple. "Your honeymoon, huh? Where's the lucky guy?"

"Oh, I left him at home."

"Really? So he's not so lucky after all?"

"Sure he is. I left him alive." She giggles, pulling the straw out of her glass and tipping the drink back, only to have the ice cubes and remaining colada smack her in the face.

Wincing, I hand her a napkin so she can dab the white milky drink off her cheeks. "Was he cheating, then?"

"I don't want to talk about it," she says, pointing at me with the napkin. "Except to say twenty-four hours ago, I would have told you I had the perfect life — I was about to become Mrs. Richard Tomy, we were going to spend our honeymoon here at this lovely resort, then go back home, finish saving up the down-payment on our dream house and start a family."

"And now?"

"I really don't want to talk about it," she answers, her words slurring together.

"Righto. I forgot you already said that."

"I did. And I don't," she nods firmly. Taking a deep breath, she says, "Except I will tell you a little secret I haven't told anyone." She gestures for me to come closer. I lean across the bar and she whispers, "I'm going to get him back."

I lower my voice to match hers. "Get him back as in you're hatching some sort of revenge plot?"

"No, silly. I'm going to get him to fall back in love with me." She gives me a confident look, then narrows her eyes at me. "Hey, you're making me talk about it and I already said I didn't want to. That's a bit rude, really."

"Sorry," I say, trying to look very serious. "Won't happen again."

I busy myself refilling the fridge with beer, then flick on the white lights that line the roof. The sun has set now, and I watch as couples slowly make their way from the beach and head in the direction of their rooms.

Freckles leans on one elbow. "I want to go for a swim. What time do the pools close?"

"About twenty minutes ago," Lolita answers.

"That's no fun. I want to have fun. I want to swim!" she says, whipping her arms out to the sides and knocking her book onto the floor. She looks down at it and shrugs, then her eyes light up. "Ooh! I should have another drink!"

"You're missing the word 'not,'" Lolita mutters, "as in you should *not* have another drink."

Freckles pauses, then says, "You're right. I should stop here, or, tomorrow, I'll be rebembering all over the place." When her eyes meet mine, she snickers at her own joke. Her eyes fall on the happy newly-weds, and her shoulders drop. "What the hell? One more round. But nothing too sweet. Just a shot of something hard, and only if you'll join me."

"Why not? I'm always up for some fun," I say, pouring us each a shot of spiced rum. Holding mine up, I wait for her to clink her glass to mine. When she finally manages it, I say, "To happy endings."

She bursts into laughter, sprawling her upper body and arms lazily across the bar. "Happy...hahahaha...endings...hahahahaha! God, it's been a very long while since I've had one of those." She gives me a naughty look and licks her lips. "What time do you get off work, Handsome?"

Aaaand that's my cue. I better get her back to her room before she finds some arse who will take her up on whatever she's offering. "I could leave now if you want."

Her eyes grow wide. "Won't you get in trouble?"

"Lolita will cover for me," I say.

"Really?" she asks, her mouth falling open for a second. "Wait. I don't want to get you fired or something."

"Trust me. I won't get fired," I step out from behind the bar and make my way over to her. "Besides, some things are more important than work."

"Yeah, right. Like what?"

I pick up her book off the floor and dust it off, noticing the nearly-kissing couple on the front. "Like...happy endings."

She snorts, then says, "I'm not this type of girl."

"What type is that?"

She leans in. "*Wanton*. The type that goes off with a man she doesn't know and does wild and delicious things."

When I look down, I see her hands on my chest and she's petting me like I'm a horse. "Oh, these are nice pecs. Very hard."

"You sure about that?"

"Oh, yes, they're much harder than most men's."

"No, I mean, are you sure you're not that type of girl?" I ask, glancing down at her very busy hands that are running over my abs now.

"Positive. I'm always a good girl," she says, and the way she says it, I can tell it's most likely true. "But you know what? I don't think I want to be good anymore. I want to be very, very bad!"

"Thought so. How about we start with a walk and see where we end up?" I turn back to Lolita and mouth, "Back in a few."

She nods back, knowing the routine. I generally manage to corral the overly drunk women over to the burger bar for some fries (they always want salty fried food at this stage), then take them safely to their rooms where I make up an emergency and leave them at the door with the suggestion of watching *Mamma Mia* on demand. Works every time.

Freckles lets go of me and sets off in the direction of the beach.

I bring her book for her and follow her closely in case she starts to take a header down the steps. "You know, if we're going to spend the evening together, shouldn't we at least tell each other our names?"

She hops from the third stair down onto the sand, then turns to me. "You know what? Let's *not* tell each other. It'll be better this way. That is, unless you object to being called Handsome."

"I thought I was Big Pants?" I ask, chuckling to myself. She doesn't answer because she's too busy spinning in a circle. *Okay, let's try this again.* "All right, Handsome it is. What should I call you?"

She stops spinning and giggles. "Hmm, I don't know. Gorgeous, maybe? Or Beautiful? Either works for me."

"Both fitting descriptions, but somehow missing your true essence." And making it difficult to find out her room number if she passes out.

"Oh, am I more than a pretty face?" she asks, snorting with laughter.

"Definitely. A guy can tell right away."

"You're nice. You know what? I'm going to tell you my *real* name, which is a *huge secret*." She stretches both arms out to the sides to indicate the enormity of this information. "Breeze."

"Breeze?"

54

"Yup. I had a wild, hippie mother." She does a spin with her arms outstretched while she answers.

"Cute. Is that on your passport?"

"Nope. My grandparents legally changed it when I was ten."

"To what?" I ask, but it's no use because Breeze is already kicking off her sandals and dancing toward the water.

The moon hangs low in the sky, giving a pale grey glow to the tide as it sweeps across the beach and then retreats. I pick up her sandals, then follow her down to the water just as she lifts the bottom of her long skirt and lets a wave lap over her feet.

Turning back to me, she calls, "Come on in! It's wonderful!"

I stay back a bit, thoroughly enjoying watching her.

"From now on, I'm never going to be boring again! Instead, I'll be a totally brazen adventure seeker!" she shouts into the wind. Laughing, she turns back to me. "Let's see how adventurous I can be…"

Then she tugs her tank top over her head and lets it drop.

Uh-oh. I guess I shouldn't have poured her that last drink.

Before I can say anything to convince her not to, she unties her wraparound skirt, letting it fall into the surf. She's now standing in front me in her bra and knickers — and a rather alluring set at that. Very lacy and very small.

Now, I know I should not be looking, and I promise to stop in a second, but it's really hard not to stare at those curves…

But I will stop. I swear.

She runs a few steps farther into the water, squealing a little as it hits her upper thighs. "I think this island has turned me wild! I'm the life of the party now!"

Okay, I'm still staring. I can admit it. But really, at this point, it's kind of a safety issue for her.

"Come on! What are you waiting for?" she yells, just before a wave knocks her onto her knees.

Oh, shit.

Dropping her sandals and book, I jog down to her just as the next wave hits. She's on all fours now, with water rushing over her head, soaking her from head to toe. When the water recedes, she sputters and coughs while I lift her up to standing. Her drenched hair is covering her entire face, and she flips it, whipping me in the face. I wince a little, then chuckle before I realize I'm still holding her up by the waist. And she's almost naked. And damn, it's been too long since I've held an almost-naked woman.

But, this one is not for me. Not tonight anyway.

"Never turn your back to the waves," I say. "You could get hurt."

She smiles lazily at me. "Yeah, that's a good rule when it comes to men too."

"Not all of us," I say, brushing the remaining hair out of her eyes.

Her hands are petting me again, and I don't seem to be stopping them as they work their way around my neck. She swallows hard, staring into my eyes for a moment before glancing down at my mouth.

Do not let her kiss you, Harrison. Seriously, dude.

She leans in and I pull back a little, staying just out of her reach, even though it damn near kills me. I give her a half-smile, knowing I've got about one minute to find out her name or room number before she either passes out or starts vomiting. "So, Breeze, what's the name you go by now?"

"Kiss me, and I'll tell you," she says, lifting onto her tiptoes and pressing herself against me.

I was wrong. I only had about ten seconds, because now she's completely passed out.

8

The Morning After Whatever Happened Last Night...

Libby

I OPEN one eye at time, each lid feeling like it's stuck to a very dry eyeball. Oh, that was a horrible mistake. The sun streaming in the window burns my retinas and shoots through my brain like a spike through a wood plank. I moan and shut my eyes, pulling a pillow over my face to stop the pain.

"Turn it off," I groan.

A deep voice comes from across the room. "Turn what off?"

"The sun. Shut it off."

"Best I can do is close the curtains," he says.

Wait. There's a man in my room.

Who the frack is that, and what the hell is he doing in my room? Clutching the sheet to my neck, I shoot up, causing the pillow to fall on my lap.

Urgh, that was not a good idea. Moving so quickly causes the left-over booze in my queasy stomach to slosh around. I gag, then press my hand to my mouth, breathing slowly.

"You okay? Do you need a garbage can or anything?" he says, standing.

I shake my head, then blink a few times, waiting for my blurry eyes to focus on the source of the voice as he moves toward me.

Oh, no, no, no, no! That man is far too hot to be in my room.

Suddenly, a flash of being at the bar comes back to me. The drinks. The laughing. The beach. Petting a brawny man—*him*, I guess. The almost skinny dipping. The kiss. Did we kiss?

I gasp loudly. *Did we have sex?*

Oh, lord, please don't tell me I was naked in front of this scruffy Adonis. Oh no! I could be naked at this very moment and he's walking over here!

"Stay back!" I order, unable to stand the thought of him getting any closer when I'm in this condition—insanely hungover, possibly nude, and most certainly reeking of booze from every pore. I cautiously lift the sheet away from me, only to find I'm in a white T-shirt I've never seen before. Reaching down, I feel the side of my bottom and feel a wave of relief that I'm wearing my knickers.

He stops in place, looking more entertained than I'm comfortable with given the circumstances. "Come on, sweetie, after everything we did last night, I'm surprised you're so shy this afternoon."

"What do you mean, *everything we did*?" I ask, narrowing my eyes. "And why did you say it's the afternoon?"

"I'd call one forty-five afternoon, wouldn't you?" He strides over and lays his incredibly muscular body across the bottom of the enormous bed, propping his head up on one hand.

"Oh my God...did we...?" I press the sheet to me again, gripping it so tightly, my knuckles turn white.

"You don't remember? It was amazing. The earth moved. And you—you were loud enough that we probably cleared out the entire resort." He grins at me, then rolls off the bed and starts across the room, giving me a view of his muscly back and behind. Those are some seriously tight shorts.

No, Libby! Do not focus on his taut buttocks! You are not that kind of girl.

"I'm very sorry, but I'm afraid I don't remember any of it."

"None of it?" he asks.

When I shake my head, he says, "That's a real crime because it was the best night you've ever had. You told me as much right after round three." Opening the mini-fridge, he grabs a bottle of water and takes off the lid. "At least I have it all on video."

"What?!" My pulse speeds up, and I suddenly feel both hot and dizzy. *What have I turned into? Some kind of hussy? Or worse—my mother?*

"I didn't think it was a good idea, but you were pretty insistent." He shrugs, then crosses the room and holds the bottle of water out to me.

I take it cautiously, then shrink back from him a bit. Why would a man *this hot* do whatever predictable, boring old Libby Dewitt said to do?

In an instant, it all makes perfect sense. My heart sinks and I let out a loud groan. "You're a gigolo, aren't you?"

"What?"

"Listen, I don't know what I told you last night, but I can't afford to pay you. I'm a little low on cash at the—"

"I'm not a gigolo."

"Then why would you…?" I don't really know how to put this. *Why would someone as hot as you sleep with a very plain Jane like me?*

"Why would I what?" He folds his arms across his broad chest.

My words come out rushed. "Sleep with someone like me."

"Are you kidding right now?" he asks, raising one eyebrow.

"No, I'm afraid not." I shake my head, then wince because my brain is pounding and because I really don't want to hear his answer. I've had enough rejection for one weekend. Before he can say anything, I take a wild stab at it. "Now I get it, you're one of those guys with extremely low standards. The type who'll sleep with anything with a pulse." I gasp again. "Oh my God. I probably have an STD by now, don't I?"

"Ouch," he says, rubbing at his chest. "You're pretty mean when you're sober."

"Sorry. I don't mean to insult you. I'm honestly just very confused." I sigh and close my eyes for a second, unable to stand the look of hurt in his strikingly brilliant hazel eyes. "Maybe it would be best if you just left. I'm really not myself at the moment."

"Okay, but it might make more sense if you left."

"Why?" I ask, opening my eyes again.

"This is my room."

I glance around, only to realize for the first time that this room, although decorated in exactly the same white linens and dark wood as mine, is much larger. This one has a sitting area and a desk off to the left, and now that I look out the patio doors, I see we're in a beach-front suite instead of a standard garden-view room. My eyes fall on a chair in the corner, upon which are my clothes, folded and piled neatly. "We came back to *your* room."

He nods. "Yup. It's a villa, actually."

"Well, then *I* should leave and *you* should stay." I shimmy to the side of the bed, then stand, tugging the sheet so it comes with me.

"Okay." He crosses to the large mahogany desk and sits down.

Picking up the pile of clothes, I hurry into the en suite, then shut and lock the door behind me. Leaning against it, I try to process everything I've just been told, but it's all too bizarre. And how can I not remember any of it?

Because you were stinking drunk, you idiot.

I let the sheet fall to the floor, remove the foreign T-shirt, then dress as quickly as possible, stopping only to pee—a loud, long pee that seems to go on forever. Oh, God, I hope he can't hear that. He probably never pees because that's something only mortals do.

When I'm done, I stare at myself in the mirror while I scrub my hands. My red curls are sticking up wildly at all angles. Oh, that is some seriously sexified hair. I try to run my fingers through it, but it's so tangled, I settle for smoothing it down as best I can. Spotting a bottle of mouthwash, I take a swig, then rinse my mouth while I try to figure out my next move.

My fuzzy-headed brain cannot seem to come up with a plan — only problems, the first one being the sex tape. My face turns bright pink and my stomach drops when I think about it. It's not like the old days when you could make a sex tape, and it would literally mean one copy of a VHS tape that could easily be destroyed.

Oh, this is really a new low — pining for the days of old, when sex tapes were difficult to share with the world.

Gah! Focus!

The video is digital, therefore is most likely on a device that is connected to the Internet, meaning it's already in 'the cloud.'

THE CLOUD!? How could you have gone and made a sex tape with a stranger!?

I pace for a moment while I try to get myself under control and think. I know! I'll just ask him to delete it off his device and the cloud. He doesn't seem like a horrible person — slutty maybe, but not otherwise nasty. I'm sure he can be reasoned with.

I pick the sheet up off the floor, then straighten my back, take a deep breath, and open the door. When I walk out into the room, I see my god-like sex partner sitting at his desk, talking on the phone. I quickly cross the floor and place the sheet on the bed, then slide my feet into my waiting sandals.

"It should be a lot more. Like one and a half times that, at least." He turns and gives me a little nod. "I have to run. Something important's come up. I'll ring you in a bit." With that, he hangs up the phone and leans back in his chair.

Clearing my throat, I try to sound very no-nonsense. "Listen, about that video…"

"Relax, there's no video."

"What?"

"I was just winding you up a bit. Sorry." He suppresses a guilty smile. "In fact, nothing happened," he says, standing. "Well, I did have the pleasure of finding all your wet, sandy things in the dark and then carrying you all the way here from the beach."

"Was I…" lowering my voice, I whisper, "*naked?*"

"You were in your undergarments. But don't worry, I wrapped your skirt around you for the walk back. Nobody saw anything. Except me. I actually saw a lot." He rubs the back of his neck and gives me a guilty grin. "That lacy fabric gets pretty see-through when it's wet."

My entire body flames with embarrassment at the thought. "Okay, well, I'm sorry for…your trouble last night. And I'm sorry for suggesting you were a gigolo earlier."

"And for assuming I gave you an STD?"

"And that," I say quietly. "I'm going to go now. You don't happen to know where my room key is, do you?"

"That's why we're in my room. You must have lost it on the beach."

"Right. Brilliant. I'll just walk over to the front desk and get a replacement one, then."

"Do you want me to call for a driver?"

"No, I don't want to inconvenience you any further than I already have," I say. "Besides, I need to stretch my legs."

"You sure? It's about a fifteen-minute walk to the main building from here, and it's about a thousand degrees outside."

"I'm positive. I love the heat...and exercise," I say, hoping he can't tell that both of those statements are absolute rubbish. I hate sweating full stop, but I really must get away from Mr. Perfect before I make an even bigger fool of myself. Besides, dying of heat stroke doesn't seem like such a bad option at the moment.

"Suit yourself," he says, picking up my copy of *One Hundred Promises* and handing it to me. I take it, trying not to notice the spark of energy when my fingertips brush against his.

He walks to the door with me and opens it while I try to think of some way to end this conversation that will leave me with a shred of dignity. But that ship has sailed, hasn't it?

Yes, Libby, you spectacular idiot, it has.

I walk through the doorway, then turn and say, "Okay, well, thank you for taking care of me last night...and today, I guess. Sorry for your trouble...er..." My heart sinks as I realize I don't even know his name.

"Everyone calls me Reef." He gives me such an insanely gorgeous smile that it's all I can do not to titter into my hand and flutter my eyelashes.

"Reef. Well, thank you for being a gentleman. I'll see you around." Because apparently my life has turned into a string of humiliations...

9

Now, Where Did I Put My Knees?

Libby

I'M SITTING on a large boulder on the beach, waiting for the sun to start setting while I talk to Alice via FaceTime. Oh, the miracles of modern technology.

I was surprised to get her IM since it's almost three a.m. in Valcourt, but she was awake with Maisie, who's cutting a new tooth. Thank God, because if there's anything I need right now, it's advice from my bestie.

Maisie finally dropped off on Alice's lap about ten minutes ago, and the two of them look so cozy curled up in the rocking chair in Maisie's room that I feel suddenly homesick. It also reminds me how beautifully close I was to having what she has — the perfect life — and now...my future is my worst nightmare: an unknown.

I've just told Alice the entire story about last night, ending off with me rushing out the door this afternoon. When my thoughts turn to Reef, my face suddenly feels strangely hot. "What is wrong with me, Alice? I almost kissed a total stranger. I was like a wildly irresponsible, hot-to-trot woman last night! How am I going to explain this to Richard when we get back together?"

"Umm, I wouldn't worry about it. Honestly."

"We *are* getting back together," I say in a haughty tone.

"Sure, hon, and if you do, you'll probably want to keep that from him."

Biting my thumbnail, I say, "But it's a really bad way to start over, don't you think? With a big lie?"

"Nothing happened, Lib. You drank too much and wore what is basically the equivalent of a bikini while on the beach. There's not much of a story there when you really think about it."

"Oh my God, Alice," I say, gasping a little. "You're like an evil genius with the justifying. You don't do this to Jack, do you?"

"No, of course not. I just meant if you *do* manage to patch things up with Richard, you probably won't want to lead with the full disclosure of something that in the end turned out to be nothing." She yawns, and I feel a pang of guilt for keeping her on the phone at this hour.

"I should let you get some sleep."

"Yeah, I better. Colby will be up in three hours."

"Goodnight, Alice."

"Goodnight, Libs. And seriously, don't worry about last night. Chalk it up to needing to let loose. You never let your hair down, and you really should. There's a very fun person inside of you that needs to be let out once in a while, so while you're there, among strangers, just go for it, okay? Do all the things you normally won't let yourself. You deserve it."

"You mean channel my inner Penny? No, thanks. I did that last night and look where I ended up."

"Okay, so maybe don't have quite so many drinks next time. But honestly, Libs, you're not going to turn into your mother if you live it up for once. If anything, you'll come back *more capable* of reining in your wild side because you won't be so exhausted from always staying in control."

"I think I follow your logic, but I'm still not going to take your advice. I'm happy the way I am. Even if the love of my life left me because I'm boring." I sigh, my shoulders dropping at the truth. "Oh, God, I am totally dull, aren't I?"

"Would I hang out with someone boring?"

"I'm your cousin."

"True, but I also really like you. So does Jack. You're funny and smart and caring and…you've been through some horrid shit. So, just get out there and have some fun."

"Okay, I'll think about it."

"Thank you," she says, yawning again. "That's all I ask."

"Love you."

"Love you too. Stay safe."

We ring off, and I stare out at the sunset, thinking about Alice's words. Maybe she's right and I should let loose for once. I mean, what's the worst that could happen if I have a little fun? Not 'drink 'til you pass out' fun, but 'take a walk just outside your comfort zone' fun. Come to think of it, maybe letting out my wild side would actually be a good thing — maybe if I had done it a little more often instead of trying so hard to stay in control all the time, Richard and I would be married right now.

It's kind of the perfect place to try it — no one knows me here. Hmmm…actually, that's not true at all, is it? I'm here for work, and if I blow this, I can kiss that promotion goodbye — and quite possibly my job, too. I better bloody well keep 'Brazen Breeze' tucked away where she belongs.

Glancing to my right, I see the silhouette of a man running along the shore. He's moving quickly, with an obvious sense of determination. Is he running from a cop? Or an angry husband, maybe?

Hmmm…I don't see anyone chasing him. Maybe he's running for the sake of running. Strange.

I notice he has quite possibly the most sculpted physique I've ever seen. Maybe *that's* why he's running. Wow.

I should probably stop gawking so shamelessly, shouldn't I? *Okay, eyes, look away. He's getting closer. Seriously eyes. Look away.*

Dammit, they aren't listening. *Neck, a little help here?*

Oh, but look at those muscly arms and the way his torso is so ripped. Mmm-mmm. Nice.

Wait, is that…? Nooooo!!! It *is* him — Mr. Not-A-Gigolo.

Scrambling off the rock, I tuck behind it, hoping he hasn't

seen me already. I hold my breath and try to make myself as small as possible, crouching with my head wedged between my knees.

How long should I wait here? He was running pretty fast, so he should pass right about…

"Did you lose something?"

Oh crap. I unfold my head and give him a surprised smile. "Oh, hello. Yes, I…did…" My voice trails off because I really have no ending to that sentence.

Giving me an easy grin, he says, "What'd you lose?"

I stand, trying to look casual. Glancing down, I scramble to think of something reasonably believable that I could have lost. Nuts! Now, my sunscreen-soaked knees and shins are covered in sand. "My knees," I say with a nod.

"You thought you lost your knees?" he asks, plunking himself down on my boulder.

"Yes," I answer, bending at the waist to brush the sand off my legs. "It's all right, though. They're both exactly where they should be now. Did you notice the sunset this evening?"

"Yes. They only make 'em like this in the Caribbean. But back to your knees, do you misplace them often?"

Nodding, I say, "Once before. Scariest ten seconds of my life."

He breaks into a loud laugh, and oh, my, I had no idea that when a perfectly sculpted, shirtless man laughs, his muscles all ripple in a most pleasing way. I stare and bite my bottom lip, momentarily forgetting to be embarrassed about my knees or forlorn about my lost fiancé. Richard. Right. I have to stop gawking at Mr. Not-A-Gigolo's body.

When he stops laughing, he gives me an amused expression. "You were trying to hide from me, weren't you?"

"Maybe," I murmur.

He pats a spot on the rock next to him, gesturing for me to sit. "Come on, I won't bite. Unless…" He raises his eyebrows suggestively.

I give him a dirty look. "Trust me. I don't want you to."

"Well, in that case, sit and watch the sun go down with me."

"To be honest, I'm not really up for entertaining company at the moment."

"I promise I won't expect you to entertain me," he says, then that playful grin returns. "Your Bob Marley attempt last night took care of that."

I laugh in spite of myself. "Fine." I settle next to him, feeling the warmth of his damp skin. "So, you're a runner."

"Just when I need to burn off some extra energy." He turns his gaze to the sun, which is almost low enough to touch the water.

We sit in silence for a moment, and I find myself wondering why he needs to burn off extra energy. I'm not going to ask, though. That would sound like a come-on, and we've come dangerously close to flirting already, which is a terrible idea for someone who was supposed to be married two days ago.

"How are you feeling?" he asks.

"Really great, thanks," I say, nodding.

"Liar." He bumps my shoulder with his, causing me to feel all warm and tingly.

"Okay, I suppose I am a little hungover. A lot hungover, actually. I haven't eaten yet today. And since you asked, I guess I'm still stinging a bit about being here solo."

"So not quite 'really great.'"

"Not quite."

"In that case, maybe *I'm* here to entertain *you*." He looks down at my lips in a way that makes me swallow hard.

"Somehow I think you're very good at entertaining women," I murmur, my voice coming out all flimsy.

"Was that a euphemism?"

I straighten up my back. "No, I'd never talk about sex with a strange man. It wouldn't be proper."

"No, of course not. But don't worry, most people who know me don't find me all that strange," he says. "I have my quirks, though, like everyone else."

"Like what?"

Rubbing what looks like three-day stubble, he says, "If I tell you, it would have to be under the cone-of-silence rulebook."

"Who would I tell? You're the only person on this island I know, and come to think of it, I don't actually know you."

"Still. A man in my position can't afford to have his secrets get out." His face is deadly serious when he says this, so I'm not sure if I should laugh or not.

I squint my eyes, pretending to be taking this entire thing very seriously, just in case. "Well, if it's a horrible quirk, I suppose you could get kicked out of the Society of Mixologists. Then where'd you be?" I'm flirting, aren't I? I should really stop.

"Mixologists? Oh, right," he says. "Because of the bar." A look of understanding crosses his face.

Does he *not know* he's a bartender? Oh my God, *that's* why he's still tending bar even though I'm quite sure he's over thirty. He's a good-looking dullard. But he doesn't seem dull...

"They're a fickle bunch, the mixologists. Very exacting standards, so you can see why it's important for me to get your commitment before I tell you anything," he says with a grin. "If I'm going to share a secret with you, I'm afraid you'll have to offer one up in exchange."

"I don't have any juicy secrets. I'm afraid I'm an exceedingly boring woman."

"An exceedingly boring woman who occasionally strips down to her very sexy red underwear on the beach?"

My face flames. "Oh, that's not an occasional thing. That was unicorn-rare. It's never happened before and never will again."

"Never again? That's a shame. You seemed so happy," he says. "In that case, I'll consider myself a lucky man to have gotten a front row seat to the show."

Lucky? The show? "Wait a minute, I thought we promised not to bring that up."

"I don't remember promising that," he says.

"Then I must have forgotten to get you to promise it."

Reef laughs, then stands and picks up my sandals. "It's getting late. You must be starving by now."

I take the sandals from him, letting my fingers brush unnecessarily against his, then slide off the rock. "Oh, right. I remember you saying something about being clairvoyant last night."

"I wish. That would be a huge help in business," he says as we slowly start back toward the resort.

"Sure. You could just bring people their drinks and food without having to take their order."

"Think of the tips I'd earn."

"It would be like the best party trick ever."

Maybe it's okay if I flirt a little. I mean, *Richard* left *me*. It's not like he's back at home crying in his soup.

Bumping Reef on the arm, I say, "Okay, cone of silence. Quirk me."

He smiles down at me. "All right. This is a biggie. It's one I rarely tell anyone because the consequences are too big." He pauses, letting the tension build. "I can't stand The Beatles."

"Beetles, as in the insect, or the iconic rock 'n' roll band from the sixties?"

"The second one."

I freeze, grabbing his arm as though I need to steady myself. "No! That can't be true."

"But it is."

I let go, and we start walking again.

"Not even the brilliant 'Give Peace a Chance' by John Lennon?"

"Not even John."

"Surely you must like Paul. Everyone loves Paul."

Wrinkling up his nose a bit, he says, "He seems a little smug."

I laugh. "I can see why you don't want that to get out."

"Exactly. I mean, love of The Beatles is practically an entry requirement for bartenders."

"That, and knowing all the words to 'The Piano Man.'"

"That, too."

We walk for a moment, then I say, "Not even "Let It Be"? Really?"

"This is why I never tell anyone."

By the time we near the resort, I've found out that Reef has a younger brother who's filming some sort of adventure/nature program, a sister who's in culinary school in the states, he loves peanut butter and pickle sandwiches but only eats them when he's alone because other people are so grossed out by the combination, and he's a total insomniac who only sleeps three hours per night. Meanwhile, I've admitted to being the world's biggest ABBA fan, hating the smell of cucumber, and having watched *Bridget Jones's Diary* over twenty times.

As we walk along, I glance around, realizing how little I can actually see under the light of the low moon. It occurs to me that I'd be very uneasy making this trek alone. Huh, now that I think about it, maybe I should be uneasy making this trek with *him*. After all, he did seem like he would have slept with me when I was very drunk last night.

"Last night, were you really going to..." My voice trails off.

"Really going to what?"

"Nothing. It's just that I was very...drunk last night...and, well..."

"You're wondering if I was actually going to take advantage of you," he says.

"Yes. I'm sorry, I don't want to insult you. It's just that..." How do I word this?

"You're trying to figure out if you should be walking alone with me on a dark, deserted beach."

"Sort of. Sorry." I look up at him, trying to determine if I've totally insulted him.

"Why are you sorry? If I were you, I would want to know the exact same thing."

"Do women often take advantage of you when you're drunk?"

"They try. Believe me, they try," he says with a dramatic sigh that makes me laugh.

"You poor, poor man."

"Everyone has their cross to bear, I suppose. Mine is having women constantly trying to get me into bed," he says, his tone light. "But seriously, the answer to your question is no. Definitely not with you in that state."

"Okay, good. I didn't think so, but it seemed wise to ask." I let out a sigh of relief. "Although, if you were a predator, you wouldn't tell me you were one."

Reef stops walking and turns to me. "I suppose that's true. If I were a smarmy predator-type, I would say exactly what I just said. But in my case, I really mean it. I took you for a walk down to the beach so you could let off a little steam. My plan was to help you find your way back to your room and leave you there, alone. The way you were talking last night, you would have taken Ringo to bed if he showed some interest."

I laugh, then cover my face with both hands. "Oh, God, I'm so embarrassed. I've honestly never stripped in front of a stranger before. Or propositioned a man like that. I'm a total play-it-safe kind of girl."

He gives me a sexy look and puts on a voice that sounds very much like Nicholas Cage. "Playing it safe is just about the most dangerous thing a woman like you could do."

"Did you just quote *Moonstruck?*" I ask, my eyes growing wide.

"Maybe?" he says sheepishly.

"Oh my God, you did!" I say, laughing. "You just quoted a *Cher movie!*"

"It's an Academy Award-winning movie, thank you very much," he says, sounding a little defensive. "Anyone with a soul loves *Moonstruck*. It's one of the very few perfect films ever made."

"I totally agree. I'm just so surprised that you'd like that sort of movie."

"Why? Did you figure me for some buffoon who only likes super-hero movies?"

I pause and stare at him just long enough to confirm his suspicion, then burst out laughing at the incredulous look on his face.

"Wow. I don't think I've ever been insulted so many times in one day." He shakes his head, clearly trying to force himself to look upset. "You've assumed I'm a gigolo, or at the very least a total slut with multiple STDs, a creepy predator, and now — and possibly worst of all — that I've got horrible taste in movies."

"Sorry, I was just messing with you. About the movie thing, anyway."

He laughs as we walk up the path that leads from the beach to the resort grounds. Glancing down at me, he says, "You were wrong earlier, when you said you were boring. You're anything but."

"Thanks. And I guess you're probably not a creepy slut."

We both laugh, then when the moment ends, he gives me a look I've only seen on a movie hero's face. It's almost like he's trying to hold himself back from kissing me. I swallow hard, staring into his eyes for a second. Oh, wow. He's just so gorgeous I can hardly look at him. Oh, and I *am* in love with another man.

I quickly turn and start along the path again, and he continues beside me until we come to a fork in the path where we'll be heading in separate directions. Turning my gaze to the sidewalk, a feeling of dread sets in, knowing I'm in for an evening alone to wallow. Unless…

"Do you have to work tonight?" I blurt out.

"No, I have the night off, actually."

"Oh, that's nice," I say, suddenly realizing I should not be having dinner with an extremely attractive man, not when I'm basically still engaged, or at the very least on the rebound. Glancing down at my ring, I feel a pang of guilt. *Do not ask him to have dinner with you.* "Well, thanks for walking me back. Enjoy the rest of your evening."

"Thanks. You too," he says.

"Goodnight," I say, giving him a quick wave and turning very slowly toward my building. I mentally congratulate myself for making the right choice. Now I'll have a quiet evening of reading in the tub to look forward to. *Good for you, Libby. Smart decision. Now make your feet move.*

"Do you maybe want to eat dinner together?" His voice tells me he's still much closer than I thought he'd be by now.

I spin on my heel and nod. "I'd love that."

"Can you give me a few minutes to shower first?" He glances at my growly stomach.

Do not picture him in the shower. Do not picture him in the shower. "Sure. I should freshen up a bit, too."

"I'll pick you up in your room in, say, twenty minutes?"

"Perfect. I'm in Building A, Room 402. See you then."

He smiles again, and just the sight of it warms me from finger tips to my toes. "See you soon, Breeze."

The sound of my real name stops me in my tracks. "Oh, I forgot I told you that. I actually go by Libby now."

His smile fades. "Libby…Dewitt?"

"Yes. How did you know my last name?"

72

Holding out his hand to me, he's suddenly very stiff and formal. "I'm Harrison Banks."

———

IM conversation between Libby and Alice:

Me: *O. M. G. Turns out hot bartender is the guy who owns the resort!*

Alice: *WTF? Are you freaking kidding me?*

Me: *I wish. We met up again right after I hung up with you, then he walked me back to the resort and asked me to dinner. I said yes, against my better judgment, then we finally introduced ourselves. #totallyhumiliated*

Alice: *Did you two still go for dinner together? And exactly what does this guy look like? You said hot, but I really need a visual.*

Me: *We did not go for dinner, and I think you're missing the point. Tomorrow morning I'll be going into his office dressed in a suit, trying to convince him to sell his property. As if he's going to take me seriously after seeing me stinking drunk, then having me passed out in his bed all day. Gah! He's seen me in wet knickers!*

Alice: *Seriously, how hot is this guy?*

Me: *Crazy hot. Completely sculpted with a smile that could melt an iceberg in under a minute.*

. . .

Alice: *So, Chris Hemsworth as Thor?*

Me: *Affirmative. Oh, Alice, what the hell am I going to do?*

Alice: *Pretend none of it ever happened. Just go in, be professional, and get the job done.*

Me: *I guess that could work.*

Alice: *It'll have to work. If he brings it up, just laugh it off and make up something about that being Vacation Libby and now you're Business Libby.*

Me: *You make me sound like a Barbie doll.*

Alice: *It's the best I can do at 5 AM when I've only had four hours of sleep in the last two nights.*

Me: *Remind me never to have kids.*

Alice: *Never have kids. Speaking of which, Colby just woke up so I'm on duty.*

Me: *Good luck with that. I hope you manage to get a nap.*

Alice: *Thanks. Good luck with your meeting! Just be breezy about it. ;) ;)*

10

Thinking Outside the Box. Way Outside

Libby

EMAIL FROM QUENTIN ATLAS TO LIBBY DEWITT
  RE: Progress Update

Libby,
  I trust your first few days at Paradise Bay have been going well, and that you aren't allowing your situation with Richard to interfere with your work. I've set up a call with you at 10 AM my time to get your progress report and see if you require any ground support.
  Regards,
  Quentin

"You sound tired, Libby. Have you been out partying too hard down there?" Quentin laughs.

"No, it's just that it's 3 AM here, so I set my alarm for this call." I do my best not to sound completely annoyed.

"Oh, well, I figured you wouldn't be asleep at this hour anyway. Who goes to bed before three on a vacation? Am I right?"

"Totally. It would be crazy for someone to go to bed by, say, eleven, when they could be out partying." I really shouldn't be sarcastic with my boss, especially when I'm definitely *not* the front-runner for the senior analyst job that's opening up at the end of the year. But Quentin has a talent for bringing out the snark in me, day or night.

Did I mention that the promotion is not only a move up, but would also get me out from under Quentin (which I quite obviously need to be)? If I can get on the senior team, I'd have a chance to cut deals with much bigger properties (which means much bigger bonuses), and I'd get to work under the queen of Mergers & Acquisitions, Karen Crawford. She was named one of the "Five Powerhouse M&A Superstars in 2017" by Forbes and is sort of my idol when it comes to analytics. Everybody respects Karen, and if you're on her team, the world is a much kinder place (read: no Quentin).

The problem is I'm up against four other analysts for the job, including Alan the Architect (that's what they call him because wherever they send him, he designs the perfect deal). He's closed on four resorts over the last year while I've managed two, but also had two deals go bad. (I can't prove it, but I'm pretty sure Alan and Quentin set me up for failure on at least one of those, sending me to a place that the head office really wanted to acquire but they both knew was dead in the water.)

"Great news. Alan's back already from Atlantis Cove."

"His poor wife. I'm sure she was hoping it would take another few months."

"Ha ha ha! She got you good, Alan!"

Dammit! Alan's there? I close my eyes while my face heats up. "Hey, Alan! I thought I heard you on the line, so I figured I'd have a go. Hope you don't mind."

"Nah, not at all," he says, his voice booming too close to the speakerphone. "You're right about the old ball and chain, though. She was annoyed when I surprised her last night, but to be fair, I did wake her up by playing "We Will Rock You" by Queen at full volume." He bursts out laughing, and I distinctly hear Quentin chuckling along as well. Lovely. "Hey, a guy's gotta celebrate his success, right, Libby?"

"Righto, Alan," I say while trying not to gag.

Quentin finally cuts in. "So, Libby, since Alan is a total shark, I figured I better bring him in on this call so he can tell you how he did it."

"Super!" I say, cringing. "Thanks, Alan."

"Happy to help any way I can…even if, say, you need someone to come down there to help lather on your sunscreen."

Eww!

The sound of laughter fills the line again, but then I hear Quentin murmur something about 'me too' and Alan say something that sounds like 'right, shit' before he says into the speakerphone, "I was just kidding. You know that, right, Libs?"

"Of course." I yawn and blink slowly as I stare at my computer screen in the darkened room.

"All right, Libby, do you have a pen and paper to jot this down?" Quentin says.

"I have a Word doc open on my laptop. Go ahead, Alan."

"Brilliant. So, basically, this is what I do: I hang around for a few days checking everything out — the restaurants and bars and all that. Then I get the owner shit-faced drunk, sometimes up to three nights in a row, which leads him to admitting some gold nugget of information. The trick is when you're out drinking, you got to pretend you hate your job, or your wife, or both — pretty much whatever he hates — so he'll start to trust you and unload all kinds of private stuff."

"Gotcha. Get owner very drunk, pretend to have mutual dislike for a spouse, boss, etc.…." On my laptop, I'm typing, 'Alan the Arse-chitect is a blowhard.'

"Yup. You're a quick study. But here's where the brilliant part comes in — once I get the guy talking, I tell him some lie, like I got a DUI or spent some time in prison for assault, that kind of thing. This gets him to unload some big secret. This last one actually admitted he hasn't paid his back taxes in three years, and he's so far overdue, his wife'll leave him if she finds out."

"What a moron," Quentin says.

"Totally, right? He never should have told me that."

"Definitely not," I say, trying to sound dazzled instead of disgusted.

"So, the next morning, when he's super hungover, I go see him and tell him I'll report him if he doesn't do the deal. Done and done!"

"Five days—a new record," Quentin adds, his pride evident.

"Brilliant, Alan. So, let me just recap your strategy to make sure I've got it: You get the property owner super drunk several times until he admits something you can then use to extort him into selling."

Alan says, "Yes" at the same time Quentin says, "No, no, no. Not *extortion*, Libby. Don't write that down, okay? Do *not* write that word down. Nobody wants you to extort anybody. Alan here is just demonstrating that he's thinking outside the box when it comes to getting the deal done. That's why he's closed four in a row while you've only managed two. But if you don't need his advice, we should just let you go you can get back to sleep." The way he says it, it's as though sleep is the most preposterous idea anyone could have at three in the morning.

You need to keep your job, Libby. You need to keep your job. You have already possibly lost your fiancé and your home. Do not lose your job on top of that. "Sorry, I didn't mean to sound ungrateful for your time and advice. I was just a little confused. But point taken, Quentin. I need to think outside the box, get close to the owner, and use whatever inside edge I can."

"Exactly. Whatever edge you can," Quentin says.

"Got it. Will do."

"Are you sure? Because I could have Alan down there within twenty-four hours to take over if you don't think you can close this one. Paradise Bay is going to be our gateway to the Benavente Islands. It's crucial that you make this deal happen."

"Not to worry, I've got a really great feeling about this one. In fact, I've already been drinking with the owner."

"Seriously?" Quentin asks, bordering on sounding impressed.

"Oh yeah. We got totally hammered the first night I was here. Hit the beach, even."

"And here I thought you would've been crying by the pool for the first two days."

"Because of that whole wedding thing?" I scoff. "God, no. I've never been better. Okay, well, thanks for the tips, guys. If you don't have anything else to add, I'll let you get on with your day so I can get back at it."

Did that sound confident? Christ, I hope so because there is absolutely no way I can put up with having Alan offer to rub sunblock on my back for the next few weeks.

"All right, we'll let you go," Quentin says. "Just keep me updated every couple of days, okay?"

"And seriously, Libs, if you need me, I'll be there," Alan adds.

"Thanks for the offer, Alan, but I promise I won't need to take you up on it." With that, I ring off.

I growl and snap my laptop shut, then get up and storm over to the mini-bar. Grabbing a half-litre bottle of champagne, I pop the cork and take a long swig without bothering to pour it into a glass. The bubbling rage in my gut blends with the cold liquid, and instead of popping the anger bubbles, the champagne causes them to multiply.

Somehow that giant bell-end Alan, who doesn't know a spreadsheet from a sheet of arse wipe, manages to best me at every turn. I take another drink, cursing the injustice of the world.

My stomach churns as I think about how far I am from closing the deal. For one, Harrison never responded to my phone calls or correspondence. And despite what Alice said, after the drunken, almost-naked Breeze debacle, I'm pretty sure he'll never take me seriously. I'm certainly not going to lower myself to extortion, but I *do* have to find a way to get Harrison Banks to see reason and agree to sell Paradise Bay so I can go home and get my life back.

I walk over to the patio door and slide it open, then step out onto the balcony. Leaning against the railing, I stare out at the night sky, noticing how much brighter the stars are here than in Valcourt. I watch as some clouds pass by the big round moon and start to feel a sense of calm settling in. The warm breeze fills my nostrils with a flowery scent and dances across my skin, assuring me that I'll figure this out, just like I always do. I won't fail. I'm not a failure. I'll figure out a plan, and it will work.

A splashing sound distracts me, and when I look down, I see a man swimming in the pool in front of my building. I watch him while he cuts through the water with perfect form. Oh my…that's Harrison.

I watch him long enough for my thoughts to cross over from admiration to creepy woman on the prowl, then wonder what he's doing swimming at this hour, especially after doing all that running earlier. For someone who seems so carefree, he obviously has something that keeps him awake half the night. All I need to do is find out what it is and hope I can use it against him.

11

No Means No, Ladies...

Harrison

JUST WHEN I meet a cute girl I actually enjoy talking to, it turns out she wants to screw me, but not the fun way. We didn't go to dinner last night. The moment we introduced ourselves, things got awkward. We both just stood and stared at each other for about twenty seconds before either of us said anything.

She was the first to call off our evening's plan, saying, "You know, now that I think about it, I should probably get some rest so I can be at my best for our meeting tomorrow morning."

"Sure, yeah. Have a good night, Ms. Dewitt."

"You too, Mr. Banks."

So now I'm in my office, it's 9 a.m., and I'm just finishing my second cup of coffee while I try to figure out the most polite way to tell Libby Dewitt to P.F.O., because no matter how sexy she is in red lacy underwear, there is absolutely no way she's getting her hands into my file cabinets.

I get up from my desk, brushing past the enormous potted palm Rosy had brought in 'to make me feel more like I'm outside.' I stand at the window, staring out at the carefully manicured grounds surrounding the building that holds both the lobby and the main offices.

I watch as Victor, our head gardener, teaches one of our new members of the landscape crew, Marcela, how to trim back a jasmine shrub. He patiently points to a spot she missed, bringing back memories of when I worked under him as a teenager. I can remember his quiet, reassuring voice as he showed me what to cut and what to leave. He was never hurried and took the time to show me how to correct my mistakes, instead of just doing it for me. I learned so much more from him than gardening — he taught me about patience and how to be a good leader. Nostalgia gives way to a sense of dread, and my chest feels tight at the thought of losing this place. Victor is closing in on seventy, so I doubt a big company would keep him around long, even though he has a lot left to give.

There's a knock at the door, and I hurry back over to my desk to sit down and pick up a pen before I call, "Come in."

Rosy opens the door, giving me a quizzical look. "There's a woman here from GlobalLux?"

"Thanks, Rosy. Please show her in."

She narrows her eyes at me and doesn't make a move.

"I'll explain later," I murmur.

"Fine." Stepping to the side, she lets Libby into my office.

Today, Ms. Dewitt is dressed exactly as I expected — dark grey pencil skirt, white button-up blouse (with too many buttons done up), and a suit jacket that matches the skirt. Black, close-toed heels and a tight bun finish off the serious businesswoman look. Between you and me, it's sexy as hell, and part of me regrets throwing on a rumpled T-shirt to show her how little I care about this meeting.

Having been taught some basics in chivalry by Uncle Oscar, I stand and walk to the front of my desk to greet her. "Ms. Dewitt, I trust you slept well last night?"

She gives me a small nod, and an even smaller smile as she moves in the direction of the chair in front of my desk. "Just fine, thank you. I trust you didn't sleep at all, Mr. Banks?"

She's referring to my admission that I'm an insomniac, which in hindsight, I wish she didn't know. "Actually, I slept like a log last night for a change," I lie. I was up most of the night — in fact, I even went for a 3 a.m. swim.

Wanting to get some space in-between us, I sit back behind my desk again and wait while she fumbles with the clasp on her leather briefcase. Part of me feels sorry for her — she's trying so hard to be professional even though we both know there's very little chance I'll be able to stop thinking of her *breezy side*, if you get my drift.

Oh damn. Now her cheeks are turning bright pink. She's embarrassed. I instinctively want to let her off the hook by saying something encouraging, but strategically, that seems like a foolish move. I have to stop thinking of her as the cute redhead who played the starring role in my dreams when I finally fell asleep last night.

Note to self: She's the devil incarnate. The devil in light pink glossy lipstick that brings out those lusciously full lips. The devil with makeup that doesn't quite hide those adorable freckles across her nose. The devil whose cowardly fiancé jilted her at the altar. But the devil, nonetheless.

She finally succeeds in getting her attaché open and pulls out a wad of papers, looking momentarily relieved. "So, Mr. Banks, as you know, I've had a couple of days here at Paradise Bay to get a sense of the resort and what you have to offer. Although I haven't taken the opportunity to go on any excursions, utilize any of the spa treatments, or try out the à la carte restaurants yet, already from what I've seen, I'm certain that the property would benefit greatly from having the backing of the world's leading luxury hotel chain."

She gives me a confident smile and a little nod, but her smile quickly fades as she takes in the dead-eyed look I'm giving her.

Clearing her throat, she says, "Yes, umm, well, I've prepared a packet for you detailing GlobalLux's purchasing process, FAQs, as well as the employee handbook and benefits package so you can see your staff will be in good hands should you decide to sell."

She holds out the packet, but instead of politely accepting it, I sit back in my chair, clasping my hands behind my head. It's a bit of a prick move, but sometimes it's best to let your body do the talking, and right now, my body is saying a pretty strong "hell no" on my behalf.

"You can read that at your leisure," she says, placing the packet on my desk. Then she sighs. "Listen, I know how difficult this can be. I mean, I don't know from personal experience, but I *can* put myself in your shoes and I know I'd be hesitant about handing my family's property over to some faceless corporation. So I'd like you to think of *me* as the face of GlobalLux, because, should you chose to partner with us, I'll be with you the entire way." She smiles again, then fidgets a little. "Unless you don't want me here, that is. If you wanted someone else, I can definitely make that happen. But if you want me, I could be here."

"Nothing personal, Ms. Dewitt, but I really don't want you here." Another lie. I absolutely do want her here, so badly I can almost taste it.

Come on, brain, do not think about what she would taste like. That's a massive mistake.

Damn, now she looks sad, and all I want to do is make her smile again. I soften my tone a bit. "I assure you, Paradise Bay is doing just fine on its own. We really don't need anybody to back us."

"Sometimes when a person is too close to a situation, we see what we want to, instead of what is real," she says, her voice quiet. "Paradise Bay has been losing money for some time now. I'm not saying it's anyone's fault. The Benavente Islands were hit particularly hard by last year's hurricane season. Couple that with the recent economic downturn, and it's sort of a recipe for disaster, really."

"Not for us."

"Harrison, I know about the loan on the property, and I understand that up until last weekend, you were two months behind on your payments. Inexplicably, you've managed to get caught up, which I'm sure is a well-timed relief. But the turnaround isn't likely to last. Not at the rate things are going.

"In my few short days of being here, I already noticed four pretty major inefficiencies that are robbing you of profits. And that's without me opening the books or doing any type of real assessment of your processes. Those were just my observations during the check-in procedure and, well, at the beach bar."

I raise an eyebrow and smirk a little at the thought of her

managing to assess anything at the bar other than the quality of rum used in our piña coladas.

She must be able to read my mind because she adds, "*Before* I started drinking the other night."

"Listen, Libby, I have no doubt that you're a highly intelligent, very organized, competent person. I'm sure you're very good at your job, and if given the opportunity, you could streamline the hell out of this place. But I like things the way they are around here, and more importantly, so do the staff and our many return guests. Things you may see as 'inefficiencies' might actually be why people come back to Paradise Bay every year," I say, looking her straight in the eye as I talk. "You may not be able to see that because you're a numbers person, but when I walk around out there, I see the opportunity to give my staff a good living and a great place to work until they retire, and I know we're giving our guests a truly memorable experience — not the kind of one-size-fits-all, 'what was the name of that resort we stayed at last year, honey' sort of place. I know big corporations like yours don't see the value in that, which is why, no matter what you offer me, GlobalPutz cannot have this place."

I finish on a confident note, despite the GlobalPutz dig (which I know was childish, but I couldn't help myself). Although I know she's not going to just pick up and leave like I want her to (sort of), I don't expect what comes next.

Setting her shoulders back and crossing her legs, she says, "With all due respect, Mr. Banks, what I see is someone who's trying so hard to hold on to his home that he's got a horrible case of tunnel vision."

I open my mouth to object, but she raises her hand to stop me and continues.

"If you don't get with the times — and trust me, you aren't — you'll end up losing everything. So, you can either take what I'm offering, which is your very last opportunity to sell and have something left for yourself and your family, or you can choose to keep your blinders on and hope for the best over the next eight to ten months max while you sink deeper and deeper into debt. But by then, I'll have moved on to another property, the bank will own everything, and you'll walk away with nothing."

Well played, devil woman. Well played. Now that she brought up my family and painted such a grim picture of our future, it would be ridiculously short-sighted of me to not at least see what the offer is. But I'm one step ahead of her. "If you're so sure the end is coming, why not just wait for me to go bankrupt? Why would your company waste time on this now, only to spend a lot more than you need to buy up my property?"

"Because GlobalLux is looking to expand into the Caribbean *now*. It's our belief that the smart money is to get in during the aftereffects of Irma, turn things around, and within fifteen months, have this place making a tidy profit. Harrison, I'm offering you a great opportunity, and I promise if I didn't believe what I was saying, I wouldn't be here. If you take us up on our offer, it'll benefit you as well as your employees."

"Sorry, but I'm not buying that one. I highly doubt you or your corporation could give two craps about the people here. It's all dollars and cents to you. You said it yourself, you're going to have this place turning a profit in nine months. How exactly are you going to do that? It's the whole 'do more with less' thing that grinds people into the ground," I say with disgust. "I may be foolish to think I can keep things going, but I'd rather go down fighting then just lay down and die."

"I'm not asking you to lay down and die. I'm asking you to say yes to what could be the greatest opportunity of your life. I could make you rich, Harrison, your brother and sister, too. After all, isn't that what your uncle would have wanted for you?"

Whatever goodwill I ever held toward this woman has now vanished. "I really don't think you're qualified to know what my uncle would have wanted—or what *I* want, for that matter," I say, my tone sharp. "You don't know me, Ms. Dewitt, because if you did, you'd know I'd never sell my soul — or the people I care about — no matter the price."

Her eyes fill with regret and she opens her mouth to speak, but I stand quickly and cut her off. "I don't want to lead you on here. The answer is no. Not maybe. Not we'll see. It's one hundred percent no. So, we're done here. You're welcome to stay and enjoy the rest of your non-honeymoon, or you can pack up and head back home today. It makes no difference to me."

Libby stands and picks up her briefcase, avoiding eye contact with me. "I'm sorry to hear that. I think this is a huge mistake."

"That very well may be, but it's my mistake to make," I say, walking toward the door.

When I open it, I see a very happy but tired looking Fidel poised to knock. Next to him is his wife, Winnie, who started working here as a receptionist when she finished college.

Fidel smiles. "Hey, Reef, would you like to meet my son?"

I look down to see a tiny bundle of human in Winnie's arms. He has huge brown eyes, chubby cheeks, and thick black hair sticking up in every direction. "Well, you're not cute at all, are you?"

"Here, hold him," Fidel says.

Winnie hands the little guy to me before I can tell him I'm not used to babies.

Once he settles in the crook of my arm, I go from feeling completely agitated to calm and happy in an instant. Huh, who knew babies were magic? I gently pick up his tiny hand with my thumb and forefinger, only to have him make a fist around my thumb. "Nice grip, kid."

Winnie comes to stand by me, and I lean down to give her a kiss on the cheek. "Congratulations, Win. You look great."

"No, I don't. I look like an exhausted whale."

Shaking my head, I say, "Your mirror must be broken because you look like a happy new mum."

"Hello," Libby says, looking over my shoulder at the baby. "Oh, he's absolutely perfect."

"He is, isn't he?" Fidel says with a wide grin. "I'm Fidel. Are you a new hire?"

Libby shakes her head. "No."

"Too bad. You should hire her, Reef," Winnie says. "She seems to have a good eye for perfection."

Libby laughs, and I find myself smiling at the sound of it. Jesus, between turning to mush over a newborn and letting myself get all affected by a woman, I'm really starting to lose it.

"Oh, sorry. Allow me to do the introductions," Fidel says, trying to sound very formal. "Harrison Banks, meet Harrison Malcolm LeCroix."

My head snaps back in surprise, and when I look down again at little Harrison Malcolm, I can't help but feel a lump in my throat. I clear it away and say, "You named him after…"

"The original actor who played Han Solo, yes," Fidel answers.

"Fidel!" Winnie says, sounding slightly irritated. She turns to me. "We named him after *you*, Harrison. We wanted to thank you for everything you've done for us over the years."

"Well, this is…" I blow out a big sigh, unable to finish that thought. Instead, I say, "It's one hell of a smart way to ask for a raise."

12

Shake Those Money-Makers, Girls (A.K.A. The Desperate Girl's Guide to Mergers and Acquisitions)

Libby

FOR THE PAST HOUR, I've been sitting on my balcony nursing a Corona and picking at some insanely delicious salty fries I grabbed down at the burger bar while I try to figure out what my next move should be. Unfortunately, I'm coming up blank.

Granted, I have been distracted. The sight of Harrison holding that adorable baby made me all gooey inside, and that image keeps popping into my head and muddling my thoughts.

Dammit. I swear it's easier to be a man. Alan would certainly never have this problem — going all gaga over seeing a man holding a baby. A sculpted, gorgeous, strong, stubborn, principled man...

Focus, Libby!

I need to hatch a plan to save my career, because I seriously cannot go home without closing this deal. First of all, if I don't manage it, I can pretty much kiss my leapfrog off Quentin's team good-bye, and without that, my past few years of work at GlobalLux will have been for nothing. There's no way I can handle Quentin's crap much longer, which means I'll need to find a new job and start at the bottom rung of the corporate ladder. Again. Second, if Richard and I really don't get back together, the home I can afford and the one I want to live in will be drastically different, especially if I'm job-hunting instead of cashing a bonus cheque. Third, and quite possibly the worst thought at the moment (even though it shouldn't be), is that if I can't even convince Harrison to *at least* let me to do an assessment of his resort, it would be an all-time low for anyone in our department. Alan and Quentin will never let me live it down. The buggers.

Think, Libby, think.

Okay, what would Alan do?

Oh Christ, I'm clearly desperate if I'm using Alan as the new gold standard of decision-making. I have to go back to the basics. Business is all about relationships. It's about two people who need something from each other who find a way to exchange goods or services in order to satisfy both of their needs. All I have to do is figure out what I have that Harrison wants.

I grab a pen and a blank piece of paper out of my briefcase and jot down HARRISON at the top of the page. Drawing a line down the centre, I write ME on the other side of the line. Under his name, I write, 'Wants to keep resort.' On the other side, I write, 'Wants to keep job.'

Oh, you're a regular brain surgeon, there, Libby.

Crumpling up the paper, I toss it in the bin and grab a new sheet. Let's try a different angle...what are Harrison's weaknesses and how I can use those against him?

I jot down HARRISON'S WEAKNESSES at the top. He really liked seeing me in my red undies down at the beach. I write 'Me in lacy knickers' and stare at it for second. Honestly at this moment, I'm not entirely certain I *wouldn't* put that offer out there.

Oh my God, have some dignity, Libby!

I tap my pen against my lips as I think. He definitely has a hero complex — he did, after all, save me from myself the other night. Two nights in a row, really.

I write down, 'Hero complex.'

And that adorable baby. That baby and his parents matter to Harrison, too. 'Attachment to Staff.'

All at once, a solid plan comes flooding into my brain. I stand, causing the chair to scrape loudly against the concrete balcony, and gather up my things. I catch my reflection in the sliding glass door and smile at the woman who finally knows exactly what to do.

Now I just have to find him.

———

Okay, so finding Harrison was a lot harder than I thought. This resort is *enormous* and I've been wandering around for over forty-five minutes in the blistering heat. I'm now dripping with sweat, and even though I have an SPF 100 zinc oxide sunscreen covering every bit of exposed skin, I am definitely going to burn.

In my excitement, I threw on my turquoise bikini and a sarong so I could try to 'use what I've got.' I figured I might as well attempt to turn his brain to mush too, since he had the nerve to look so dreamy holding that newborn.

If I could only find the damn guy…

I've asked just about everyone in the Paradise Bay uniform of a white golf shirt and khaki shorts if they know where Harrison might be, but apparently, he's as elusive to them as he is to me. Either that or he has so many strange women asking about him that they've learned not to tell.

I make my way down to the excursion desk, which is located next to the one of the swimming pools, but no one is there. I stand for a moment, tapping my fingernails on the counter, then I notice a clipboard sitting right out in the open where anyone could read it. It's today's schedule for all of the boats and tours. There's a sunset cruise leaving in five minutes and the captain listed is none other than Harrison himself.

"Gotcha," I mutter as I hurry off in the direction of the resort pier.

I arrive just as a young man is starting to lift the ramp connecting the catamaran to the pier.

"Is there room for one more?" I call to him.

He smiles and gives me a nod while he lowers the ramp. "You just made it. It must be your lucky day."

"Let's hope so," I answer.

He offers me his hand to help me climb aboard, and I accept, noting that his name tag reads 'Justin.' Feeling slightly unsteady as the catamaran rocks a little with the tide, I look around and see there's a surprisingly small group of people aboard — all couples, of course. Blech. One pair has already claimed spots on the net. They lay there cuddling and smiling at each other as the boat pulls away from the dock. I quickly find a spot to sit down and look around but don't see any sign of Harrison.

Before long, Justin offers me a beverage. He holds a cooler open so I can choose for myself. Channeling my inner Alan, I grab two cans of Corona. "Thanks. Say, where does the captain do all his... captaining from?" I ask, cringing inwardly at the fact that I can't think of the actual terminology.

"Up those steps," he says, pointing to my right.

"Do you think it would be okay if I go up and say hi?"

"Yes, you're exactly the kind of guest he likes."

I squint my eyes. "How so?"

"You're pretty and you like beer."

Something about the way Justin says this bothers me, even though it shouldn't. And if I were smart, I'd use this knowledge to my advantage instead of wondering if it means Harrison found a different beer-drinking, pretty woman to keep him company last night. "Well, maybe I'll go up and say hello then..."

I stand and grab hold of the railing as I make my way to the steep staircase. Checking my bikini top to make sure everything's where it should be, I then adjust my sarong and do a quick breath audit. Passable. This is about as good as it gets for me. Glancing down at my chest, I mutter to myself, "All right girls, at the moment, you're all I've got."

Well, that's not true. I have my brains...and these beers, so let's go give this a try.

When I reach the top deck, I give myself a second to take it all in — the crystal-clear water, the late day sun hanging low in the sky, and the very shirtless, very chiseled man behind the wheel, who is barefoot in a pair of low-slung swim trunks. He's got a ball cap on, which gives him a laid-back, sporty look. He turns with a smile that fades as soon as he realizes who I am.

"Hi, Harrison." I steady myself as I walk over to him. Then, trying to look very relaxed, I grip the railing just to the left of where he's standing. "Peace offering?" I say, holding up one of the beers.

"What's the fine print?" he asks, glancing down at the Corona, and if I'm not mistaken, his eyes are also doing a little bit of a swipe across my chest.

"No fine print. But it does come with an apology. I shouldn't have suggested that I knew what your uncle would want. Or you. You were right, I don't really know you at all."

For a moment, I worry he won't accept my apology, and I feel my throat start to tighten. Then Harrison reaches out to take the drink, his fingers touching mine for the briefest of seconds. I exhale as he cracks it open, then takes a swig of beer. "You're not going to change my mind, so you might as well quit now."

"You mentioned that earlier," I answer with a playful grin. Letting my smile fade, I say, "You're not like the other owners I've met."

"No? What are they like?"

"Well, none of them have employees who name their firstborn after them, so that should give you a bit of an idea."

His face turns a bit red and he looks slightly embarrassed. "That's not exactly a regular occurrence around here. I actually don't think they should have done that. I'll make a terrible role model."

I chuckle a little at his self-deprecating remark. Clearing my throat, I say, "It helped me understand how much you care about your employees and vice versa. It also made me realize how much is at stake for you."

"Which is why I hope you can see I'm never going to sell."

"Not even if we were their last resort?" I ask, then add, "No pun intended."

He looks out to the horizon as he turns the wheel slightly with one hand. "You're not our last resort."

"And you're willing to gamble the future of everyone you care about on that?"

"It's not a gamble. I've been here for over twenty years, and you've been here for three days. Between the two of us, I'd say that makes me the expert in what is and isn't good for Paradise Bay."

"Fair enough. You do know more about this resort than probably anyone. But between you and me, I'd say I'm the expert when it comes to the hotel and resort industry around the world, and that matters. You can't ignore the changes that are happening everywhere else — not if you want to stay afloat," I say.

"I knew I never should've accepted the beer."

I give him a small smile. "What if I make a deal with you, completely off the record, both of us agreeing to go total cone of silence on it?"

"I hope you didn't think you could throw on a bikini, bring me a beer, and I'd hand over the keys to the resort," he says. "Because if you think I'm that much of a cliché, that would be more insulting than thinking I have terrible taste in movies."

Why, yes, actually. That was phase one of my four-part plan. Shaking my head, I do my best to look shocked. "Of course not. I know you're much smarter than that. And I completely respect why you turned me down earlier, too."

"But?" he asks with one eyebrow raised.

"But, what if I promise that at the end of my assessment, if I think your people are better off with *you* as the owner and I can find a way for you to turn things around without needing the backing of GlobalLux, I promise to tell you — full disclosure, not holding *anything* back. I'll even give you a copy of my report, including plans for fixing every inefficiency I find. That's a hell of a deal, by the way. If you hired an independent analyst to come in and do that, it would cost you over 30,000 pounds." I stop while I'm ahead (I hope).

He narrows his eyes. "Why would you do any of that for me?"

Here's the part where I have to channel my inner-Alan and try not to throw up. "Because I need you as much as you need me. If I can't get you to at least agree to the assessment, I'll lose my job, which, now that I think of it, will go well with my no husband and no home." I chuckle a little at my own dark joke.

A look of sympathy softens his hard edges, but only for the slightest second before he throws the wall back up.

"If I can't go home having convinced you to *at least* let me do a preliminary assessment, it means I'm shit at my job. And to really lay it all out there, my last two deals didn't exactly work out, so you're my strike three."

I hold my breath while I wait for him to respond. His shoulders drop, and I know that I'm getting closer to hitting my mark. He stares at me for a long moment, his eyes searching for the truth.

"You have my word, Harrison." I place one hand over my chest. "I'm just asking for a chance to do my job, that's all. There is literally no risk here at all for you. Not even a hint of a risk. You're not committing to sell, just giving me a chance to help you figure out what's really best for Paradise Bay."

He sips his beer, making me wait for a reaction. "And you'll *actually* tell me the truth? If you come to the conclusion that the resort is better off *with me*, you'll say so?"

I lift my hand, palm out. "My hand to God. If I believe your property will be better off without GlobalLux, the report is yours and I go away forever. It's a no-lose situation, Harrison. You should take me up on it."

"And what if you don't think the resort is viable on its own?"

Ready. Aim. Fire. "Then I'll make sure the offer I recommend will be so generous, your family and staff are taken care of."

I swallow, praying for a yes that I don't get. Instead, he gives me a hard look. "How do I know I can trust you?"

I look up, trying to think of a good reason. "Because I haven't told a soul about your Beatles thing."

Chuckling, he says, "That's only because I have some pretty juicy knowledge about you."

"Another reason to trust me." I smile and blink, trying not to notice how the setting sun is bringing out the green flecks in his eyes.

He takes a long drag of his beer, then gives me a roguish smile. "Okay. I'll let you have a peek inside my files."

"Really?" I squeal, hugging him before I can think better of it.

Oh my, but that's a nice hard, naked torso. And the way he smells, it's like soap and delicious male. *No, Vacation Libby, no!*

I quickly pull back and lower my voice, trying for a sophisticated look. "I mean, brilliant. You won't regret it."

Much better. Well done, Business Libby. You got a yes.

He gazes down at me and his eyes flick to my mouth for a second. "It's almost not fair, you know."

"Why's that?" I say, my voice sounding much breathier than I intend.

"Because I'm going to show you such a good time, you'll be willing to agree to anything just to stay a little longer."

"Go ahead. Do your worst."

———

Apparently, his worst is pretty damn impressive. About a minute after we made the deal, he stopped the catamaran, anchored it, threw on a snorkelling mask, then dove into the water, coming back up a minute later with a lobster in each hand. Then, he repeated this until he had one for each guest. And I have to say, seeing him climb back aboard that boat all wet almost made everything I've gone through up to this point worth it because — *ha cha cha wow*. There are no words to describe it.

The atmosphere on the boat turned into a bit of a party, with the music turned up and another round of drinks served while Harrison made us the best tasting lobster of all time. He boiled them right there, then added a bit of pepper and a sprinkling of lime. Justin plated rice and warm cheese biscuits, with tiny cups of melted butter, before Harrison added the main event. Maybe it was the beer or the sunset, or the fact that Harrison said yes, but I honestly can't remember a better meal in my life.

He sat next to me on a soft bench while we ate. "How's this meal for cost-efficient?" he asked.

I gave him a grin. "What's the fuel efficiency on this beast?"

Harrison shook his head and laughed. "You're going to give me a run for my money, aren't you?"

"I just might."

Now I'm back in my room, wide awake even though it's well after midnight. I feel all giddy and stupidly happy. Then I feel horribly guilty for feeling stupidly happy because – let's be real here – it has very little to do with me getting him to agree to the deal and much more about the man who said yes. But, please don't judge me too harshly. I'm sure it's just a reaction to being so utterly rejected at that church the other day. I'm clearly in need of a major ego boost, and the way Harrison looks at me is *definitely* enough to boost the hell out of any girl's ego.

I let out an exasperated sigh, then grab my phone and scroll through my pictures. While we were eating, Justin grabbed my phone and said, "Let's make everyone back home jealous."

He snapped a few photos of me sitting next to Harrison, our delicious meals on our laps, the orange and blue sky behind us. With the angle of the shots, I actually don't look bad in my bikini. In one of the pics, I'm laughing because Harrison just said, "Say Breeze!"

I stare at his gorgeous face, and the thought pops into my mind that I could literally stare at that face forever. But that's a crazy, confused thought. I'm just transferring romantic feelings from Richard onto Harrison. It means nothing.

But, if I'm smart, I could use this to activate the 'I want what I can't have' response in Richard. Yup. That's what I should do. Before I overthink it, I post the pic on Instagram with the caption 'Dinner in Paradise #happiness.'

Putting my phone on the pillow next to mine, I close my eyes and wait for sleep to come.

––––––

Text from Alice to me: *Holy spitballs! Just saw your IG post. Is that HIM?!?*

· · ·

Me: *Yes, ma'am.*

Alice: *Forget Dick and marry him IMMEDIATELY so you can make gorgeous babies. Also, does he have a brother? Jack really pissed me off last night, and I wouldn't mind relocating to the other side of the planet with the kids.*

Me: *There's seriously nothing going on between us. It's just business with a side order of using him to make Richard jealous. Could work, right? Also, oh no! What did Jack do?*

Alice: *Completely forgot our anniversary and came home from work expecting dinner on the table instead of "surprising" me with our usual dinner at Chez Lawrence.*

Me: *Oh. Doghouse time.*

Alice: *Yeah. Indefinite stay in Maison de Dog for him.*

Me: *Oooh! Fly here and hang out with me for the next week!*

Alice: *SO tempting. But here's my week: Take Maisie for vaccinations tomorrow, volunteer at Colby's play-school class on Wednesday afternoon, then cut up enough orange slices for his entire tot football team and get him to practice by five p.m., Music Together class on Thursday morning with both kids, and round out the week by hosting a four-course dinner for the oral surgery partners and their wives to celebrate their ten-year anniversary (do you see the irony there? Because my husband doesn't).*

· · ·

Me: *In that case, DEFINITELY get on a plane immediately and come.*

Alice: *Only if Hot Harrison has a single brother who loves children (and has a chiseled bod).*

Me: *I'll have to get back to you on that.*

Alice: *Please do.*

13

Breezy Breeze and Dolphins with No Sense of Shame

Harrison

"I'm coming home," Emma says for the third time in the two minutes since she called.

I'm standing in my bathroom, dripping wet from the shower, drying myself off while I simultaneously try to calm my hyper sister down. Glancing at the clock, I see I have exactly six minutes to dress and be all the way on the other side of the resort if I'm going to beat Libby to my office. And I absolutely *must* get there before she does because if Rosy greets her, everything could fall apart. I haven't exactly had a chance to tell her about the whole GlobalLux thing, and Rosy isn't the kind of person who embraces change easily. She *is* the kind of person who will chase off anyone she thinks is a threat, though, and she won't be nice about it.

"There's no reason for you to come back. Seriously, I've got it handled, Emma, and there's absolutely no way I'm letting you give up your dream just because there's a teeny financial squeeze at the moment." I toss my towel onto the floor and grab my boxer briefs off the counter.

"A teeny financial squeeze? Are you kidding me right now? I know it's much worse than that because nothing short of bankruptcy could ever make you sell Matilda to Stogie Stew."

I wince, then curse under my breath. "I take it Wikileaks called you?" Pulling my polo shirt over my head, I then quickly slide my arms through and reach for my bottle of cologne.

"*I* called *her*. Unlike Will, I feel like I owe it to Rosy to stay in touch."

I'm not even going to touch that one — Emma and Will butt heads like a couple of mountain goats. Something about being a year apart and complete opposites seems to have doomed their relationship. "Listen, I have to run. I need to be over at the office in about half a minute. Just promise me you're not going to do something stupid like quit school."

"I'm not going to sit here in New York and let you spend thousands of dollars a month on my education while you're there struggling."

"We've talked about this, Emma. I'm making an investment in your future that is going to have huge returns for all of us. If you come home now, we can't add that we have a Culinary Institute-trained master chef to our promotional material. I need you to stay put. And I've really got to run."

"Harrison, do not hang up on me!"

I grab my keys off the counter and rush out the door, hopping into my golf cart and starting it up. "I need to hang up. I could get a big ticket for talking on the phone while driving."

"How is it possible someone with no children has nothing but dad jokes in his repertoire?"

"You know, if you're going to be mean, you should just stay in New York. In fact, stay anyway."

"Not a chance. I'll see you in a few days," Emma says.

"Do not—" I don't finish my sentence because she's already hung up on me.

"Son of a bitch," I murmur. I hit the accelerator and zip around tourists who are meandering along the wide path on their way to breakfast. One of them is leaning down, feeding a pastry to an opossum but I don't even bother to try to stop her. Redialing Emma's number while I weave my way to the office, I then wait for her to answer, but her phone goes directly to voicemail.

"Hey, this is Emma. I'm busy perfecting a soufflé right now, so leave me a message. *Beep.*"

"Do not come home. I repeat, do *not* come home. Stay exactly where you are. Finish school. I will see you next year when you are a fully certified chef and not a moment sooner. I promise the resort will still be standing when you get here." With that I hang up, feeling a knot in my stomach caused by the possibility that, even though the resort will still be standing, we may no longer be the owners.

I round the next corner as fast as the 48 volts of power in the batteries will take me and slide into a parking stall in front of the office. Hopping up the steps two at a time, I rush into the building, only to see Libby has arrived ahead of me. Rosy goes from glaring at her to glaring at me. Shiiiiittttttt.

"Good morning, ladies. I'm sorry I'm a few minutes late." Giving Rosy a sharp look, I say, "I was on the phone with my very panicky sister, who's insisting on moving home."

Rosy gives me a sheepish look and backs down just slightly from her previous aggressive, mother bear stance.

I smile at Libby. "I haven't had a chance to bring Rosy up to speed on our conversation from yesterday."

"I gathered that," she says, looking utterly uncomfortable. "Rosy was just telling me where GlobalLux can stick our proposal, in rather graphic detail."

"I wanted to be sure *GlobalLux* got the message," Rosy says, narrowing her eyes.

"So, then I take it you already know that Libby is a business analyst who's going to…well, analyze our business and save us from ourselves." That may not have been the best way to word it, because Rosy looks utterly pissed at the thought of me bringing in an outsider for advice when I won't listen to hers.

Libby holds out her hand. "Oh, no, I'm not here to tell you how to do your job, Rosy. I'm more of a process person. I look at all the procedures in place and offer solutions to make improvements where needed."

"That sounds suspiciously like you telling me how to do my job," Rosy says, raising one eyebrow.

Libby nods and chews on her bottom lip. "Yes, I suppose it does."

I decide to step in and save her. "Do you want to go grab a coffee, Libby? I think it might be beneficial for Rosy and I to have a quick chat."

"Sure," she says, sliding the strap of her briefcase onto her shoulder and turning to the front of the building.

I usher Rosy into my office and shut the door.

"Have you completely lost your mind?" Rosy asks, her tone rising with each word.

I hold up my hand before she can start yelling. "Hear me out. This just may be the most sane thing I've ever done."

"You better have an ace up your sleeve because it sounds like you're about to sell everything Oscar spent his life building just so it can be dismantled for parts."

"It's not...they won't..." I shake my head, horrified by the idea. "Listen, I cut a deal with Libby. She's going to do her assessment, then tell her bosses we aren't selling. We get all her ideas for how to get out of the considerable hole we're in free of charge, and she goes home." Okay, I may be bending the truth here a bit, but it's for the greater good, so...

"Really? And just what exactly did you offer her to get her to agree to that?"

I give her a devil-may-care smile, but she doesn't buy it. Sighing, I say, "She's desperate to do the assessment. If she can't, she'll be fired. I said I'd agree to let her look around so she can go back with that much at least. There's literally no risk involved for us."

"Don't be so sure. Once these companies get their talons in you, they don't let go until they shake the life out of you and pick the meat off your bones. Then they leave the bones for the vultures to snack on while you rot."

"Well, that was a disturbing metaphor," I say. "You really don't have to worry though, because I'm going to use her to get what we need and then say no."

Raising one eyebrow, Rosy crosses her arms and does her signature stare-down, which, as children was guaranteed to make us confess to any crime, whether we did it or not.

I sigh and continue. "You said it yourself, Rosy. We're in some serious trouble and we need to make some major changes. I'm hoping we can use Libby to figure out the right moves."

"But, *GlobalLux*? Have you forgotten what they did to Mooncrest Hills? They bought them, and when they couldn't make a profit after six months, they shut it down and sold off everything piece-by-piece."

"Which is why I'd never sell to them." I say, putting my hands on her shoulders and giving them a squeeze. "I'll do whatever I have to in order to keep this place." Letting go of her, I give her an impish grin. "Even if I have to take one for the team and sleep with Ms. Dewitt out there."

Rosy rolls her eyes and opens her mouth to say something, but I beat her to the punch. "I know what I'm doing, Rosy. I promise I'll do whatever I have to do to protect what's mine. I am Superman, after all."

———

"There's been a slight change of plans today." I usher Libby out of the building just as she's walking in.

"I thought that might happen. She hates me, doesn't she?"

"More like she hates change, and you represent what could possibly be a massive change. So while we're giving Rosy time to get used to the idea, I thought I would take you out for the day so you can examine Paradise Bay's most popular activity — the snorkelling and parasailing excursion." I give her my weatherman smile, hoping my enthusiasm will detract from what just happened.

She chews on her bottom lip, adorably conflicted. "I really wanted to get started looking at the books today…"

"Tomorrow will be much better. Maybe Monday."

"Doesn't Rosy work for *you*?" she asks, looking very confused.

"She works for the resort, yes, but she also pretty much raised me, so we have a bit of an unusual power dynamic."

Her face softens and she nods. "All right. So, what do I need to bring for this boat trip?"

Letting out a sigh of relief, I say, "A bikini, some sunscreen, and definitely a giant hat to keep you from burning. The catamaran leaves in forty minutes."

"Okay, but Harrison, you need to know I'm really not there to have fun. I'll be bringing my notebook so I can start my assessment. I'm also not parasailing or snorkelling."

"But Ms. Dewitt, how are you supposed to properly advise your employer if you don't try all of our activities?"

"That's my problem to solve, not yours."

———

I help Justin and Fidel finish stocking the boat with drinks and food for the day. Then we double check to make sure we have the right number of snorkel masks and flippers, but to be honest, my mind isn't really on the tasks at hand. Instead it keeps wandering to the all-important question of whether or not a certain someone will be wearing a certain bikini again today.

"What's that smile about?" Fidel asks with a knowing grin.

"Nothing. I was just thinking of a funny video I saw on Reddit last night." I avoid eye contact with him and try to order my face to stop blushing.

"It's that woman from last night, isn't it?" Justin says as he tucks a box of crisps under the bar counter. "The one with the blue bikini."

"Who?" I ask, trying to look completely confused. Then I feign boredom. "Oh, *her*. She's just doing some work for the resort for the next little bit."

"I don't know, man. I saw the way you looked at her."

"Really?" Fidel asks, his face spreading into a big smile.

"No, not really," I say. "Don't listen to him, Fidel. I seriously am not interested in Libby."

"Oh, good," Justin says. "If you're not interested in her, maybe I could see what she's up to later."

"Nope. Bad idea," I say with a much sharper tone than I intend.

Both guys start laughing and Fidel slaps me on the shoulder. "He likes her!"

"I do *not* like her. Not even a little bit. She's irritating and…way too quirky. Besides, I think she has a fiancé, sort of, although he sounds like a total dickhead." When I look up, both guys are looking far too amused for my liking. "That doesn't mean I like her. I just feel sorry for her, okay?"

"Sure you do," Fidel says. "And I bet you'd like to be the guy to help her *feel better*." He and Justin high-five each other while I straighten up and cross my arms.

"There's nothing going on between us. She's here for work. End of story. Now, if you two boneheads could drop it, we have a boat to prepare."

———

We're halfway through the morning, and so far, Libby has made good on her word to work while she's aboard. As much as I hate to admit it, I'm kind of disappointed she hasn't come up to the top deck while I navigate our way over to our destination, Playa Blanca Cay.

The tiny island has a beach that looks and feels like someone dumped a cargo plane full of icing sugar on it. My uncle bought it, along with a few other very small, uninhabited islands, back in the early nineties. We use this one for day excursions because there's a nice wide reef surrounding the entire island, which means the water is always calm and it's perfect for snorkelling. We dock a speedboat there for parasailing and have bathrooms, showers, and an outdoor kitchen with a wooden plank floor, a bar, and a grass roof for some shade. We also have lounge chairs and umbrellas we bring out when we arrive. It's an experience people never fail to mention when they post reviews on TripAdvisor.

Normally I'm completely confident that things will go off without a hitch, but somehow just knowing Libby's on board is causing my heart to race a little. I'm sure it's because she's evaluating me — well, not *me*, the resort. It's definitely not because I find her attractive. I've met hundreds of attractive women, and they never cause my heart to race.

She's wearing the cutest sundress today — a short yellow number with some flowers on it — and I can see she's wearing a bikini underneath, but this one has white straps. I'm itching to see what it looks like when it's wet, which tells me it's been *way* too long since I've been with a woman.

When we reach Playa Blanca, I dock the catamaran as close to the beach as possible, then turn off the motor and jump down the steep steps to the main deck where Fidel is giving the guests the itinerary.

"...have lunch and then whoever didn't have a chance to do the parasailing this morning will get to do it in the afternoon while the other people are enjoying their time snorkelling or relaxing on the beach. At around 3 o'clock, we'll start our trip back to Paradise Bay. So, don't forget your sunscreen and to have the time of your life."

The guests move in the direction of the ramp while I scan the small crowd, looking for Libby. I spot her sitting on a bench, shaded by the wall of the cabin. She's writing something in her notebook with one hand while she taps a few numbers into her calculator with the other.

"You coming, Reef?" Justin asks. He jabs me in the ribs and lowers his voice. "Or are you going to stay aboard for a little alone time with Miss It's-Just-Business?"

I shoot him a warning look. "I'll be down there in a minute. I just want to see if she has any questions first."

"I bet," he says with a laugh.

A moment later, we're alone on the boat. She must know I'm staring at her because she looks up from her work.

Rubbing the back of my neck, I say, "So? Did we fail?"

"You really don't expect me to answer that, do you?" she says with a smile, snapping her notebook shut.

"Well, I kind of hoped..." I give her a boyish grin.

"It will be much better for you if you stop hoping, because I have no intention of telling you *anything* until I've made my final decision."

"In that case, are you ready to go parasailing?"

"I already told you, I'm not going parasailing." She shakes her head and tucks her notebook and calculator into her beach bag.

"Why not? Been there, done that?"

"Never been there, never going to do that." She pulls on her enormous straw hat and walks toward me. "I have a pretty good life and see no need to end it at the tender age of twenty-eight."

I step aside and gesture for her to disembark ahead of me. She gingerly makes her way down the wooden plank to the shore while I watch her skirt sway. Being a gentleman has its advantages. Except I guess the fact that I'm staring at her bottom doesn't exactly make me a gentleman, does it?

I follow her down the dock, trying not to ogle her backside anymore. "Are you afraid of heights?"

She turns and looks at me over her shoulder, then says, "I'm not afraid of heights. I'm afraid of *falling*, which, if you ask me, is just good common sense. If humans were meant to fly—"

"—we would've been born with wings?" I say with a wry smile.

"Yes. Exactly." She stops just as she reaches the end of the dock. Sliding off her sandals, she picks them up and steps down onto the white beach.

"Then how did you manage to get to the Benavente Islands all the way from Avonia?" I ask.

"That's different."

"How so?"

"Because that was necessary for my job. Plus, I wasn't dangling from the back of a boat in some dodgy harness. I was tucked safely into a very large jumbo jet, wearing a seatbelt and sitting on a very sturdy chair."

"I'll have you know, none of my harnesses are dodgy. They're very well-made and safety-tested regularly."

"And yet, I'm not about to strap myself into one."

"Come on. That girl I met on Sunday night certainly would've gone parasailing."

"That girl doesn't exist," she says, tucking an errant lock of hair behind her ear.

"Sure she does. I saw her in person — a *lot* of her."

Laughing, Libby covers her mouth with one hand, then shakes her head. "I'm *not* going parasailing. I'm just going to find a nice spot in the shade where I can observe everything."

"How about I make you a deal: you go parasailing with me, and I'll ask Rosy to add up all our utility and fuel costs since the start of the year, which ought to save you quite a few hours of calculations."

"Seriously? You're trying to negotiate this? Why do you even care if I go parasailing?"

Good question. I have no idea why I care, I just know I do — very much. "Because in the unlikely event that you decide the resort is better off with your people than mine, I want to make sure to drive the price up on you," I say.

"And you think getting me to dangle from a harness is actually going to drive the price up?" she asks, looking completely unimpressed.

"I happen to know for a fact that when you see the view of these islands and this water from that vantage point, it's going to add at least one zero to the price. Maybe two." I bump her shoulder with my arm, hoping she'll say yes. "I'll even go with you, tandem, so you won't have to do anything, and I'll be right there to make sure you land safely. I promise, I won't let anything bad happen to you."

When she looks up at me, the expression on her face tells me I've won.

———

"When you said tandem, I thought you meant we'd be side-by-side," she says, leaning to the right and turning so she can look back at me.

"This is the safest way for a beginner. It means you don't have to balance yourself back here while the boat hits full speed." We're standing on the stern of the speedboat, strapped together, with me behind her, and I have to say, I did not think this through. If I thought I was having trouble keeping my mind on business before, it was nothing compared to now.

She's clearly very nervous, which makes me want to wrap my arms around her and pull her in until she relaxes. She's also wearing nothing but a bikini, which made it hard for me to help get her strapped in — hard on account of trying not to get hard while I was tightening the straps so close to her ample chest and her cute behind.

Fidel starts the motor and gently increases the speed, and her hair blows toward my face, bringing with it the scent of her shampoo and sunscreen. She smells like apples and coconut, and the combination makes me feel a little drunk.

"You all right?" I ask her.

She nods, but doesn't say anything, which makes me think I may be pushing her too far with this one.

"You sure? We don't have to do this if you don't want to."

"No, I think it'll be good for me. I should try new things," she says, her voice sounding anything but sure.

One of the other guests has Libby's phone and says, "Say cheese!" to us.

I lean to the left and smile, hoping I don't look like a total arse grinning away while the woman in front of me is so scared, she's trying not to pee herself.

The boat speeds up and Libby loses her balance. I catch her, holding her by the waist, trying not to notice how soft her skin is against my rough palms. She giggles nervously, then squeals as we're lifted into the air.

"I think I changed my mind!" she shouts as we go up in the air.

I force my hands to release her and enjoy the sound of her laughter as we ascend up one thousand feet into the sky. She grips the cords that attach us to the sail and says, "This is really friggin' high! I didn't think we'd be so far from the water!"

"Too high?"

"Yes! And no! I'm not sure, but I think I kind of love it," she yells, laughing some more. "It's scary and wonderful at the same time!"

I chuckle, thoroughly enjoying being here to experience this with her.

"What happens if we fall?"

"Don't worry, I'll catch you on the way down."

"Is that even possible?"

"Absolutely. The impact will likely break most of the bones in my body, but you'll be just fine."

"Okay, good. That's all I really care about anyway," she teases.

The boat curves to the right, making its way around the first turn of the tiny island. Libby points down to where a pair of dolphins can be seen jumping and swimming along next to each other. "Do you see that?"

"We call them Fred and Wilma. Watch, they'll try to race the boat!"

We watch for a minute, but the pair seem completely disinterested in the boat. They continue to swim side-by-side.

"They're not doing it." Libby says.

Then suddenly, one of them flips onto its back and they connect at their bellies.

Libby cocks her head to the side. "Are they…?"

"Yep, they're doing it, all right."

We both burst out laughing while we pass over the pair.

"Let's give them some privacy," I say, tapping Libby on the shoulder and pointing in the other direction. There's an excellent view of the snorkelling bay, and you can make out the brightly coloured fish swimming around the coral.

"This is amazing," Libby says, letting go of the cords and holding her arms out to the sides.

"Are you glad you agreed to try it?"

"I'll tell you when I'm safely on the ground," she says.

The next few minutes go by far too quickly for my liking, and I'm already filled with regret before we even land in the water. *Okay, idiot, snap out of it already. Nothing is going to happen. She's going to do her report and go back home, and you're never going to see her again.*

The boat slows and we start to drift down toward the sea near the beach. Libby grips the chute cords again and I know she's nervous.

Leaning forward a bit, I say, "It's okay, just remember what I told you. All you have to do is relax and I'll take care of everything."

"You sound like my first boyfriend," she answers, looking over her shoulder with a grin.

"And?"

"He did a most thorough job of taking care of himself."

I don't know why I say the next thing — well, actually, I do — but I know I shouldn't. "Don't worry, you won't have that same problem with me. Your happy ending is my top priority."

Fidel cuts the engine and everything grows quiet as we finish our descent.

"You ready?"

"No," she says, curling up her knees.

We float down into the water, the sail landing behind us and tugging on the cords a bit as I start to tread water and unhook myself. Once I'm free, I push myself under the water and out of the harness. I swim around and come face to face with Libby while I unhook her, trying not to think about how close my hands are to her chest right now as it rises and falls with exhilaration.

"So? Are you glad you tried it?" I ask, looking her right in the eyes.

Her gaze meets mine and there is enough heat to bring the entire sea to a low boil. Swallowing hard, she says, "Yes. Thank you for taking me."

"You're welcome. That was fun." *Do not kiss her. Do not kiss her, Harrison. That would be a very bad idea. No matter how full those lips are or how she's looking at you.*

Licking her lips, she says, "I'm almost sorry it's over."

Me too. I brush some wet hair from her cheek and tuck it behind her ear, letting the back of my hand graze her skin. She closes her eyes and I start to lean in, lowering my face to hers.

Something shifts in an instant, and her eyes spring open with fear. In a very formal voice, she says, "Thank you again, Mr. Banks. I'll have to make Richard try it sometime. He'll love it."

Oh, shit. I'm going to get crushed, aren't I?

———

Text from Will: *Hey, bro. Heads up - Emma called a few days ago. She's super pissed that you sold Matilda, so maybe don't pick up when she calls for a while. On a side note, you should totally come to Antarctica — the cold weather makes the women here desperate for someone to keep them warm. ;)*

14

A Week in Un-Paradise

Libby

HAVE you ever been so confused and befuddled emotionally that up seems like down, and right is left, and wrong is right (even though you know it's *really wrong* but it feels *so right* that you start to believe it actually *is* right)?

Yeah, that's me right now.

I'm supposed to be here on my unhoneymoon/business trip, proving I can do this job just as well as Alan-the-Arsechitect and figuring out a way to get back the love of my life, who is definitely still Richard even though he left me at the altar. Right? Yes. Definitely. We have a perfect future together back home, and I must not forget all the good things, even though he did abandon me on the most important day of my life.

Oh, God. This is just so terribly confusing, isn't it? What I *should be* doing and what I *am* doing are wildly different. I've been letting myself get totally carried away by a certain sculpted resort owner, which is a *huge* no-no. That's why I made the comment about wanting to take Richard parasailing — to firmly apply the brakes on whatever is not happening between Harrison and me. And it may be wishful thinking, because my self-esteem is so badly in need of a boost right now, but I could have sworn he looked disappointed when I said that. Hurt, even.

But he couldn't be hurt.

The truth is, we're both just using each other. He needs me to like him, so he's being all, "I'll take care of you. You're beautiful, Libby." Okay, he hasn't said that bit about me being beautiful, but the way he looks at me could turn a rock into lava. I mean, seriously, it's like he wants to devour me with those gorgeous hazel eyes of his. And part of me, the very naughty part, wants to let him. (Naughty me really wants to let him. Badly.)

But, no. That would be an enormous disaster, both personally and professionally. I'd be throwing away my career and my future marriage in one long, lusty afternoon. Or night. Or an afternoon that would stretch into an all-nighter, because, let's be honest, Harrison does seem like the type to have stamina to spare. Plus, he's an insomniac, so the chances of him falling straight to sleep after he orgasms are pretty much nil. In fact, I'd probably have trouble keeping up with him, what with all his running and swimming and doing all that sweaty active work every day.

So, now I'm walking back to my room, getting my land legs back after a day at sea. I have to say, things were so much more fun before I brought up Richard's name. After that, Harrison got very busy with hosting duties the rest of the afternoon. He didn't even sit with me at lunch, but opted to eat with Justin and Fidel, which left me awkwardly alone with my mind racing. Which it's obviously still doing.

As soon as I push the door open to my room, I drop my bag and get straight in the shower, turning the water as cool as I can stand it. I can't go with hot or even slightly tepid water on account of needing to cool down my raging hormones. I shampoo quickly and get out as fast as possible, deciding to get right to work on my assessment. I have a lot of data to put into my spreadsheets, which is terrific. It'll keep me busy all evening and keep my mind off you-know-who.

My phone buzzes and I see I have a new like on my Instagram account. It's Richard. Huh. What's he doing up at this hour looking at my IG pics?

Now I'm *very glad* I posted all those shots this afternoon at the beach and of me parasailing with Harrison. My plan could be starting to work. Maybe Richard will see I'm turning into Unpredictable, Super-Fun Libby, and he'll change his mind about us. Plus, he's bound to be wondering who that very attractive man is in two of my pics. If this doesn't lead him to get on the next plane here and sweep me up in his arms, nothing will.

But between you and me, I like my chances…

———

Five Days Later

Did I actually say I liked my chances? Because if I was really that cocky, I have to tell you, I was wrong with a capital WRONG.

In the past several days, I've posted an obnoxious number of photos on Instagram, trying to make it look like I'm having the time of my life. Photos of me at each restaurant (where I was actually doing inventory and making process observations), at the beach, on my balcony, at the pool (where I walked in up to my waist, took a few selfies, then went back to my room to get changed and get back to my laptop, which is where I am right now).

I know it's pathetic, but I even went so far as to pose for a few activities I didn't do — like paddleboarding. That was a production, let me tell you. First, I had to get into my bikini and do my hair and makeup, then I had to walk all the way over to the beach from my room, and by the time I did that, I was all sweaty, so I had to find a bathroom and freshen up. Then I had to ask the paddleboard rental guy if he could help me out by coming down to the shoreline to take a picture. I had to set up the shot to make it look like I was out on the water (which involved some serious camera trickery), then stand on the board (which was still firmly attached to the beach), and make an open-mouthed, 'wow this is awesome fun and kind of hard at the same time' face.

After making sure he got a good shot, I told the rental guy I changed my mind and didn't want to paddleboard after all. He was not impressed, by the way. And, now that I think about it, I could have totally just Photoshopped something, which would have been much less time-consuming, not to mention less humiliating.

The worst part is, all that effort hasn't yielded *any* results on the Richard front.

Not one little like.

Not a phone call.

Not him showing up here, desperate to find me and rushing down the beach (because of course I'll be at the beach in a lovely sundress staring pensively at the setting sun over the sea). He'll lift me into his arms and pledge his undying devotion, then out of thin air, a minister will appear and two witnesses (probably Alice and Jack, who he begged to come with him) …and we'll be married immediately and live happily ever, our relationship becoming a legendary love story like Romeo and Juliet (except without the double suicide ending).

Instead, *nothing* has happened. Well, except for Richard liking a video Alice posted of Maisie in her Jolly Jumper, as well as one of his brother Tom's posts, giving a thumbs-up while holding an empty pint glass. I mean, Maisie *is* adorable and she's laughing her head off while she jumps, so that deserves a like. But Tom celebrating the fact that he's just had a beer? Really, Richard? That gets a like, but me suspending myself thousands of feet in the air with nothing but a harness to prevent my death gets *nada*?

I'm starting to think it's over, and I'm sure to you that sounds insane, because like Greta from Germany, and Lolita the barmaid, and Alice, you probably thought Richard and I were through the moment he sent that text. But, honestly, how can I throw away the *six years* I've invested in a man who is normally a very stable and terrific partner?

Just because he ditched me on our wedding day like a total coward?

Just because he basically said being with me was as exciting as being with an eighty-year-old retired librarian?

Well, the joke's on you, Richard, because I can be a total thrill-seeker! At least I can make it look like I am, anyway, which is basically the same thing in the end, isn't it? I mean, really, don't most people do crazy, adrenaline-rush-inducing things just so they can *say* they did it? Nobody *really* likes to 'live on the edge.' Not even Richard, whose middle name isn't exactly Danger. The most thrilling thing he's done in the last few years is to order a curried chicken with a three-hot-pepper rating on the menu at Tandoori Tavern. And he couldn't even finish it, he was sweating so much. I mean, honestly, it wasn't even that hot. I had a bite, and at best, it was White People Spicy. Hypocrite.

I pull out my mobile and dial Alice, who is probably cleaning up from dinner at the moment. As soon as she picks up, I say, "You know, I'm not even sure I want Richard back."

"Hello to you too. How's paradise?"

"Hot and worky," I say. "It just really hit me that Richard's sort of a hypocrite for calling me dull when he can't even handle spicy food."

"Hold on…let me change rooms." In the background, I can hear the firetruck Alice's older brother bought Colby as a revenge gift for the drum set she and Jack bought his daughter. Alice covers the phone, and I hear her muffled voice telling Jack to watch the kids for a few minutes. I can't hear his response, but I hear her say, "She *needs* me right now."

A minute later, silence fills the line, then Alice comes on. "Sorry about that. Just finishing up the after-dinner dishes. Okay, first, let me say, *thank God* you got past the denial phase of this. I've been wondering how long it would take."

"I haven't been in *denial*. I was just completely positive we'd get back together." I take a deep breath, then say, "Oh, shit. That's denial, isn't it? And now I'm angry. Does that mean…"

"You're grieving, yes. But don't think of it as a bad thing. It's a healthy, normal process."

"Right. I guess so. I just thought that maybe…"

"…He'd see all those fun Instagram photos and come running, only to find you looking gorgeous on the beach for an ultra-romantic reunion?"

"Maybe."

"Yeah, thought so. Did you even go paddleboarding?"

"Did I actually stand on the board with a paddle in my hands? Yes. Was I on the water? Not as much as the photo makes it look."

"Oh, wow. So, Denial River runs deep in you."

"Not my proudest moment, but I was a woman on a mission." I stand and walk to the balcony door, slide it open, and step outside into the hot afternoon air.

"Oh, hon. You're definitely going through the grieving process. Denial, anger, bargaining, and closure. Wait — is that right? Closure?"

I gaze out at the property, secretly disappointed not to see Harrison, whom I haven't set eyes on for days. "That doesn't sound right."

"But it *is* denial first, and I think anger is next," Alice answers.

I nod to myself. "I should Google that. So, if I *am* grieving, does it mean my relationship with Richard is really over?"

Alice's tone is gentle, like she's afraid if she speaks too loud, I might break. "Yeah. I think it's safe to say it is."

"Oh God. What do I do now?"

"Start with that hottie resort owner. Do him first. Then move on to whoever you fancy next — but use protection. The last thing you need is a rebound baby. You're going to have enough on your plate with needing to find a new place to live and all."

"Right. Solid advice, Alice. Thanks," I say sarcastically.

"You're welcome, Libs," she says, clearly ignoring my tone.

I roll my eyes. "I'm not sleeping with Harrison. Or anyone else for that matter."

"Why the hell not?"

"Because I'm a professional. And not *that* kind of professional, so don't even say it."

The sound of a wailing child gets louder. "Christ, they found me," Alice says. "Gotta run."

She hangs up and I flop myself down into a chair in the shade, then Google 'stages of grief.'

Might as well know what's coming, right?

15

A Rosy by Any Other Name
Would Still Scowl at Me...

Libby

THE NEXT THREE days are a less-than-fun extension of the week before. I barely see Harrison at all, which is good I suppose, since I am one angry bird. The fact that I'm angry means I'm right on track according to StartingOver.com, so at least I'm on schedule on something. I even took off my engagement ring last night and put it in my room safe, which has made my left hand feel oddly naked. I keep trying to turn the band with my thumb, only to discover it's not there. Then I get in a loop of thinking about *why* it's not there, which reminds me that I'm really pissed off at anything with a penis at the moment, including Handsome Harrison (for no reason at all, really).

As much was I wouldn't mind being distracted from my feelings by his sexy abs, I'm not even sure *he'd* be safe from my rage, no matter how many packs he has on his abdomen. (It's eight. Not the usual impressive six-pack. Eight. With a man-V. Not that it matters.)

Anyway, I spend long days in the office with Rosy, who frankly isn't all that helpful. And I've been around her enough now to know I *should* take this personally, because she's super wonderful to pretty much everyone who comes to the back office for anything, even the

FedEx guy. Now that I think of it, it's more like *especially* the FedEx guy.

But when I ask her for even the tiniest thing, she chews her gum for an inordinate amount of time while making direct eye contact, not saying anything. It's like a game of 'chicken,' only with staring. Just when I'm about to cave, she shakes her head, sighs deeply, and gets what I need. I know she basically raised Harrison and his brother and sister, and I definitely get the feeling she's über-protective of them, so maybe it's not *completely* personal. I just wish I could find some way to get her to lighten up on me because this whole thing is becoming as awkward as the time I congratulated my neighbour on her pregnancy, only to discover that she had just been stress-eating because she was sure her husband was cheating on her. My punishment was a forty-five-minute conversation in which she listed all the 'red flags' and gave me *way* too much info about someone whose last name I can't remember. (In case you're wondering, it turned out he'd been sleeping with anything that moved, and when she finally confronted him, he blamed it on the extra weight she'd gained. You can see why I hate everything with a penis at the moment, yes?)

Grrr. But back to work. My scan of the financials is a preliminary one — nothing too in-depth — but I need to get enough of a picture of how the resort operates, so that if we should come to an agreement in principle and GlobalLux sends an entire team down here to do our due diligence, it won't be a waste of time and money. So far, things aren't looking great. It's not that the management hasn't been properly running things — it's more like a string of bad luck lately that has them trying to dig out of a deep hole. There are definitely things they can do to cut costs and ways to increase their revenue, but the hole they're in is so deep, it's a wonder they've been able to stay afloat as long as they have. At this point, I'm confident I'm going to have to recommend that GlobalLux take over the property. We won't have to do a major renovation because that's been done already (and quite nicely at that), and there's no evidence of anyone skimming off the top or any other major causes for us to abandon our offer.

What there is, however, is a plethora of evidence that Harrison is a dream boss. It's like he's a god around here the way the staff go on and on about him. One would almost think he coached them all on what to say, but I've seen him in action myself, and I have to admit, I'd love to work for someone like him (even though he has a penis). He's just so reasonable and calm and generous.

A few days ago, I was evaluating the resort's Brazilian Steakhouse, and I couldn't help but overhear the sound of some dishes breaking, then some yelling coming from the kitchen. It was very quiet because the restaurant was closed for their dinner prep, so it wasn't hard to get the gist — not when you hear words like 'butterfingers' and phrases like 'what will we serve the meals on if you break all the plates?'

A young woman in a dishwasher's apron (let's call her Butterfingers Girl), came out crying and sat down at a table in the corner for about ten minutes. Then, in walks Harrison with a warm smile on his face. He sat down with her and had a chat. Pretty soon she was laughing and nodding. Then she took off her apron, handed it to him, and gave him a big hug. On his way out, he glanced over at the table I was at, looking genuinely surprised to see me there. He stopped to see how things were going with the assessment, and when I asked about what had just happened, he shrugged and said, "Not everyone's cut out to handle breakable things, so I found a more suitable position for her."

On my way back to my room, I saw Butterfingers Girl folding towels by the swimming pool and swaying a little to the music, looking like she didn't have a care in the world. I have to admit that the business analyst in me had a tug of war with my soft side for how to feel. Business Libby was shaking her head, because that girl most definitely didn't have to pay for all those dishes she broke. If she had, she wouldn't have been hugging Harrison and dancing. But Just-Being-A-Human Libby felt all gooey inside because that was just about the sweetest thing I'd ever seen an employer do.

And how do you put a monetary value on happiness? I mean, technically there *is* a formula you can use that has to do with staff turnover, paid days off, employee theft, and a few other variables. But still, a spreadsheet isn't going to capture the look I saw on that girl's face or the boost Harrison gave to her sense of self-worth.

See? Dream boss.

Also, did I mention he's on the handsome side of the 'looks spectrum' and he has an eight-pack? Oh, I think I may have…

Anyway, today there's been no sign of Harrison, with or without his shirt, and it's been a particularly rough day with Scary Rosy. I can't help noticing that somehow the air conditioning in the tiny office I'm in has 'broken.' So basically, I'm sweating my ovaries off here. My Annabel dress from Hobb's Suit Yourself line has big wet spots under my arms, and worse than that, my hair doesn't react well to the heat and humidity, so it now looks like I had a grandma perm done. The curls are so tight, I could store stationery supplies up there without them falling out. In fact, I have two pens and a pencil in there right now.

I'm bored out of my mind because I've been waiting for Rosy to get me a file I asked for thirty-eight minutes ago. I can hear her flirting with the FedEx guy again. Rosy could give my mum a serious run for her money for the Cougar of the Year Award—the guy can't be more than one-third her age.

She finally appears in my office doorway with a thin file folder she sets down on my 'desk' (and I use that term lightly because I'm pretty sure it's a room service tray with the wheels taken off).

Rosy smacks her lips together, then says, "This ought to be everything you need to know."

I open the file and see it has one page in it, on which is written, *You can't have this resort, so go home.*

My shoulders drop and I look up at her. "I get it. You don't want me here, and I understand why, but—"

"No, you don't," she says, folding her arms across her huge boobs. Seriously, they're extremely intimidating — like she could use them as weapons, possibly trapping and smothering an attacker and rendering him unconscious if needed. And she knows it.

I put my pencil down and sit back in my chair. "So tell me. I want to understand."

"You think this is just another property to take over — a bunch of rooms and a beach — but it's a community. We're a family, and if somehow you manage to pry this place away from the Bankses, everything that makes this place special will be gone."

I stare at her for a second, my heart breaking a little for her. "You're not wrong. It *would* be different and it wouldn't feel the same anymore if the Bankses are no longer the owners. But at least it'll still *exist*. If Harrison turns down our offer and we move on, the resort could go bankrupt, and it could be sold off piece by piece. GlobalLux definitely wants to keep it operational, which would mean everyone would still have jobs."

"*Puh-leeze.* Don't try to tell me you're the good guys here," Rosy scoffs. "I know what happened to Mooncrest Hills."

"That was a completely different situation. They were a much smaller boutique hotel without a solid return client base." I pause, but she just stares me down instead of answering. Sighing, I say, "I know it's hard, but you'll have to trust me. I'm only trying to help keep the resort going in the long term — with or without the Banks family."

Rosy purses her lips. "The Banks' kids *belong here* and they wouldn't be in danger of losing this place if big damn companies like yours weren't buying up everything they can and making it impossible to compete," Rosy says, lifting her chin.

"You're right about that, too. That's the case in virtually every industry in the world. But I'm not the person who started globalization, so this" — I hold up the paper — "isn't going to change reality, no matter how much you or I wish it would."

"You still don't get it. This is *home* for all of us. These people are *our family*. My husband and I never had children of our own, so when those three beautiful lost kids showed up here..." Her voice cracks and she shakes her head.

I nod, hoping my face conveys the empathy I'm feeling for her. "Would it surprise you to know I can see how special this place is? Not as an analyst, but as a regular person. I see how Harrison looks after everyone — guests and staff included. He's somehow everywhere at once, making everybody feel like everything's going to be all right, even though to look at the books, it's clear it won't be."

"It's just a blip," she says defensively. "We've come back from the brink of bankruptcy before and we'll do it again." Her pride shows on her face.

I shake my head and say, "Not this time, Rosy. I'm sorry." And I am. Somehow, what should have been an easy in-and-out deal has become so complicated. I honestly don't know what's right or wrong anymore, but I *do* know what's right for GlobalLux (and for me, for that matter) isn't what's right for Rosy or Harrison or for Butterfingers Girl.

Sitting down on the folding chair opposite me, Rosy sighs. When she looks up, her eyes are filled with tears. "Well, can you help us, then? You promised Harrison you'd tell him if there was any way he could keep this place going on his own. Are you a woman of your word or were those just lies so you could get him to sign over the resort to GlobalLux?"

My throat feels thick with guilt, because deep down, I know how this ends and I'm just telling them what they want to hear so I can get what I need. But, it's just business, right? "I made Harrison a promise, and I intend to keep it."

"Then find a way to make this work, *please*, because if Emma, Will, and Harrison don't have a place to come back to, they won't have roots anymore. They'll just end up drifting all over the world alone, I know it. And I can't protect them if they're not here. Our little family will just slowly disappear instead of staying together and the thought of that…" She blows out a puff of air and blinks fast.

As I stare at Rosy, I see a woman who wants nothing more than to protect the children she loves and keep them with her. I'm suddenly aware of how much I've missed out on in my life, and the thought of tearing apart a family that wants to be together is suddenly unthinkable. Dammit. My voice comes out all shaky as I tear up. "I'll try, okay? I promise. But I need your help."

16

A Wild Night Out

Harrison

It's Friday evening and Nelson's on his way here to pick me up. We're heading to a local pub called The Turtle's Head (seriously, I could not make that up. It's owned by an English ex-pat who decided he wanted to spend the rest of his days pulling pints somewhere sunny and hot). As I finish getting dressed and grab my wallet, I feel a sense of relief washing over me. I'm badly in need of an evening out with my best friend, sipping cold beer, playing billiards, and watching sports on big screen TVs. It's Nelson's turn to drive, and I intend to cut loose. It's been one hell of a week.

Ever since the whole parasailing thing, I've been carefully avoiding Ms. Dewitt. She's clearly not for me — or for anyone at the moment, really. She's a hot mess who's still clinging to a strand of hope that she and her dickhead fiancé are going to live happily ever after. She's also the one person who's either going to help me save this place or will head up the charge to ruin everything. Why I ever let my libido take over when I was around her is beyond me. So, she's cute as hell. So, she's got curves for days. So, she has a sexy, smooth voice, and she's funny and smart and quirky. She's not for me. Period. End of story.

When I get to the parking lot, Nelson is standing near the lobby, chatting with one of our security guards, Mateo. Mateo went to school with us—in fact, almost half of our graduating class has ended up at the resort over the years, so for Nelson, popping by is like a bit of a reunion.

"Hey, guys," I say when I reach the pair of them.

"There he is. You all set?" Nelson says, punching me on the shoulder.

"More than." Glancing at Mateo, I say, "We'll be at The Turtle's Head. Stop by if you get a chance."

"Wish I could. It's Jolissa's birthday weekend. I'd never hear the end of it."

"Birthday *weekend?*" Nelson asks, laughing. "I bet you're so glad you got married."

Mateo gives a deadpan expression. "Every day is better than the last. Especially when her mother is in town for a month."

"Oh, wow," I say, slapping Mateo on the arm. "Have fun with that."

Nelson and I start for his Jeep when someone from the other side of the lot calls my name. It's Fidel, coming from the lobby steps. I consider pretending I don't hear him, but then he hollers, "I know you can hear me, Reef!"

Sighing, I turn to him and call back. "Can it wait? I've got this thing in town, so I really better get going."

"What? Going out to get wasted with that guy?" Fidel asks with a grin. "Sorry, dude. We need the Opossum Whisperer in A 102."

"I prefer Opossum *Wrangler*, thank you very much." Glancing at Nelson, I say, "Wanna help? It'll be quicker with another set of hands."

"Oh, I'll come, but I'm not touching some rabid giant rat," Nelson answers.

"You're coming just so you can laugh at me, aren't you?"

"You know it," he says.

As the two of us start toward Fidel, Mateo calls out, "Hey, Reef, have fun with that!"

I flip him the bird over my shoulder as we walk away.

———

"We may have to wait until she's done eating her Pringles," I say, as the opossum hisses over her shoulder, then continues digging in the can of crisps again.

She already bit Mr. Vaughn, the genius who lured her into his suite with a trail of mango pieces. He's sitting on the bed with a towel wrapped around his hand while his wife oscillates between shrieking at him for being 'an utter idiot' to shrieking at me to 'catch that bloody thing' to shrieking every time the opossum makes the slightest move. So if nothing else, Mrs. Vaughn has a healthy set of lungs.

A small crowd has formed outside around the suite's patio doors, waiting to see what's going to happen. Libby is among them, notebook and pen in hand. When she arrived, I told her to stay outside for her own safety, and I may or may not have been giving her a smoldering 'firefighter doing crowd control' look. Nelson gave me a 'what the hell was that?' face, then smirked and introduced himself to her.

I glance out at them and see the pair peering in through the glass door, chatting. Nelson calls out, "Go get 'em, Opossum Whisperer!"

Libby covers her mouth, but I know she's laughing.

I give him a dirty look, then turn back, trying not to think about what she's writing down on that damn notepad. GlobalLux probably has some sort of policy about handling wildlife, like calling Animal Control instead of doing it themselves, which would probably be the sane thing to do. Except here on the island, Animal Control takes one business day to respond to all wild animal complaints, and since it's Friday evening, that means someone wouldn't get here until Tuesday. Mrs. Vaughn would surely die from Excessive Shrieking Syndrome by then, and that wouldn't be good for our TripAdvisor ratings.

Note to self: make sure to explain that to Libby the first chance you get.

Fidel, who is the only one brave (or stupid) enough to join me in the room, stands on the opposite side of the bed from the little creature. We're waiting for Justin to bring a cage. Until then, all we can do is watch her nibble away on the crisps. We exchange a 'well, isn't this fun on a Friday night?' look, then Fidel says, "Oh, hey, I keep forgetting that Winnie sent a thank you card for the onsie you got Harrison Junior."

"Oh, don't worry about it. It was nothing."

"No, it wasn't. It was very thoughtful, and you guessed right, he is a boob man," Fidel says with a grin.

"How is the little guy?"

"He's amazing, the other day during his bath—"

Mrs. Vaughn clears her throat. "Excuse me! We're in the middle of an emergency here. Can we save the chitchat for a time when there isn't a wild animal poised to attack?"

We both glance at her, then at the opossum, who quite frankly looks like she'd only be a threat if you were a potato-based snack.

Fidel lifts his walkie-talkie to his mouth. "Any E.T.A. on that cage?"

The radio crackles, then I hear Justin's voice. "Found it. I'm just leaving the shed now."

Ingrid, our on-site nurse, walks in through the open patio door, medical kit in hand. "I hear we've got a biter on our hands."

"Yes, we bloody well do!" Mrs. Vaughn screeches.

Ingrid peers across the room at the offending biter, then wrinkles her nose up sympathetically at Mr. Vaughn. "Thought you could feed her and maybe get a few photos?"

"You've seen this before, then?" Mr. Vaughn asks sheepishly.

Mrs. Vaughn cuts in before Ingrid can answer. "Is it really necessary to point that out? He already knows he's a bloody idiot who's ruined our vacation!"

Ingrid tilts her head to the side. "It's not necessarily ruined. Are you up-to-date on your tetanus shot?"

He looks blankly at his wife, who rolls her eyes and nods. "Yes, he is."

"Good." Ingrid nods. "In that case, we'll get him cleaned up and you two can get back to having a good time." She gestures for Mr. Vaughn to follow her. "Let's head into the loo so I can have a look."

I glance over my shoulder at Fidel. "Say, why don't you take Mrs. Vaughn over to the pool bar for a cocktail?"

Fidel gives her a warm smile. "Would you like to do that? No sense in staying here in harm's way."

Mrs. Vaughn glares at the opossum again, then nods and follows him out the doors muttering, "Not sure why I got married at all, really. He's probably going to die of rabies, the daft man."

I let out a sigh of relief, now that the shrieker and the bleeder are out of the room. Staring down at the little creature, I say, "Well, it's just you and me now. You almost done with those crisps?"

She looks up at me as though trying to decide whether I'm competition for the food or not. In my right hand, I'm holding a large towel I grabbed out of the bathroom. I could throw it over her if she tries to attack, but otherwise, my plan is to wait for Justin.

I crouch down a little, keeping a safe distance. "I'm not going to take your food, I promise. But I am going to put you in a cage and drive you up the mountain to a very lovely nature sanctuary. There are no crisps there, so you should probably enjoy those last few, but there's a lot of fruit and…other things that'll be better for you." I rub the back of my neck while she stares at me, nibbling away at the crisp she's holding. "Who knows? Maybe you'll meet the opossum of your dreams there…"

Outside, I hear a cart pull up, and a moment later, Justin walks in with the cage. He hands it to me, slaps me on the back, and says, "Good luck, Opossum Whisperer."

"Wrangler," I correct him.

When he's gone, I open the cage and set it on the floor, then say to the animal, "Here. I'll even put in a towel so it's a cozy ride."

Folding the towel in half, I tuck it in the kennel, and put a trail of peanuts from the middle of the cage out toward her. She's no longer interested in the can, so I'm pretty sure she's finished her dinner.

"How about some dessert?" Standing slowly, I wait to see if she'll go for the food. She must be full, though, because she doesn't even sniff around with her little pink nose, but just watches me.

Damn.

"We're going to have to do this the hard way, aren't we?"

I put my arms out to the sides and make a low growling sound, taking a couple of menacing steps toward her. She freezes, faints, then falls over onto her side.

I quickly walk over, pick her up with one hand, and hold her up to the smattering of people out on the patio, who start cheering. I smile at them, feeling quite satisfied at managing to avoid some violent alteration ending with Ingrid bandaging me up.

Placing the opossum in the kennel, I pet her little head and say, "Sorry about that, but I promise it's for the best."

I shut the cage, then go check on Mr. Vaughn.

Knocking on the bathroom door, I open it and poke my head in. "I got the opossum, and Mrs. Vaughn has gone for a cocktail. How's it going in here?"

Ingrid continues working on his hand without looking up and says, "No need for stitches, so he can go join his wife in a few minutes."

Mr. Vaughn lets out a sigh of relief. "Thanks, both of you. I'm really sorry about all of this. I had one too many margaritas this afternoon, and suddenly, feeding the wildlife seemed like a good idea."

I give him an understanding smile. "That's all right. It could happen to anyone. Enjoy the rest of your stay."

With that, I pick up the cage and walk out of the room to the waiting crowd. Libby looks gobsmacked, and I grin inwardly at how impressive that must have been.

Then she wrinkles her nose at me and says, "What did you do to that poor thing? Did you scare her to death?"

"No," I say, taken aback. "She just fainted. That's their first response to a threat."

"She fainted?"

I nod. "It's an adaptation to predators. She'll be out for a bit, and when she wakes up, we'll release her at a nature sanctuary on the other side of the island."

Nelson's head swivels toward me. "Hold up. You don't mean 'we' as in *us*, do you? Because we've got plans, dude, and that'll take hours."

Shrugging, I say, "I'd rather drop her off myself. You know, make sure she's okay."

"Seriously?" Nelson says, groaning. Looking at Libby, he says, "More often than not this guy ruins my night with his Superman routine."

I roll my eyes, pretending to mind him telling Libby I'm a bit of hero around here. Pointing to the rigid opossum whose eyes and mouth are open, I say, "Sorry, Nelson, but I'd kind of like to be the one to free her, you know. I mean, I did scare her into…that."

Libby stares up at me, and I swear to God, her eyelashes are fluttering.

Nelson glances back and forth between us, then says, "Sure thing. Nothing I like more after a long week at the bank than a drive up the mountain instead of hitting the pub."

"Thanks, man." Turning to Libby, I say, "I used to call Animal Control in these situations, but it takes them a full business day to come out here, so…"

She nods and looks in the cage. "They're kind of cute, aren't they?"

"Yeah, they are." *Not nearly as cute as you, though.* Clearing my throat, I glance at Nelson. "We should get going so we can be on our way down the mountain before dark."

Nelson's shoulders drop as he spins his key ring around one finger. "Yeah, okay. Nice to meet you, Libby."

"You too," she says with a smile.

"Have a good night," I say, giving her a little nod as I walk past, careful to inhale her perfume on the way by.

———

"So, you going tell me about what you and that redhead have going, or what?" Nelson says as he winds his way around a curve.

Instead of answering, I take a long swig of beer. Yeah, I know it's illegal in most places, but I'm not driving and he's not drinking, and island life is a lot more relaxed than most places.

Nelson chuckles and shakes his head at my silence. "I knew you two had a vibe."

"No vibe. Definitely zero vibage," I say, a little too forcefully to be in any way convincing.

"Really? Because you were totally swaggering," he says, then puts on a Texan accent. "Well, little lady, I'm here to wrestle down this here wild animal. You stay back. This ain't no place for a delicate thing like you."

"Ha ha. Very funny." I look out the passenger window, avoiding his gaze. There's no point in talking about whatever *isn't* going on between Libby and me. It's a dead-end and I know it. "She's a business analyst from GlobalLux. They sent her to check out the resort and see if they should make an offer."

When I glance over, Nelson's mouth is hanging open. "Shit, man. I totally read that wrong. Sorry."

"Easy mistake. She's hot as hell, so I can see why you'd assume," I say, lifting the beer back up to my lips.

"Are you actually thinking of selling? I thought you'd fight to the end," he says, weaving around a slow rental car filled with some elderly tourists.

"This might be the end," I say, feeling my gut tighten at the thought. "Emma's quitting school and coming home to try to save me the money."

"I bet you're thrilled about that."

"Oh yeah, what's there not to be thrilled about? She's going to abandon two years' and thousands of dollars' worth of education with only six months left. I'm sure you can imagine the conversations we've had about it."

"Yes, but when Emma's mind is made up…"

"There's no chance of changing it."

We're both quiet for a moment, then he says, "You caught up on your loan payments. That ought to buy you some more time."

Nodding, I say, "I hope so, man. Things could still work out. I actually cut a deal with Libby. If she thinks she can find a way for me to turn things around on my own, she's going to give me all her recommendations and tell her boss not to pursue the deal."

Nelson raises one eyebrow. "And how exactly did you get her to agree to that?"

"Played hard to get," I say with a grin. "Works every time."

"Do you think you can trust her?" he asks.

"I better be able to, because if not…" My voice trails off.

"You're totally screwed?"

"Yup."

17

A Little Flattery (and a Plate of Drop Doughnuts) Will Get You Everywhere...

Libby

IT'S BEEN two days since I saw Harrison, the Impressive Opossum Wrangler. I keep hoping I'll run into him so I can ask how things went when he and his friend dropped her off at the nature sanctuary. Truth be told, I kind of wanted them to invite me along. But only because it would have been nice to see more of the island, and not because I want to spend some time with a certain sensitive, caring, sculpted resort owner.

It's now Monday morning, and I'm making my early morning commute to the office via a relaxing stroll through the tropical gardens to the main building, which is much nicer than my normal twenty-minute bus ride through rush hour back home.

One of the gardeners, an older gentleman in a wide-brimmed hat, looks up from the flower bed he's weeding and smiles. "Good morning!"

"Good morning," I answer, returning his friendly wave. Yes, this is a lovely commute. He's the third person to say hello to me already. It occurs to me that I hope he'll be as happy working for GlobalLux as he is for the Banks family. My gut twists when the answer pops into my mind.

I spent most of the weekend crunching numbers and trying not to think about Rosy pleading for my help, because every time I think of her, I'm filled with a sense of dread. The future for an independent Paradise Bay is not looking so good, and even though the math involved is completely objective, my feelings somehow aren't.

When I walk through the open-air lobby and into the back offices, I'm greeted by a mouth-watering aroma. I inhale deeply, trying to figure what it is. Freshly baked pastry, maybe, or...oh, doughnuts! I spy a plate of them on Rosy's desk as I pass by her office toward my broom closet.

"Good morning, Rosy," I say, giving her a small wave as I continue on.

"Oh, there you are! Good morning, Libby," Rosy says cheerfully. "I made you a special Caribbean treat."

I stop short and turn, eying the doughnuts hopefully.

She stands, picks up the plate, and walks over to me. "I woke up early, so I thought, 'Why not make Libby some Benaventean drop doughnuts? She's been here for almost three whole weeks, and she's hasn't tried one.'"

I hesitate, wondering if maybe this is some sort of trick — like maybe they're filled with some sort of truth serum custard or...oh! just straight up poison. That's probably her game. She's going to kill me, then put some sunglasses and a huge hat on me and prop me up in a seat on one of the catamarans like that dead guy on *Weekend at Bernie's* (oh right, *Bernie*). Everyone will be partying around me, and she'll distract them with some dirty dolphins port-side so she can dump my body in the sea off the starboard-side.

"What? Are you gluten-free or something?" she asks.

"No, I just don't want to eat alone," I answer with what I hope is a convincingly warm smile. "Let's each have one."

I select one, then wait to put it in my mouth until she pops one in hers.

The second I bite into the scrumptious treat, I moan in delight. Honestly, if this does contain poison, it wouldn't be the worst way to go. The sumptuous textures of a crunchy outside and a pillowy soft inside dance across my tongue. "Mmm, is there some orange...and nutmeg in this?"

"That's an old family secret," she says with a wink. "But I could be persuaded to share it with someone willing to save our resort." Rosy nudges my stomach a little with the plate of doughnuts. "Here. Take them. They're all yours."

I stare at the offering, feeling a little concerned that I'm letting myself be bought for a plate of sweets. They're almost delicious enough that it would be worth it, but still, a moment on the lips, a life-time of...not having a career or being able to pay the bills.

"Go on, Libby. No strings attached, I promise," she says, giving me an apologetic look. "I wanted to make up for being sort of unco-operative before."

Sort of? That's like saying ABBA songs are sort of catchy-slash-awesome. "Thanks, this is really thoughtful of you," I say, taking the plate and starting down the hall.

"Oh, I have you set up in here today." Rosy points toward Harrison's office. "He never uses the damn thing, so someone might as well."

Moments later, I'm seated in a proper office chair (instead of a wobbly folding metal one) at a real desk (instead of an out-of-commission room service cart) in a wonderfully air-conditioned office. I pop another doughnut in my mouth, then flip through the stack of files Rosy had waiting for me.

I don't want to jinx it, but this morning feels like a tremendous new start.

———

Or not.

It's only been a little over twenty-eight hours since the Drop-Doughnut Campaign began, and I'm already feeling a considerable amount of pressure. All day yesterday, as well as today, Rosy's been making frequent 'pop-bys' to see how things are going. She stands by the door (or even worse, by my desk), watching me. Smiling. Nodding hopefully. Saying things like, "How does that look? Good, right? It all looks good? What do you think now?"

I don't want to complain because being fed delicious treats by Fangirl Rosy is *so* much better than being scowled at by Scary Rosy, but beyond that, having her watch me work all day with an expectant grin is a little…unnerving.

I've basically had a fake smile plastered on my face for most of the last two days, which has resulted in sore cheeks. Even worse, I've been sort of (read: definitely) pretending everything looks fine even though it definitely (read: 100% without a doubt) does not.

It's clear the resort is walking a fine line between getting by and going bankrupt, with the difference being decided by the weather gods. Another huge hurricane anytime soon, and they're sunk.

I'm also starting to think Rosy has a bit of a big mouth, because she's not my only fan around here. I mysteriously have become the belle of the ball at Paradise Bay. Everywhere I go, the staff smile and wave and say things like, "Hi, Libby! Let me know if you need anything!" or "There she is! The woman of the hour!"

What?

On my walk over here this morning, I was greeted by no less than ten happy staffers who called me by name like we're the oldest of friends. I was even stopped by the two main actor/singer/dancers in the resort's nightly shows to see if I wanted a part in *Mamma Mia* tonight. Obviously, I Do I Do I Do I Do I Do (want to), but I had to turn them down. I don't have time to learn all the moves to "Dancing Queen" in the next five hours.

To be honest, this is all starting to get a little creepy, and even worse, it's enough of a strain to cause a brain hernia (well, if that were a thing, that is).

All these people look at me like I'm Luke Skywalker and I'm the only one that can prevent the Evil Empire from blowing up the resort. And I gotta say, I'm no Jedi. I'm C-3PO at best. I can spit out a lot of very accurate data and worry with the best of them, but I'm no hero, and when they figure it out, they're going to turn on me faster than the crowd would turn on Luke Skywalker at a Sith Lord convention.

In an effort to escape the unrelenting pressure, I told Rosy I needed to head over to the burger bar because I haven't had a chance to evaluate it yet. The truth is, I just need some salty, greasy carbs.

Spotting a group of restaurant servers on their way to start their shift, I decide to take a left instead of a right so I can avoid another round of 'all our hopes are pinned on Libby.' I find myself near the main pool and beach bar, and instead of going back to my room to change out of my suit, I decide to shrug off my jacket and go sit at the bar. Lolita's there, so I know I'll finally have some time alone to think — there's no way she's going to strike up a conversation with me.

She's taking an order from a couple sitting at the far table when I arrive. I seat myself at the same stool I did the first night I was here and drop my briefcase next to me — a not-so-subtle sign that I'd like to be alone.

The breeze picks up, providing the tiniest respite from the suffocating heat. Grabbing a napkin off the bar, I dab at my face and neck, although there's basically no point because I know it will be dewy in a matter of seconds. I really should just go back to my room, get out of this suit, and go for a swim.

"Hey, girl!" Lolita says as she steps back behind the bar. I look up to see who she's talking to, only to discover *I'm* said girl.

"Hey?" I say, momentarily confused before I realize Rosy must have gotten to her too.

"Piña Colada? It's on the house," she says with a wink.

A wink? Seriously? "I think I should just stick with water. I have a lot of work to get done."

"In that case, would you like an iced coffee to keep you going?"

"That would be lovely. Thank you."

"No, thank *you*." She gives me a grateful look and reaches out to pat my hand.

"This must be Libby!" a female voice calls out from behind me.

Well, isn't this craptastic? More fans. I turn to see a young woman hurrying toward me with a big smile. She's dressed in a long sleeveless black-and-white striped maxi dress, and her dark hair is pulled back in a high ponytail. Even though I'm in a bad mood, I like her immediately.

"I'm Emma, Harrison's little sister."

Oh, so *that's* why I like her.

She holds out her hand, and we shake.

Lolita makes a *tsk*ing sound. "I heard you were coming back, but I didn't want to believe it."

Emma laughs and says, "Some welcome home, hey Libby?"

"We'd all be a lot happier to see you if you finished school, young lady," Lolita says as she adds two squirts of vanilla syrup to my iced coffee.

"As if I could stay in New York learning how to pipe icing into pastries when my family's in trouble."

"Your brother's got it handled. Besides, Wonder Woman here is going to help us get everything back on track, so you should get your cute little behind back on a plane to school."

"Wonder Woman? Pfft!" I scoff even though I'm completely flattered. "I'm just crunching some numbers. It's not like I have a lasso of truth or something." I chuckle a little at my own joke. "Seriously, though, I'll do what I can, but I honestly can't promise any miracles here."

"That's not what Rosy told me," Emma says, plunking herself down on the stool next to my stuff. "She says you're basically a genius and if *anybody* can save the resort, it's you."

"That's very flattering." And very terrifying because there's no freaking way I can save this place.

Lolita pops a straw in my drink and passes it to me. I take a long sip, suddenly wishing it was a piña colada.

Emma smiles at me. "So? Rosy also says she thinks my brother might fancy you."

"Oh, no. I don't think so. He's just being polite. And even if he weren't, I'm practically married."

"The arse ditched her at the altar," Lolita says with a quick purse of her lips.

Huh. Apparently, 'I Like Libby' Lolita still has a lot of bite to her.

Instead of seeming shocked, Emma nods. "Yeah, men'll do that. That's why they suck, generally speaking."

"Amen, sister," Lolita says with a firm nod.

"Except Harrison. He's one of the good ones." Emma leans one elbow on the bar and faces me. "So, does that leave the door open for you and my brother?"

Now I'm basically just pouring with sweat. I really should have changed out of this suit. That way, my armpits wouldn't feel like they're part of some sweaty grease fire when Harrison's little sister started interrogating me about my potential for being his everything. "Umm...Harrison is...he's...he seems really great, but we have a strictly professional relationship. It would be completely inappropriate for me to..." My voice trails off as my cheeks heat up.

"Uh-oh! You like him," Emma says, her face lighting up. She turns to Lolita. "Is it just me, or does she like him?"

"Oh, yeah. You should've seen her the first night she was here," Lolita says. "She was rubbing his abdomen like he was a Buddha statue. Then she stripped down on the beach in front of him." Looking at me, she adds, "Not that I blame you. Harrison's a fine piece of man candy."

"Eww," Emma says, shaking her head and sticking her tongue out.

"In my defence, I was kind of in the middle of a breakdown at the time, and I had no idea who he was."

Ignoring me, Emma asks Lolita, "Is Rosy right about Harrison liking her back?"

"He doesn't—" I start, then stop because part of me is dying to hear Lolita's answer.

"Oh, yeah. You should see his eyes when she walks by. They practically pop right out of his skull and follow her wherever she's going." Lolita raises and lowers her eyebrows at Emma.

I certainly don't hate hearing that a man like Harrison can't keep his eyes to himself when I saunter by. Inner Teenage Libby does the Macarena while Business Libby shakes her head and says, "No, seriously. There's nothing going on between us."

"But you wouldn't kick him out of bed for eating cookies, would you?" Lolita asks.

"No, I wouldn't—"

"Oh, snap, girl!" Lolita says, holding her hand up for a high-five before I can explain.

I decide not to leave her hanging and raise my hand, not as a sign of admission that I want to sleep with Harrison, but because leaving someone hanging is the height of bad manners. After I put my hand back down, I hear a familiar voice behind me.

"Wouldn't kick who out of bed?"

Freezing in place, I give myself a second to get the first flame of humiliation out of the way before I turn around.

"You, you big dummy," Emma says, getting up to hug her brother.

"No, I didn't—" I mumble, but clearly there's no point in interrupting their family reunion.

Harrison hugs Emma, lifting her off her feet, then sets her down and ruffles her hair. "I told you not to come home, you brat."

"I had to come meet your new woman," she says, pointing at me with her thumb.

Harrison gives me an eyebrow raise, accompanied by a sexy half-grin. Then he turns back to his sister and his face grows serious. "Nice try, but you can't distract me that easily. I'm putting you on the first flight back to New York."

"I'm not sure if you are aware of this, but you're my brother, not my boss," Emma says with her chin lifted. "Now, you're being rude to my future sister-in-law. You haven't even said hello to her."

"We're not done with this conversation," he says to Emma before turning to me. "So, about those cookies…"

My stomach does this flipping thing that only happens when he's around, but this time it's a much bigger flip (like a quadruple somersault) because of all the stuff Lolita said about Harrison liking me. Is it hot out here? It feels really hot. "Those were fictional cookies. Very fictional."

"Oh my God! You two are so cute together," Emma says, clapping her hands excitedly. "That's it. You're going to have to dump the jilting arse and marry Harrison. You'll have the best story to tell your grandkids of how Libby saved the resort and you two fell madly in love and lived happily ever after."

Shit. The resort.

My heart drops, and I suddenly feel the weight of the entire land mass Paradise Bay sits on press down on my shoulders. A familiar wet sensation starts in my nostrils. *Oh, no. Not now…*

I cover my face with one hand and reach for a napkin with the other, quickly shoving it under my nose.

Harrison squints his eyes at me. "Are you okay? Are you bleeding?"

"I'm totally fine, thanks. I'm a stress bleeder. My nose," I say with a little nod, as though it's the most normal thing in the world.

"A stress bleeder? Have these two been winding you up or something?"

"No, not at all. They've both been lovely. It's…something else entirely." I stand and try to pick up my coat and briefcase with one hand while keeping the napkin in place.

Harrison picks up my things. "Let me get you back to your room."

"No, you don't need to. I'm fine, really. This happens all the time."

"And yet, I'm still going to make sure you're all right."

Emma pats my shoulder and whispers, "That's because he likes you."

He gives her a dirty look. "It's because it's the right thing to do." Then looking back and forth between the two women, he says, "And no more gossiping. Libby is practically married. There's nothing going on between us."

Lolita and Emma exchange a look, then Lolita says, "Oh, that's over, trust me."

And I swear for the briefest second, Harrison's eyes flicker with hope.

18

Excuses for Touching Eight Packs

Harrison

"So, that was your sister, huh?" Libby asks as we get in the golf cart.

"Yes. I'm sorry about her. She wants to marry me off for some reason." I back out of the stall and head in the direction of her building.

"That's okay. It was kind of flattering, in a slightly off-putting way."

Laughing, I say, "I have no idea if that's a good thing or a bad thing."

"Me neither," Libby answers.

I stop where the two main paths intersect to let a group of guests walk by, then continue on much slower than I normally drive (for some unknown reason that has nothing to do with wanting to spend more time with Libby, so stop thinking that).

Libby looks over at me. "Did she really quit culinary school to come back and help out?"

"Unfortunately. I told her I've got it handled and to stay put, but instead she packs up and flies all the way back here with one semester left in her program," I say, shaking my head. "Do you know how hard it was for her to get in at that school? She applied for *over two years*. Two years. And she gives all that up to come back here and try to bail out a sinking ship."

"Do you really think it's sinking?"

Giving her a sideways grin, I say, "You tell me."

When I look at her, Libby's face is filled with concern. "I really shouldn't say until I've had a chance to finish crunching the numbers."

Shit. That isn't the face of someone who has happy news to share in the near future. "I know. I was just testing," I say. "But I owe you an apology. I'm supposed to be helping you, not adding more stress to you by going on about my own problems."

"This?" she asks, pointing to her nose. "Don't worry about it. It happens so much, I've started called it Old Faithful."

Her entire face turns pink. "That sounded sexy," she says in a sarcastic voice. Then her eyes grow wide and she blinks quickly. "Not that I'm trying to be sexy around you. At all."

God, she's cute when she's embarrassed. "Somehow I don't think you can help being sexy. It just happens."

Libby giggles a little, then waves her free hand dismissively. "You're just trying to butter me up so you can get some intel on my findings."

"As much as I'm dying to know, I'm being completely honest about the sexy thing. Probably too honest."

She swallows hard, then says, "In that case, while we're being overly honest, it's not looking too great so far." Her expression goes from worried to hopeful. "But maybe there's something I haven't seen yet that will help move things in the right direction for you."

I nod and do my best to act like that didn't feel like a gut punch.

"I mean, you never know, right? Sometimes things look like they're going one way and something can come along and turn everything around."

Giving her a small smile, I say, "It's nice of you to try to make me feel better. Especially since my loss is your gain."

"Right. I almost forgot. I'm supposed to be working on a hostile takeover." She says it like it's the last thing she wants to do.

"Can I ask you a question?"

"Sure," she answers, her tone tentative.

"Do you like your job?"

"Some things about it. I love the investigation part of it, and I like it when a deal comes together — that bit is very exciting. But this time it feels...different."

"Is it because you kind of like me and you can't stand the thought of seeing me ruined?" I bump her shoulder to let her know I'm sort of joking.

"No, you're a total nightmare. I can hardly stand to be around you," she says, grinning up at me. "The rest of the people here are pretty wonderful though, and *they* seem to like you, for whatever reason..."

"Must be Stockholm Syndrome."

Laughing, Libby says, "Oh, now it's all making sense." She changes to some clean tissues, then dabs her nose and drops her hand to her lap.

"All better?" I ask.

"All better," she says.

A couple walks past us, and Libby points at them. "Are you aware of how slow we're going right now? We just got lapped by some senior citizens."

"I'm trying to conserve battery power."

"Liar. You just want to spend more time with me."

"There may be a little of that too, but it's mostly about saving the earth," I say, giving her a mock serious look.

She laughs again, then her face falls. "Harrison, have you thought about what you're going to do if this doesn't have a happy ending for you?"

"Nope," I answer, rubbing the back of my neck. "It'll be okay, though. At the end of the day, a person has to learn to roll with the punches, you know?"

"Makes sense." She fiddles with the handle on her briefcase, seeming so vulnerable, it makes me want to forget she's in love with someone else.

Before I can stop myself, I say, "Speaking of rolling with the punches, have you heard from Dick lately?

"It's *Richard,* and no, I haven't."

"Whatever his name is, he's a total coward," I mutter.

"He's not a coward. He just got——"

"——so scared of getting married, he didn't show up for your wedding?" I ask, trying to cut the sarcastic edge out of my voice but failing miserably.

"I think I'll walk the rest of the way. I'm not enjoying this conversation very much anymore," she says, turning her head away from me.

"Sorry, that was out of line."

She glances in my direction. "*And* it's none of your business."

"That too," I say, feeling shitty for having upset her. "It was a total arsehole thing to say. I'm just in a really bad mood, but that doesn't mean I should take it out on Dick."

She levels me with a steely glare.

"*Richard,* sorry." I give her a little grin that seems to soften her up some.

We pull up to her building long before I'm ready, and I stop by the front door.

"Well, thanks for the ride," Libby says as she gets out of the cart.

"Are you going back to the office today?" I ask, trying to draw out the conversation just a little longer.

"I don't think so. I have enough numbers to crunch at this point, so I can probably stay in my room for the next day or so and finish up most of my work."

She turns and starts toward the door while I sit, thinking about the fact that things 'aren't looking great.' Then her words pop into my head about how maybe there's still something she hasn't seen that would make a difference.

Before I can second guess it, I get out of the cart and follow her. When I catch up, I say, "Hey Libby, there might be something that will change your mind after all."

"No, it's fine, Harrison. Really. I don't think you're an arse, even if you did make unwanted comments on my love life."

"Not that. I mean about the resort," I say, barely able to contain my nervous excitement. "I've had a crazy idea for a long time. Well, I'm actually not sure if it's crazy or a stroke of genius, so I've never told anyone about it before. But you're the perfect person to ask. You'll know right away if I should do it."

Her eyes light up. "What is it?"

"Are you game for another boat ride?"

———

Thirty minutes later, we're taking off in our fastest speedboat, normally used for water-skiing. Since I dropped her off at her room and told her to get changed into hiking clothes, I've managed to shower, shave, and pack a picnic dinner for us to share once we reach our destination. It's a long trek, and it's getting late in the afternoon, so I hit the throttle.

Libby sits in the seat to my left, holding on to her ball cap as the wind whips her ponytail around. "Just how far is this place?"

"About another twenty minutes," I shout over the loud engine.

"This place better be magical!"

"That's the perfect word to describe it."

By the time we arrive, Libby looks like she's so rattled, her teeth might've come loose. She's also adorably sexy in that girl-next-door way in her hiking outfit — skinny cropped yoga pants, a tank top and running shoes. I anchor the boat as close to shore as I can get without hitting the rocks, but it still means wading through the water to get to the beach.

"What's this place called?" Libby asks, her eyes scanning the beach that rises up into a dense, tropical rainforest.

"It doesn't have a name yet. I thought maybe you could help me come up with one."

"How about 'terrifying jungle that's probably full of deadly bugs' island?" she asks, looking very tense.

Tapping one finger against my lips, I say, "We may have to finesse that a little. I'm not sure it sounds enticing enough."

I toe off my runners and peel off my socks, then stuff them inside my shoes and toss them onto the shore. Picking up my backpack, I hop out of the boat and into the knee-deep, clear blue water.

"Oh, are we wading in?" she asks.

"I am," I call back to her. "Wait there a second. I'll come get you."

"Sure. Okay. I'll just be right here…waiting to go on to the scary deserted island. Can't wait."

I toss the pack onto the sand and turn back, fully enjoying the sight of her in the soft early evening sun. Somehow, inexplicably, I've almost forgotten everything that's been bothering me lately, and when it does pop into to my mind, none of it seems so bad.

She climbs up onto the side of the boat and balances there in a crouched position. I hold my hand out to her, and she takes it, the warmth spreading through me. Huh. Every damn time. Crazy.

"Okay, you have to choose between being professional and being dry," I say.

"How so?" she asks with an adorably confused look on her face.

"I could carry you, in which case you'll be dry, but it's not all that professional. Or you could make your way on your own, in which case your pants are going to be pretty much soaked, but you may feel a little more professional."

"Having soaked pants is hardly professional," she says, letting a small smile escape her lips. "Plus, you've already carried me across the resort in my undies, so I choose dry."

"Okay, then," I say, tugging on her hand. She falls sideways with a squeal and I catch her in my arms. I'm not even going to try to pretend I'm not enjoying this, because I damn well am.

"Oh, I didn't think you meant like this. I thought maybe you'd piggyback me," she says, her voice taking on a breathy quality.

"Is piggybacking considered more professional?"

"Obviously. Everyone knows piggyback rides are considered the height of sophistication."

I laugh as I start toward the shore, but after a few steps I'm all too aware of the heat running through me at holding her like this. The way she's blushing and looking everywhere but at me tells me she's feeling it too. I set her down sooner than I'd like.

Once her feet touch the white sand, she clears her throat and straightens her T-shirt. "Thanks for the lift."

I keep my reply casual. "Any time." And I mean *any time*.

We walk side-by-side down the length of the beach, then turn onto a sandy trail that's been cut through the jungle. An iguana steps out of the brush, and Libby steps in front of me and holds out her arm in front of my stomach.

"What are you doing?" I ask.

"Protecting you," she whispers. "Stay back. The brightly-coloured ones are poisonous."

"No, they're not," I whisper back.

The iguana gives us a long stare before disappearing back into the brush again, and Libby pats my stomach before putting her arm back down. "It's safe now."

"Uh-huh. You sure you didn't just use that as an excuse to touch my abs?"

Shaking her head vigorously, she turns a little red. "I certainly did not. That was a...maternal instinct thing."

"Say what you want, but I know the truth. It's okay, really. I totally understand and don't mind, even if it was a bit pervy of you."

She grunts a little, then says, "Agree to disagree on the topic of me wanting to touch your rock-hard abs. On to more important topics. Now that I see iguanas live here, I'm more than a little curious about what other deadly animals are lurking in the bush that I'll need to save you from. Poisonous spiders, maybe? Giant snakes?"

"Seriously, you can just go ahead and grope me all you like. I already told you I don't mind."

She gives me an exasperated look. "So, is that a yes to the deadly fauna?"

"It's a no. None that I've ever seen, and I've been coming here since I was a kid," I answer.

She nods, seeming to relax a little as we walk on.

"Do you want me to take a picture of you hiking to send home?" I ask.

Libby blushes a little and shakes her head. "I've given up on that. I posted at least a dozen shots, and none of them seems to be attracting the attention I was hoping for."

I do my best not to smile as a wave of hope hits me. "I'm sorry to hear that."

"Somehow I doubt that," she says with a wry grin. After a moment, she says, "I was so sure we were going to have the perfect life together…" Her words are slightly laboured as we go up the steep part of the climb to the top of the mountain.

"And now?"

"Full disclosure? For the first time in my life, I don't have the first freaking clue where I'm heading, and it's completely terrifying."

"Well, you know what they say: when one door closes, a window opens."

"Except this particular window seems to be on the tenth floor and there aren't any firefighters holding one of those big trampoline things for me."

"I know this'll sound strange, but I can relate. I mean, it's not as bad because I haven't just had my heart broken. But I can relate to the whole uncertainty thing."

"I actually think your situation is worse — no offense. With me, I just have to figure out what I'm going to do for myself. In your case, you have the lives of over a hundred people riding on your shoulders."

"That's why I'm hoping to sweet talk you into helping me," I say with a little smile.

She looks up at me but doesn't smile back. "Is it hard? Having all that responsibility all the time?"

"You know, it's funny, people have been asking me that my entire life. When we lost our parents, I took over as sort of a parent for Will and Emma. Grownups were always asking me if I minded having so much responsibility, and I never understood why. The truth is, there's really nothing I'd rather do than look after the people I care about. I suppose that's a weird goal in life," I say, feeling strange about admitting this to her. "Maybe it makes me unambitious."

"I think it's beautiful." Her voice cracks a little, and I stop walking and turn to her, only to see she has tears in her eyes.

Unable to help myself, I put my hands on her upper arms and rub them up and down a little bit. "Hey, what's wrong?"

"Nothing," she says, her face screwing up with emotion.

Pulling her in for a hug, I feel her sob against my chest, and it nearly breaks my heart. I hold her close, running one hand over the back of her head, trying to soothe her.

"Shh, it's okay. It'll be okay."

After a minute, she pulls away, wiping her eyes and looking embarrassed. "I'm sorry, that just got to me for some reason. I don't think I've ever had anyone who thought taking care of me was anything more than a burden."

"Then you've been hanging around the wrong people all your life," I say, stopping just short of telling her I wouldn't mind applying for the job.

She looks up at me, her face full of emotion. "Yeah, maybe I have."

I lose myself in her deep blue eyes and let all my feelings for her bubble to the surface, knowing I can't hold them back anymore. And I no longer want to.

Cupping her jaw with my hand, I lean down, closing the space between our mouths, waiting for her to meet me halfway. She licks her lips and closes her eyes, then moves so her mouth just barely skims against mine.

19

Welcome to Fantasy Island...Bow Chicka Wow Wow

Libby

OUR LIPS BRUSH against each other, and I feel my entire body heat up in a way it never has before. Suddenly, I don't care about my job, I don't care about Richard, I don't care about my mum and her stupid young boyfriends. The only thing I care about is this moment right here with this man.

Letting his backpack fall off his shoulder and onto the ground, he kisses me gently at first, and when I press myself up against him and grip his muscular back with my hands, he gets the idea that I want more. He crushes his mouth to mine, giving me the kiss I've been waiting for my entire life. It's filled with passion and honesty, and somehow it feels like love, even though I know it can't be.

We stay like this, just kissing and letting our hands roam over each other's clothes for so long, it makes me completely crazy with lust. I let out a moan that speaks a thousand words of desire.

Suddenly, his hands are on my bottom and I feel myself being lifted into the air in what I'm pretty sure is every woman's fantasy move. He holds me up while we kiss some more, with only the sound of the wind rustling through the trees and the song of some birds I don't know the name of (and at this moment do not care because the thing he's doing with his tongue is complete magic).

A gentle rain starts to fall. It's refreshing, and it feels as though it could cleanse away all my pain and disappointment. The rain intensifies, but we don't stop even though we're both drenched. At this point, we're both so far gone, it would take a force of nature to stop us.

A huge crack of thunder booms, shaking the ground. Well, there it is. Hello, Mother Nature.

Harrison pulls back and says, "That's not good."

I stare at him with what I'm sure is a dreamy expression on my face. "I completely disagree. That was very good."

"I meant the thunder. What *we* were doing just now was better than very good." He sets me down and grabs my hand. Picking up the backpack, he swings it over his shoulder and we start running even though I don't know where were running to.

"You don't happen to have a house here, do you?"

"More like a rustic cabin, but it'll get us out of the storm."

The ground is wet and slippery under our feet as we run and slide our way along the path, laughing a little at ourselves as the rain beats down on us.

"I'm glad you're enjoying this!" he yells over the sound of the rain.

"I've honestly never felt so alive in my entire life!" I shout, suddenly shocked by the fact that it's true. I feel like a new woman, suddenly — a brave, adventurous one who parasails and kisses gorgeous men in the jungle.

"Okay, so the next part is going to be a little scary," he shouts as we round a corner and come to a sudden stop where the ground drops off into a steep, lush valley below.

On the other side of the valley sits a tiny cabin, and my heart jumps to my throat when I realize the only way there is over a rickety bridge. When I give it a hard look, I see it's really more of a rope and wooden plank type of thing that's rocking wildly from side to side in the wind.

Aaaaand Adventurous Libby has left the island.

"No," I say, shaking my head as my pulse pounds in my ears. "I can't do that. Nope. That's not for me."

A clap of thunder causes me to jump, and Harrison looks down at me. "There's not much choice. The trick is —"

"Don't look down? Yeah, *you* don't look down. I'll be just fine over here on solid ground because I'm not going to get on that thing. In fact, I think I'll just head back towards the beach." I turn and call, "I'll see you later," over my shoulder.

Harrison grabs my wrist and stops me. "It'll be okay. I promise you."

"I can't, Harrison," I say, trying not to sound like I'm about to cry but failing miserably.

"Do you trust me?"

"It's not *you* that's the problem. It's me. There's no way I can make it across that thing without falling. In case you haven't noticed, I'm not all that athletic."

"You don't need to be. I've got it from here."

He slips the backpack onto my shoulders, then clips it across my chest and tightens it. "You ready?"

"No." I shake my head vigorously.

"Just close your eyes and trust me."

I close my eyes tight, deciding that actually *does* seem like an excellent coping mechanism at the moment. Suddenly, I feel myself being lifted into the air, fireman style, and I clutch his back with both hands, feeling utterly terrified.

"Whatever you do, do *not* open your eyes!"

"No problem," I say, wincing and clinging to him like a baby monkey to its mother.

"So, you're taking us a different way, right? A not-on-the-bridge-that-is-definitely-going-to-collapse way?" I shout.

My answer comes in the sudden swaying and bouncing up and down. Oh great, now I feel like I have to pee. *Oh God! Do not do that right now. Do not pee, Libby. There would literally be nothing worse than you peeing at this moment!*

Unless I peed and got a nosebleed at the same time.

Oh God, I just want to wake up and be at home in my bed. Maybe if I click my heels together and say, "There's no place like home," I'll open my eyes and this will be over.

We continue to bounce along, and a huge gust of wind hits. I feel Harrison freeze for a moment while the bridge swings left and right. I do my best not to scream even though I'm pretty sure *someone's* screaming, and it sounds both very loud and a lot like me.

"Are we going to die here?" I shout. "I don't want to die!"

Just as I'm shouting the word 'die' for the second time, Harrison's steps feel very steady. Then the rain stops. I open my eyes and lift my head to discover we're already in the cabin.

Harrison sets me down and smiles at me. "Told you we'd be okay."

I shrug, trying to look nonchalant. "I knew that the whole time."

"You're such a bad liar," he says as he unclips the backpack and slides it off my shoulders. The look he gives me makes me feel as though he's just completely undressed me instead of just removing a bag. "We should get out of these wet things," he says with a sexy grin.

I narrow my eyes at him. "Did you know a storm was coming?"

He holds up one hand. "Scout's honour, I had no idea."

"Were you ever even a scout?"

"No, but I buy their disgusting tubs of popcorn every year when they come around, so that should count for something." He peels off his shirt, and I try not to drool at the perfection that is his wet, naked torso.

He sets his shirt down on the back of a kitchen chair, and it hits me that I haven't even bothered to look around the small structure that's sheltering us from the rain. It's a one-room cabin with a hot plate, a table for two and a double bed.

I point to the bed and say, "There aren't any bedbugs, right?"

"No bedbugs," he says, chuckling a little as he reaches for me. "Now, if you don't mind, I'm trying to set the mood here, and you're kind of killing it."

Then he lifts my shirt over my head.

———

Okay, so that was mind-blowingly incredible. It was body-blowingly amazing too. Is that a thing? Because if not, it totally should be the phrase for having your entire world rocked so hard, you don't think you'll ever recover from being so thoroughly and deliciously sexified. Three times.

I lay under the sheets panting while he kisses my neck in that place that makes my eyes roll back in my head. I didn't even know I had an involuntary response like that, but it turns out I do. Several of them, in fact.

"Did I warm you up yet?" he asks, smiling down at me.

"Almost," I say, giving him a naughty grin. That's been my excuse to get him to do all the sex stuff for the last...oh...two hours, maybe? I have no idea. All I know is that it's completely dark in here now, so it must be night. It's still raining, but it's now settled into a steady, hypnotic thrum against the roof.

"If you want me to keep warming you up, I'm going to have to eat something to get my strength up."

"Oh, definitely eat, then," I say, unable to wipe the satisfied grin off my face.

"Okay," he says, but instead of standing to get some food, he ducks under the covers.

I laugh, putting my hand to my face while he works his way down. By the time he gets *there*, I'm not laughing anymore. And I disappear from the real world again for a wonderfully long time.

―――

We sit together, pillows propped up against the wrought-iron head-board, dining on a pretty decent picnic. He brought a container with olives and cheese and sliced bread that tastes like it just came out of the oven. There's a container of fruit, a bottle of red wine, and for dessert there are two thick slices of very yummy looking chocolate cake waiting for us on the table.

"Mmm, God, this is amazing."

"That sounds familiar to me. I may have heard you say it earlier," he says with a grin that would melt my knickers, if I were wearing any.

"Yes, a few times, even, but now I actually mean it. This Brie is divine," I say.

"So it's going to be like that, is it?" he says, looking amused.

"Oh, you were good, too," I say, patting him on the leg condescendingly. "But this cheese is *really* worth writing home about."

Giving me a mock frustrated look, he takes both our plates and sets them on the night stand.

"Wait, I was enjoying that."

"Then you shouldn't have thrown down the gauntlet." He pulls me down so I'm laying flat, then rolls on top of me and kisses me hard on the mouth.

When he pulls back a bit, I give him a skeptical look. "So, let me get this straight. You're trying to prove you're more satisfying than a slice of cheese right now?"

"I am. And between you and me, I like my chances."

20

The Secret to a Good Night's Sleep

Harrison

OKAY, this is going to sound stupid, but I've never been so happy in my entire thirty-two years on this planet. Not the first time I slept with a girl, not the first time I caught a swordfish, not the first time I managed a no-grab barrel roll (which is a pretty impressive surf trick, if I do say so myself). Of all the things I've done, this is by far the best moment of my life. It's like everything has just come together and my life suddenly makes sense. I feel like I could take on the world and win.

Libby and I are listening to the rain fall, wrapped up naked in each other's arms. I want to know everything about her, her opinion on every topic, even stuff I don't normally care about.

I've already told her basically everything there is to know about me, from the time of day I was born (11:45 p.m.) to how I lost my parents to the first girl I kissed (Kelly Plouffe, on the beach, when I was fifteen. Very nice girl, big rack).

I finally approach a subject I've been curious about since the night I met her — her hippie mother. I ask her about her real name, and she talks for a long time, telling me about drifting from place to place as a young child, then being abruptly abandoned by her disappointingly irresponsible mum.

I pull her in and kiss her on the forehead, wanting to kiss away any pain she's ever had. And to be completely honest with you, I've never wanted to do anything nearly that cheesy. Ever. But with her, I'd do anything — hell, I'd even take a ballroom dance class if she wanted me to.

"I think that's why I've always kept myself on such a short leash my entire life," she says. "I've always been terrified that if I cut myself some slack, I'd end up like her."

I prop my head up on one hand and smile down at her. "You won't."

"How do you know?"

"Because your mum is clearly an extremely selfish person, and you're not."

"Huh. I never thought of it that way. I've always thought she was just wild, you know? I never thought of her as selfish."

"Really?" I ask.

"Yeah, but now that you say it, I can totally see it."

Cupping her cheek with one hand, I say, "And now that you see it, you can relax. You don't ever have to worry about turning out like her again because you aren't her — you never could be." I give her a lingering kiss to emphasize my point.

When I pull back, she's smiling, and not just in that 'post-sex, I've just been totally satisfied several times' way, but with a 'happy all the way to my soul' sort of way (which is pretty much what I was aiming for).

We kiss some more, then I lay back against my pillow and press my forehead to hers.

Libby runs one finger lazily down my chest. "Did you always want to run the resort?"

I feel a little taken off guard by her question and have to think about the answer for a second. "No, never. As a teenager, I was planning to get out of here the first chance I got. I was either going to race yachts or be the biggest surf champion in the universe." I shake my head, feeling a little embarrassed to admit my childhood dreams. "I was going to see the world, taste every exotic food from every country, date the prettiest girls each port had to offer…"

"Why didn't you?" she asks, her face serious.

"I grew up," I say simply. "Will and Emma needed me, and just when they were ready to fly the nest, Oscar died."

She runs a finger along my jaw. "So you picked up the pieces and held it all together for everybody else instead of living your own dreams."

"Don't feel too sorry for me. I have the prettiest girl in my bed right now. Besides, I didn't have the talent to make it as a surfer or the cash to race yachts anyway, so either way, it would've been a short run."

"That's not what I heard."

"If you're getting your intel from Rosy, she may be a little biased."

"Did she fake those newspaper articles about you as the junior surf champ of the Caribbean?" Libby asks with a skeptical look.

"Oh, Christ, she got out the albums?"

"She may have."

"It's really not that big a deal," I say, shaking my head. "Being champion in Hawaii, South Africa, Australia, or California…now that's a big deal."

"I have a feeling you're being very modest right now."

"Nope. I have no discernible talents whatsoever." I smile playfully. "Except maybe as a wild animal wrangler."

"Are you talking about the opossum or me?"

"Both, although I have to say, you're much wilder."

We laugh for a moment, then Libby snaps her fingers. "Hey, I completely forgot that you brought me out here to show me something…or was that just an elaborate excuse to get me into bed?"

I give her a sideways grin and waggle my eyebrows. "Oh, I wanted to show you something, all right." At the incredulous look on her face, I laugh. "Okay, for real, there was an actual business-related reason to come out here, but you distracted me with your hotness."

"You distracted us *both* with all the sexing — not that I'm complaining," she says, lifting herself up a bit and crooking her arm to hold up her head. "So? What is it? Have you discovered some secret lake on the island that's the fountain of youth?"

"Oh, that would be a huge money-maker."

"You'd basically be a trillionaire within months."

"Damn. Now my thing doesn't seem like such a big deal anymore."

"I wouldn't say that," she says, all serious. "Your thing is rather impressive. Great length, perfect girth." Unable to keep it up any longer, she giggles and turns a little pink.

"Perfect girth, eh? I might have to keep you around. You're pretty good for my ego."

"I may let you," she says, blushing a deeper shade now. "Which means I've probably already succumbed to Stockholm Syndrome. Now, tell me why we're out here," she says, looking very excited.

"Okay, well, it's no fountain of youth," I say, trying to reel in her expectations a bit. "But I think this is even better."

"Better than never growing old?"

"I think so," I say with a slight nod. "Listen. Do you hear that?"

She stills her breath and waits, then whispers, "I only hear the rain."

"Exactly. Just the rain. No cars or trucks, no other people. Nothing. No one but us." I smile at her and pause for a second. "What if I built a few cabins on different parts of the island for people who want the ultimate private getaway? Rustic ones like this—nothing too fancy but much nicer, of course, and eco-friendly."

"I love it," she says, grinning at me.

"You do?"

"I really do." Her eyes light up. "That's honestly the biggest thing right now in boutique travel — ultra-private getaways, surrounded by unspoiled nature — a true escape from the entire world. I think it could be a huge draw."

"Really?" I almost sigh in relief that she didn't laugh at the idea.

"*Definitely*. I mean, it's not like finding the fountain of youth, but if you did it right, you could turn it into a huge money-maker," she says, sitting up, looking very excited. "You'd actually be able to charge a lot more if you only built one cabin — a villa. That way, you can market it as having their own private island. You'd need top-end food and service, a heated infinity pool, lots of spaces to lounge...and then you price it right — and by that, I mean disgustingly high."

"You think? We can't build a sprawling mansion or anything, though. Not on my budget. Plus, it would be really difficult to build anything too big with the terrain out here."

She reaches out with one hand and places it on my face. "It doesn't have to be huge. Just really well done. You could charge *big bucks* for it, Harrison. Exclusivity is like catnip, but for rich people. They love nothing more than having access to something no one else does." She scrunches her face with excitement, and I have to admit, it's addicting.

I glance down at her mouth for a second, then say, "Any chance you'd want to stick around and help me make it happen?"

Her face grows serious, and she lays back down, putting some space between us.

Before she can say anything, I blurt out, "You don't have to answer that. That was just the sex-brain talking."

Turning on her side, she gives me a small smile. "Is it okay if right now, at this moment, I know for sure the only place I want to be is here with you, but because my life is such a mess, I can't tell you how all of this is going to turn out?"

I nod, knowing that as much as I wish it weren't, this is one of life's 'go with the flow' moments. "Of course that's okay."

Deciding my best move is to prove what she'd be missing if she went back to Dickhead, I lean over her and give her a smoldering look. "So long as you give me a chance to convince you to stay." Lowering my face, I nuzzle her neck, then kiss her softy.

Libby giggles a little, then says, "Do your worst."

———

I wake to the sounds of the birds outside the window and the sun spilling light into the little cabin. Libby is snuggled against me, and as obnoxious as this sounds, she really does look like an angel. Her hair is messy, and she has the most peaceful look on her face.

It takes me a minute to realize I finally slept through an entire night. I don't know if I slept because of her or if because I finally feel like there might be a way to save the resort, but I just feel…happy. I literally haven't felt this good in years — since before Oscar died. Actually, probably before my parents died, if I really think about it. I haven't felt this free or calm maybe ever.

I pull her closer, inhaling the scent of her skin, then my next thought is like a blow to the chops. It's going to hurt like hell if she decides to leave in a few days, because now that I've let her fill up my entire heart, I'm afraid she'd take it with her. I think about what kind of future we could have together, the two of us working to build the resort into what it's meant to be — a piece of paradise that can weather any storm, real or financial.

Whoa, I'm definitely getting ahead of myself. I mean, this could just be a rebound thing for her. My chest aches at the thought. I stare at her, trying to figure out if there's any sign that this is nothing but a fling.

She stirs and opens her eyes. Smiling, she traces my lips with her fingertip before giving me a lingering kiss.

"Good morning, beautiful," I say, brushing off my sense of doom.

"Morning. How many hours have you been laying awake watching me sleep?" she asks.

"A couple of minutes."

Her eyes grow wide. "You mean you actually *slept?*"

Nodding, I say, "Turns out I just need to have sex for four or five hours a day."

Libby grins at me. "Well, if that's what it's going to take, I guess I'll just have to volunteer for the job."

I smile back, hoping she can't tell how badly I want to make that a permanent position.

21

Mr. Right or Mr. Right Now?

Libby

HARRISON BROUGHT me back about three hours ago. We spent the entire morning in bed, then went for a hike, which included some extremely delicious skinny dipping in a freshwater pool under a waterfall. Yeah, that's right, Adventurous Libby had sexy sex under a sexy waterfall.

Now my head is spinning with a joy so all-consuming, it really is like being completely intoxicated. I sang "Take a Chance on Me" (horribly, I might add) all the way through my shower, then floated around the room in my robe before throwing on a cute T-shirt dress and plunking myself down in my chair.

I, then, spent several dreamy minutes staring at a cream and purple stripped sea shell Harrison gave me before we left the island. It was perfectly in tact when he plucked it out of the sand and handed it to me. "This is you around the wrong people," he said.

Then opening it so the two halves opened up so the iridescent shiny inside showed, he added, "This is you around someone who cares. You go from being all clammed up to being a butterfly and revealing everything that's beautiful about you."

Tears pricked my eyes as I rubbed the smooth center of the shell with my fingertip.

"That was corny, wasn't it?" he asked.

I shook my head. "That was lovely. Thank you."

"Thank you for letting me see the real you."

Dreamy, right?

Okay, so when I'm not gazing at my shell, I've been writing not one but *two* reports on the property — and not because I'm an over-achiever. It's because while I was in the shower, I came up with what I hope will be the perfect plan to save Paradise Bay.

At this moment, I don't know if Harrison and I will end up together and live a long, happy island life. But, what I *do* know is that I can't be responsible for the destruction of this wonderful community. Rosy was right. This *is* a family, and no one should tear apart a family for profit. It's just wrong.

I sit back in my chair, having just read over the final version of each report. My heart pounds as I look back and forth between the two of them neatly stacked next to each other on my desk. The first report is for Harrison's eyes only, and it contains a very detailed how-to guide for him to take this property and make it extremely prof-itable. If my bosses saw this, it would not only get my arse fired, they would also make sure I'd never get another job in mergers and acqui-sitions again. And they wouldn't be wrong because what I'm doing is completely unethical. I'm making a decision to hide the truth from my bosses, which means a lost opportunity for GlobalLux and its share-holders.

The second report is a complete lie meant to cause GlobalLux to abandon their takeover bid. This report is so damning, it will pretty much guarantee no one ever looks at this property again unless it were to burn to the ground and only the land was up for sale. I've made it sound as though things have been so poorly managed and constructed, the cost of acquisition plus making the necessary improvements to turn a profit would exceed any potential future earn-ings for many years to come.

I tap my fingers on my lips, hoping I'm doing the right thing, even though I know this is irresponsible — reckless, even. My gut churns at the thought that maybe I am just like my mum. Because at the moment, I'm willing to throw away my career for a man I hardly know. And it's not about the amazing orgasms, I promise you.

At least I think it isn't.

Over the past few weeks, I've come to see the beauty of what Harrison has built here, and I can't bring myself to tear that apart even if it would be the boost I need for my career. The truth is, I don't actually care about my job at the moment, and I'm not sure I ever did. Other than the fact that it made me *look* like a success, I don't like what we do. It's ugly and soulless to reduce someone's dream to profit margins and efficiency ratings. There's so much more to a business than what's on paper — at least there should be.

I can't do it anymore.

I don't want to.

I won't.

Opening up my laptop, I start an email.

Email from Libby Dewitt to Quentin Atlas:
  RE: Paradise Bay Preliminary Evaluation Results

Quentin,

I've attached my full report. To summarize, I've deemed Paradise Bay All-Inclusive Resort not worth pursuing. The owner's valuation of the property is unrealistically high, and he's in no way willing to move off his position. At this time, it is my unequivocal recommendation that GlobalLux abandon the pursuit of acquiring this property.

Regards,
  Libby

. . .

P.S. Effective immediately, I quit.

I stare at the email for a moment. "After this, I have no plan," I say to the empty room.

I do a quick body-scan before I hit send. No clammy hands. No heart palpitations. My throat doesn't feel like it's going to close up. Complete lack of dizziness, nausea, and lightheadedness. Lifting my hand to my upper lip, I find it dry.

Huh.

If I don't feel like I'm about to have a panic attack, that must be a good sign, right? Or am I completely numb because this is the worst idea I've ever had?

I look down at the shell and run my fingertips along it. I am a butterfly, not a clam. I'm worth more than this job. I can do something better with my life — for example, staying here and trying to help turn things around so Paradise Bay Resort can stay exactly the way it is, only with one new person here to complete the puzzle.

My hand hovers over the mouse, I take a deep breath, then click send. I have exactly 29 seconds after hitting that button to change my mind. I watch the timer count down and do nothing as it winds its way to zero. Then, I exhale — long, deep, and slow. When I'm done, I smile and stretch my arms out to the sides, feeling free for quite possibly the first time since I was a little girl.

My phone rings, and I quickly pick it up. Thank God, it's Alice. I swipe the screen to answer.

"You're not going to believe this, but I just quit my job."

"What?"

"Crazy, right? Am I crazy? Don't answer that, I already know," I say, biting my thumbnail.

Then I spill my guts, telling Alice everything that's happened since we last talked. I tell her about Rosy and Fidel's baby and the opossum and Butterfingers Girl, and about my night on Fantasy Island.

When I get to the end of the story, I say, "I mean, none of this makes any sense. This has to be a rebound thing, doesn't it?" I pace the room, holding my mobile phone up to my ear.

"Okay, hang on a second," Alice says. "I'm just trying to wrap my head around a few of the details before I can help you sort this out. Are you sure you guys did it, like, seven times?"

"Alice, seriously, I need your help here. I'm desperate."

"I actually wouldn't call you even a little bit desperate if you got it seven times since yesterday afternoon. And that whole waterfall thing? That sounds like the kind of fantasy that could keep a girl going for the rest of her life."

"Yes, it was unbelievably perfect, but what if Harrison's wrong? What if I am exactly like my mum and I just threw away my entire life for some crazy, lust-filled relationship with someone I barely know?"

"How old is he?" Alice asks.

"What does that have to do with anything?"

"Just answer the question."

"Thirty-two."

"Well, then you're fine. He's older than you, so you're not turning into your mother."

I groan. "Alice, I don't think you get it. I am doing *the most reckless thing* I have ever done, and I have absolutely no desire to stop."

"Then don't. Where did being good and predictable get you, Libs? I mean, *really*?" she asks.

I consider her question and find myself unable to come up with a defense for sticking with my old ways. "Good point."

"Do you think you might be in love with him?"

I stop pacing and consider the question. The answer makes me sit down on the bed because my legs feel weak. "I think I might be. But it can't be real. I mean, I've known him for less than three weeks."

Alice makes a clicking sound with her tongue, then says, "There is such a thing as love at first sight, you know."

"No, there isn't. There's just *lust* at first sight, which I definitely have."

"So, that's all you like about him? How he looks?"

"No, there's so much more to him than that. He's just so generous and caring, and he's *so* great with his staff and the guests…and tiny wild animals," I say with a dreamy sigh. "And then there's the way he smells, and the way he smiles, and how he looks at me like I'm the only woman who's ever lived. It's like...he just really wants to take care of me, you know? Like, *really* take care of me."

"Yeah, I got that when you said the part about doing it seven times," Alice says. Then her voice drops. "Oh, shit. I just realized if you end up with this guy, I'm hardly ever going to see you."

"*Exactly*. Which is why this whole thing is insane. I just need to tell him my life is in Avonia and even though this has been amazing, I really can't stay." I stand and start pacing again.

"Did he ask you to stay?" Alice says.

"Yeah, actually." My entire body warms at the thought of his words and the feeling of being in his arms.

"As much as I hate to say it, I think you need to stick around there for a while and see where this goes," Alice says, sounding a little bit sad. "You owe it to yourself to see if he's the one. And based on everything you've told me about him, he sounds so perfect, I kind of hate you right now."

"I take it things still aren't much better between you and Jack?"

"You could say that. I don't know, things are just... I think we're just hitting a rough patch."

"How rough?" I ask, leaning on the desk in my room and letting worry set in.

"I don't know. I mean, I'm sure it's totally normal, but he just seems really distracted lately. The other night, I woke up in the middle of the night and he wasn't in bed. I went to go find him, and he was, umm, you know, at his computer, watching something."

I pull a face I'm glad she can't see. "Oh, well, I suppose that's probably pretty normal, isn't it?" I ask, feeling one part worried for her and one part scared for me having to get any more details than I already know about them.

"I'm sure it is. It's just that I've never known him to do *that* before, so it just really feels like he must be...I don't know...unhappy."

My heart squeezes at hearing Alice sounding so unsure of herself and her marriage. This isn't like her at all. Here I've been so caught up in my own drama that I've completely missed the fact that my best friend is struggling.

"Hey, you guys have a lot going on, you know? I mean, you barely ever get any sleep or have any time together alone. What if you leave the kids with your parents for a few nights and get away, just the two of you?"

"Yeah, that's a good idea. I should suggest it," Alice says, but her tone is not in the least bit convincing. "Oh crap, I have to run. Colby just started up the stairs with the toaster, and I think he's headed for the bathroom. I should *not* have let him watch that Bugs Bunny cartoon."

"Oh God. Yeah, go."

As Alice hangs up, I hear her shouting Colby's name.

I toss my phone on the bed and sit for a minute, trying to digest my conversation with her. I'm aching for her, and part of me wonders if I've been wrong to try to find a perfect life that looks exactly like hers, because it turns out it isn't so perfect after all. Maybe perfect doesn't exist.

If that's the case, I might as well go for crazy happy, even if on the outside it just looks plain crazy.

There's a knock at the door. Wow, that was quick. Harrison told me he wouldn't be back for a few more hours. One of the resort's trucks broke down, and he needed to go fix it.

I hurry to the door, running my fingers through my hair to tame it and straightening out my dress a little. My entire body feels all warm and tingly as I grab the handle.

I swing the door open with a huge smile on my face, planning to yank him inside and have my way with him.

But it's not Harrison standing there grinning down at me.

It's Richard.

22

Look Who's Making Plans Now

Harrison

I THOUGHT you should be the first to know that I'm completely in love. Well, I suppose Libby should probably have been the first person to know, but somehow telling her is far scarier. I've only been apart from her for three hours, and it feels like three months, which I'm guessing is a good sign. I have to guess because I've never felt this way before. I want to know everything about her, I want to hear her laugh and listen to her talk, and for the first time in my life, I can imagine why people want to have children. Because with her, having a family would be like a dream come true.

But before I can rush off and tell her how I feel, I need to get the oil leak on this truck fixed. I gave my mechanic, Charlie, today and tomorrow off so he could enjoy a long weekend with his family, and pretty much as soon as he left last night, oil started spewing all over the ground from this pickup. I'm currently in the non-airconditioned resort garage, lying on a creeper under the truck with oil, grease, and sweat covering my face. Luckily, I found the source of the problem pretty fast, but fixing it has been a real pain in the arse. It's taken me forty minutes to replace the cracked oil pan, but that's okay, because Libby is busy finishing up her report.

To be completely honest with you — and this is not something I would ever tell Rosy or Will or Emma — there is a tiny part of me willing to sign the deal with GlobalLux so I can have her here for a few extra months. I know that sounds very selfish, and I promise I would only consider it if it was actually the best thing for my staff. Well, and for Libby and me.

That has a nice ring to it, doesn't it? Libby and me. Oh, shit. Now I sound like a lovesick teenage girl. I might as well throw on some bubble gum lip gloss and write Mr. and Mrs. Harrison and Libby Banks all over the inside of my Physics binder.

Footsteps interrupt my thoughts, and it doesn't take long for me to figure out who they belong to.

"And where exactly have you been?" Rosy asks.

I slide out from under the pickup. "Right here fixing this truck," I say, holding up my wrench. "Did you need me for something?"

"Don't try to be cute with me. That stopped working when you were twenty. I meant where were you last night and all morning, and you know it," she says, staring down at me from her arms-under-her-boobs stance.

"Trying to save the resort," I say, then disappear under the truck, where it's safe.

"You went off with Libby in a speedboat and didn't come back for almost twenty-four hours."

"If you knew that, why did you ask?"

"It's more dramatic this way."

I shake my head and smile at her answer. "I have a plan, Rosy, and if it works, we might be in good shape for a very long time."

Another set of feet appear next to Rosy's, and when I look over, I can see they belong to my sister, who's wearing pink flip-flops that show off her cupcake ankle tattoo.

"You found him?" Emma asks.

"Yes, but he's being awfully vague about what's going on. Maybe you can talk some sense into him," Rosy says. "I need to go home and see my husband for a change." With that, she walks away muttering to herself about learning not to bother.

I finish tightening the last bolt and slide out from under the truck. When I stand, Emma's giving me a dirty look.

"What's up your butt?" I ask as I place the tools back in the box and close the lid.

"It was my first night back in *how many months*, and you just disappear," Emma says, planting a fist on her hip.

"Sorry about that. I thought I'd be back before dark. But I swear it was for the good of the resort." I wipe the sweat off my face with a clean rag, then peel off my coveralls.

"What's that mean? Where'd you go?"

"I took Libby out to look at a potential expansion site, then we got stuck in that big storm and had to stay the night there." I look her straight in the eye, hoping she can't tell there's more to the story, because the last thing I need right now is for her to tell Wikileaks before I know for sure what Libby's planning to do with the rest of her life.

Obviously, my poker face isn't as good as I hoped, because Emma's grinning and covering her mouth with both hands. "Oh my God! You love her!"

"It's strictly business, Emma." *Getting busy business…*

"Ummhmm." Emma raises one eyebrow.

"Strictly business." I nod to confirm my answer.

"Ha, well, that's really interesting, because 'strictly business' seems to have left a hickey on your neck."

I reach up, blushing a little and wincing as Emma laughs. "Please do *not* mention this to anyone, especially not to Rosy."

"On one condition," she says, folding her arms and reminding me of her bratty self at fourteen.

I roll my eyes. "What?"

"You admit you have feelings for her."

"I have feelings about lots of people," I say, starting toward the open overhead door. "Like you — I feel like you're the most irritating sister on the planet."

"Oh, stop trying to deny it. Everybody can tell you like her."

"What do *you* know? You've only been back for a day, and you've seen me have a two-minute conversation with her, if that."

"Yeah, but as soon as she got that yucky nose bleed, you were all, 'here, baby, let me swoop in and save you.'"

"God, you're such a child," I say, shaking my head.

"Takes one to know one," she says, sticking her tongue out at me.

"Really?"

"Yeah, well…you're the one sporting the hickey!"

"It's not a hickey. I must have walked into something."

"Libby's lips, perhaps?" she says with a huge grin. Jumping up and down, Emma claps her hands. "You're finally going to get married!"

"Am not," I say. "And why the hell are you so excited about the thought of me getting married, anyway?"

"Because once you have a wife, you'll be too distracted to nag me all the time."

"Oh, how wrong you are, little one. When I find a wife, I'll make sure she's willing to help me nag you. Now, I'm kind of in a hurry, so if you could lock up the garage for me, I'd appreciate it."

"You're going to see her, aren't you? For more smoochie woochies," Emma calls after me.

I wave her comment off and get in my golf cart, then take off before she can say anything more.

The entire ride back to my villa, I think about what I'm going to say and how I'm going to say it when I see Libby. Every nerve ending tingles with excitement as I plan out our evening together. Last night was incredible, but tonight I'm really going to sweep her off her feet. I'll swing by the lobby and get the keys to the royal honeymoon suite, then order champagne and a four-course dinner served on the terrace. We'll go for a midnight dip in the private infinity pool and make love until morning.

And if there's any justice in this world, Libby Dewitt and I will have a very happy ending.

———

Text from Will: *Bro, Emma's on her way home. I meant to text you a couple of days ago, but I got busy (with a super-hot chick, haha). #goodluck*

23

Trouble in Paradise (Bay) (Sorry, I had to do it)

Libby

"Richard?! What are you doing here?" I say as soon as I recover from the shock.

Richard's face is filled with emotion as he stares down at me. His silver hard-sided suitcase stands at attention at his side, and he's dressed in his resort-wear — a white button-down shirt with the sleeves rolled up and some tan linen pants with boat shoes.

Sweeping his left arm out from behind his back, he reveals an enormous bouquet of tropical flowers. "I came to beg you to take me back."

My entire body freezes up with shock, and all I can think about is, what if Harrison comes by right now? I can't imagine anything worse at this moment.

Except Richard kissing me, which it appears as though he's about to do because he's leaning in and he's closed his eyes...

A gush of liquid builds up in my nose. Oh, thank God. I've *never* been so relieved to have a nosebleed as I am at this moment. It allows me to avoid kissing him and taking the flowers, which, for some reason, feels disloyal. And I know that probably seems insane since

Richard has been my boyfriend for six years and Harrison for about twenty-six hours (is he even a boyfriend? I suppose not, right? Still... after everything we did and said to each other, whatever we are, it isn't *nothing*).

I hurry to the bathroom with my hand under my nose, leaving the door open behind me. I grab a wad of toilet paper and stand in front of the sink.

"Oh, sweetheart, this is all my fault, isn't it? I've done nothing but feel absolutely sick since you left. I tried to tell myself that I should just stay away after how I hurt you, but I couldn't. As soon as I realized you were really gone, I knew I'd made a horrible mistake. I don't know if you can ever forgive me, but I vow to spend the rest of my life making it up to you." He rubs my back and stares at me with a forlorn expression that almost makes me want to laugh out loud.

My only answer is a slight nod.

"Here, let me get you more toilet paper." He dashes across the bathroom and takes the entire roll off the toilet paper holder. Ripping off a long section, he holds it up to me with one hand and simultaneously crouches sideways to grab the garbage can and hold that up with his other. "Ready for a change?" he asks earnestly.

I just may be...

I have to say this is *the most attention* Richard has ever given me over a nosebleed, and ironically, this is the one time I really want some time alone because all the synapses in my brain are firing at once and I feel like my head is going to explode. Honestly, I'm kicking myself for not having come up with a 'just in case Richard shows up' plan, but I suppose I was too busy sleeping with Harrison, then trying to figure out how to save the resort to bother to do that.

I allow Richard to help me swap out the tissue, then stand, watching him in the mirror as he talks.

"I have a confession to make," he says.

I narrow my eyes, wondering if he did cheat on me, then swiftly realize how hypocritical that is, which leads me to the thought that actually, no, I didn't cheat because *he* broke up with *me* before I got here — in a very shitty way, I might add.

"It really was that picture you posted of you paddleboarding that sealed it for me. I mean, it's not just the bikini — although I do love you in a bikini — it's that you were willing to change for me. You really heard me when I said how boring our life was, and I honestly didn't know if you would. It was just such an awful moment for both of us, and I wasn't sure how much of it you were actually taking in, but then I see you posting these pictures of yourself parasailing and snorkelling and paddleboarding, and I thought, 'Wow, she's just so fun. I need to be there with her.'" He pauses and just stares at me like a sad puppy. "Say something, sweetie. I need to know what you're thinking."

"I need more toilet paper," I say, my words coming out muffled.

He shakes his head. "Sorry, sweetheart. Here you are with this horrible affliction, and I'm just rambling on about my own feelings. If I'm not careful, you're going to start thinking you were lucky to get away from me."

I let out a nervous laugh and say, "Yeah. Listen, if you could give me a few minutes, I'd like to get myself cleaned up."

"Of course. Of course you do. Okay, I'll just go sit in the room and wait for you." He nods repeatedly, then backs out like a servant leaving an evil queen. Shutting the door behind him, he leaves me alone with my panic.

Oh my God, what am I going to do? I don't even have my phone in the bathroom with me, so it's not like I can secretly call Alice or text her to get some advice. *Think, Libby, think.*

I breathe deeply while I wait for my nose to stop bleeding. Then I wash my face and brush my teeth — not because I want fresh breath for Richard, but more because I need the extra time to figure out what I'm going to say to him when I walk out there.

I stand with my hand on the doorknob for a ridiculously long time before I finally decide just to wing it. Opening the door, I find him sitting at the desk on the far side of the room, reading over my reports. It's always been a bit of a pet peeve of mine, because he tends to give me unsolicited advice even though he's never worked in mergers and acquisitions. To be fair, as a corporate lawyer, he does have a fair bit of knowledge. But still…he's quite mansplainy about it.

"Why two reports with completely different conclusions?" he asks, furrowing his brow together.

"The first one I wrote up is wrong. I got some new information last night that made me rethink the whole deal." *Not that it's any of your business.*

"Huh, well, that must've been one hell of a discovery last night for you to go from wanting to advise GlobalLux to back out to writing up a detailed plan for a major expansion project."

Oh, it was one hell of a discovery, all right. Seven of them, actually.

I set my shoulders back and stare him down for a second. "Yes, the property owner had a hidden gem that really made all the difference in the value of the property. It was a total game changer."

He shrugs nonchalantly even though I think he might suspect there's more to my change of heart than I'm letting on. Standing, he says, "I've actually got some stellar work-related news as well," smiling as he walks over to me.

"Really?" I ask, trying to sound enthusiastic.

"I'm up for partner." He stops, obviously waiting for some huge reaction from me he doesn't get. "On Tuesday, Morris told me I'm his front-runner. There are a couple of tiny things I need to do first to lock it in, but both are basically as good as done."

"That's amazing, Richard. Congratulations."

"Congratulations to *us*, sweetheart. The bonus alone will be enough for the down payment on that house on Waldorf Lane." He pulls me in for a hug, careful not to press my nose against his shirt.

Us? Waldorf freaking Lane? I've just been told everything I've always wanted is right within grasp, and instead of feeling elated, I feel... nothing. I'm numb. And that's not how I should feel, is it?

Giving me a kiss on the forehead, he pulls back and smiles down at me. "It's everything we wanted, Libby. And Morris said I can take the next week off with you to celebrate. If you want to get married here, we can. I'll go out first thing in the morning and get the license so we can be married by tomorrow afternoon. Or if you'd rather wait and do the big church wedding, I'll get Daniella on it immediately, and she can have the entire thing ready by the time we get home."

I push him away gently and shake my head, feeling uncomfortably hot. "Stop, just stop. Less than a month ago, you literally left me at the altar and told me you didn't love me anymore. Now all of a sudden, you show up without any warning and tell me you want to get married right away?"

He looks taken aback. "I thought you'd be happy. You've always wanted to get married, and now I'm saying, let's just do it."

"That was before..." I say, gesturing out to the sides with both hands.

"But you posted those pictures to show me how much you're trying to change, didn't you?"

I nod. "Yep, I did." He's got me there. A mere seven days ago, I was desperately trying to get his attention, but somehow everything changed when I got nothing back, and then...Harrison gave me so much.

Richard smiles and presses one palm to his heart. "I knew if you would do *that* for me, I had no choice but to fly halfway across the world to get you back. But if you need some time to let this sink in, that's more than fair. I completely understand."

"Yeah, that would be best." I slide on my flip-flops and grab the card key for my room off the desk. "I'm going to go for a walk. Alone. I need to think."

"Absolutely. I'll just unpack my things and get settled while you're gone."

He beams, and I stare at him for a moment, trying to figure out what exactly I feel for him. The only word that pops into my brain isn't a feeling at all. It's *nothing*.

———

I walk out of the building and straight down the path without even thinking of where I'm going. My feet take me to Harrison's villa, obviously, because my feet are attached to the rest of my body, which includes my naughty bits, which are clearly jonesing for some more of Harrison's length and girth.

How can I be thinking about sex at a time like this?! Oh, dear, I'm in some serious trouble, aren't I? I mean, Richard finally shows up and says everything I've been dreaming he'd say, which means I can still get my perfect life. All I have to do is say yes, and the entire thing will unfold before me like one of those origami swan napkins (you know the ones—you pull on the beak, and it magically fans out).

I knock on the door, not sure if I'm hoping Harrison will answer or not. Somehow, I feel like as soon as I see his face, I'll know what to do. I wait for a minute, but nobody comes to the door. Sighing, I start for the beach, hoping he's out for a run and we'll find each other like we did once before.

My head swirls with everything that's just happened, and it's hard for me to believe that in the last twenty-four hours, I've thought I was maybe falling in love with someone other than my fiancé, and now I'm faced with a choice I never thought I'd have to make. My thoughts switch back and forth between Richard and Harrison…and land on Richard.

I think about how excited he looked, and how he was saying all the right things and doing all the right things and offering me the life I've always wanted. I should definitely say yes to him. I mean, it's the safest choice, right? The responsible thing to do.

Plus, I know exactly what I'm getting into with Richard. He loves me — in spite of the whole wedding thing. After all, he did come all the way here to try to get me back. And if I go home with him, I'll be returning to the life I know — Saturday mornings at the farmer's market, fine dining, stability, my family and best friends nearby. With Harrison, it's a whole lot of terrifying uncertainty, which quite frankly isn't my comfort zone.

I should say yes to Richard. Yes to my old life. Yes to the dream house a few blocks from Alice and Jack's, where we can raise our children. It's the logical decision.

Then why doesn't any of that sound even remotely appealing to me right now? Is it just residual bitterness from the wedding? Dammit. Why can't someone just tell me what to do?

24

Dick Can Suck it for a Change

Harrison

THE SUN IS JUST STARTING to set as I hurry over to Libby's building. I take the steps two at a time and hold the door open for some of our guests who look dressed to go out for dinner.

"Have a great night," I say as I hurry past them, feeling completely alive.

When I knock on her door, my chest pounds with excitement and I think about the wonderful evening I have in store for us. I lean on the doorframe and grin as I hear the chain unlatch.

When the door swings open, I say, "Hey, beautiful" at the same time a man says, "There you are, darling."

We both stare at each other for a long moment before either of us says anything more. The guy has the phrase 'old money' written all over him, with his lame boat shoes and fancy 'I'm on a tropical vacay' pants, and I'm pretty sure he's never seen the business end of a wrench. I immediately dislike him, and not because he called me darling either.

I'm the first to speak again. "You must be Dick."

"*Richard*. And you are…?" he says, cracking his knuckles.

"Harrison Banks."

"Oh, yes. Libby told me about you." His eyes are hard enough to make me wonder if she told him *everything.* "Can I help you with something?"

"No. Is she here?"

"I'm afraid she's just stepped out. Oh, you're probably here for her report, yes? She was printing it just in time for my arrival." He turns and walks over to the desk. Picking up a stack of papers, he says, "She finished her work just in time to celebrate our future. I've been made partner at the largest law firm in the U.K."

My stomach drops to the floor at hearing Dick's happy tone and seeing the smug grin on his face. Through clenched teeth, I ask, "When will she be back? I need to ask her a few things about this report."

He walks back to me, his gait stiff. Handing the report to me, he says, "Why don't you email your questions to her? She'll be a bit busy tonight, if you get my drift."

I stare at him for a moment, pressing my tongue against the inside of my teeth while I decide whether or not I should just punch him. Realizing that's not really the best option, I say, "Yup, I'm pretty sure I know what you mean."

"We'll probably lock ourselves in our little love nest here for a few days before going back home to get married. Or if she's in a real hurry to get on with the wedding, we may just beam out tomorrow morning. Shall I tell her you said goodbye?"

What a fucking douche.

"No need. I know how to get in touch with her." I glare at him for a moment, rage coursing through my veins. "You know you don't deserve her, right?"

"Oh, and who does? Someone like you, perhaps?" he says, wrinkling up his nose. "A man who ran his business into the ground? I think she'll be better off with me, thanks — someone who can really take care of her."

"Take care of her?" I scoff. "You mean like abandoning her on her wedding day and telling her she's too boring for anyone to love? Like that, you mean?"

His head snaps back in shock, and he opens his mouth in what I'm sure would be a total douchey douche bag comeback, but I cut him off with, "Nice fucking boat shoes."

With that, I turn and walk out, letting the door shut behind me.

———

Have you ever been faced with something so horrible, the effort you put into wishing it wasn't true was enough to make you feel like you'd just finished an Ironman? Because that's how I feel right now.

I've been sitting on my couch sipping bourbon and reading over Libby's report line by line. She's written a scathing assessment that basically makes me sound like the world's most inept resort operator.

Her projections for Paradise Bay are bleak, to say the least, and I do my best to separate my feelings for her from what she's written, but it's nearly impossible. It all feels so personal because it is. The failures she sees are mine to claim.

Among the papers is a sheet I'm certain she didn't want me to see. Part of me wonders if Dick saw it and tucked it in for me to find, because I can't see her being so cruel to include it on purpose or so careless to leave it in by accident.

HARRISON'S WEAKNESSES:
- *me in lacy knickers*
- *hero complex*
- *attachment to staff*

Richard's smug face pops back into my head every twenty seconds or so, and it's all I can do not to go back over there and beat him to a pulp. I try not to think about what they might be doing right now, because the thought of his hands on her — and any other part of his body on her for that matter — makes me want to vomit.

Maybe if I'd had a few more days with her, she would have realized *I'm* the one who sees her, not him. I don't need her to be someone she isn't. I love her exactly the way she is. Or I thought I did. I stare down at the report again, and it finally hits me: I've been played.

She was just stringing me along so she could…what? Get in my pants?

Sipping my drink, I try to figure out what the hell just happened and what my next move should be. I toss the papers onto the coffee table and sit back on the couch, rubbing my eyes. How did I go from feeling so incredible to so incredibly bad in one evening?

I cringe when I think of all that cheesy shit I said about her being a beautiful butterfly, not a clam. What was I thinking? This was just business for her and should have been for me too.

Part of me can't help wondering if maybe the two of them do belong together. She'll obviously never want for anything with Dick-head, whereas she clearly sees me as some sort of…I don't know what.

The door swings open, and in walks Emma, three sheets to the wind. "Hey, brotha! Whatreyoudoinghere?" She plunks herself on the couch next to me. "I thought you'd be spending the night with your laddddayyy. Did you two get into a fight or something?"

"Not exactly. More like, I found out what she really thinks of me, and it turns out it's not all that flattering." I point to the report.

Emma leans forward and picks it up, then squints at the first page for a minute. Turning to me, she says, "Yeah, can you just give me the gist? I'm a little tipsy right now."

"You don't say," I answer, wincing at the smell of her breath. "It basically states that the resort is poorly built, has been poorly maintained, and would be a horrible investment."

Emma wrinkles up her nose. "What? That's crazy. Why would Libby say that? She seemed so nice…"

"I honestly don't know. Last night she sounded like this place was full of potential, but this…" I shake my head and sigh. "She played me."

"But why? So her company would be able to buy us for cheap?"

"That's the weird thing. She recommended they *don't* make an offer."

Emma looks up at the ceiling. "Okay, I'm not following, but full disclosure, I am actually really *very* drunk, so…"

"That's okay. I'm not following either." I rub the back of my neck.

185

"Maybe we should just sell to Stewart. We could use some of the money for you to finish school and protect the pension fund. And I could maybe buy a catamaran and spend the rest of my days taking people out on booze cruises." The thought makes me want to hurl, but then again, how much less stress would that be for me compared to this?

"Are you serious? One bad report, and you're ready to give up?" She tries to snap her fingers but misses, then gets distracted trying to snap them again and again.

I pat her leg and smile. "You should have a glass of water and get some sleep."

She finally lets her hand fall to her lap and rests her head on my shoulder. "You can't give up, Harrison. This is our home."

"You need to know when you're beat. And when you are, you have to roll with the—"

Sitting up suddenly, she points a finger in my face. "Don't say it. Do not say roll with the punches. That's just an excuse for giving up," she slurs. "And you're not a quitter. You're Super-Harrison. I know I've never told you this, but you're my hero. You can do anything. Always could, you beautiful bastard." Emma leans in and pats me on the cheek, too hard. "But don't tell Will. He thinks he's the hero, but it's you. It's always been you."

I feel a lump in my throat for some stupid reason and clear it away. "I'm not super anything."

"Yes, you are. So don't go making some stupid excuse to give up just because she hurt your feelings."

"It's not an excuse, Emma. As the guy who's been holding it all together for over a decade, I'm probably the best one to know when it's all unraveling."

"Nope. We can fix it. We're a family, which means we can fix anything if we work together," she says, nodding wildly. Then she closes her eyes and leans back on the couch. "Just give me a minute to think of a way…"

"And she's out," I murmur.

I get up and pick up a blanket off the armchair, then take off her shoes and cover her up. As I arrange Emma on her side and tuck a pillow under her head, I think of the last woman I looked after who was in this shape.

The thought twists my insides, and I realize I completely forgot my own motto: Never get too attached. Ha! I screwed that one up, didn't I? And for a brief moment, I was even willing to sell out my family for her.

Holy shit, Harrison. What were you thinking?

Lesson learned — again. And this time, I won't forget.

25

Fireworks at Night...and Not the Good Kind

Libby

I'M LYING awake in bed, listening to Richard snore. He's on a cot I had brought in. By the time I got back from my walk, I didn't feel like I could very well kick him out into the night, but I certainly did not want him in my bed either. He seemed to accept the fact that I wasn't ready to kiss and make up, and although he's made it very obvious he's disappointed, he's really not in any position to do anything other than wait.

My heart is aching, and I feel hot and sweaty, like I have a horrible fever, but it's one I've caused myself. I've never been so torn up in my life. There's no way I'm going to fall asleep, not until I've seen Harrison.

I get up quietly and pull on a pair of shorts and a sweater over my T-shirt, not because it's cold out, but because I have a horrible feeling I'll need an extra buffer to protect myself from whatever is about to happen.

Picking up my flip-flops, I pocket the key to my room and sneak out. When I step outside, I'm met by a cool breeze and the sound of sprinklers watering the grass outside the building. The combination somehow holds a hint of the relief and hope I need right now.

I hurry down the path, praying Harrison will be home this time. When I round the corner, I see the light is on in his villa, and I practically sprint the last few hundred yards (except without actually sprinting because, eww, sprinting).

I knock loudly and wait. It takes a minute before the door opens and he stands before me, shirtless, with a very serious expression that hardens his features.

Between my rush to get here and the sight of him, I'm nearly breathless. "Hi. I came to find you earlier, but you weren't home."

"Yeah, I got busy."

"Can I come in? I think we should talk."

"Well, I don't." He shrugs, seeming completely indifferent to me.

I stare into his eyes, trying to figure out what exactly is going on. "Why not?"

"I met Dick earlier."

My heart drops to my toes, and I cringe, wondering what Richard said to him.

"Harrison, I didn't know he was coming, and I didn't—"

"Is he still in your room?"

"What?"

He's gruff in a way that shocks me.

"Is he still in your room?" he asks, over-pronouncing each word. "Because if he is, it means you want him there, which means we don't have anything to talk about."

"Yes, he's there, but—"

"—then I guess we're through."

Tears prick my eyes, and I blink them back, my mind racing for what to say but coming up blank.

"Don't overthink this, Libby. We were just having some fun, but the fun's over now, which, believe me, is for the best. I was starting to feel guilty about using you to try to get some extra zeros."

My eyes scan his face, desperate to see some trace of the gentle man who takes care of everyone he meets and who held me in his arms last night while I cried about my mother, but he's not there. In his place is someone I don't know. Someone harsh and hateful.

"You're lying."

"Not this time," he says, his voice clipped.

Feeling a deep sense of betrayal and pain bubble up from my stomach, I say, "You let me see who you really are — not the super-hero you pretend to be, but the *real Harrison* who's so worried about everyone else that he can't sleep at night. The guy who'd do *anything* for the people he loves."

His face is so cold, he doesn't even look like the same man. "You're right. I would do anything for them. But you're not part of that group, so you should just...go home."

My head snaps back in shock.

He sets his jaw, then says, "The truth is, there's another investor interested in the property, and I've been using you to drive up the price on him. I went to see him today, and it turns out my plan worked. I'm going to be very rich, so thanks for that."

"Why are you saying this?" I ask, my voice catching. "Why are you lying to me?"

"Libby, listen to me, this is the first time I've told you the truth. It's just business. Everything else I've said to you was...strategic."

I shake my head. "No, it wasn't."

"Yes, it was. But try not to let it get to you. You're still going to get your happy ending. Dick flew all the way around the world to sweep you off your feet," he says. "And he's still in your room, so there's really nothing more for us to say to each other."

Tears threaten to make an appearance, but I blink them back. "Wow. I'm glad I could see your cruel side before I did something stupid like fall in love with you."

"Yeah, *I'm* the cruel one," he answers, letting out a frustrated laugh. Grabbing the door, he looks at me with such disdain, it nearly takes my breath away. "Have a good life, Ms. Dewitt. I'm sure you and Dick will have a long, happy future together of corporate domination."

———

I wait until I'm halfway back to my room before I allow a sob to escape my chest.

Spotting a bench along the path, I sit down and curl my legs into my chest, tucking my head to my knees and wishing I could just disappear from this place and from this moment. I feel dirty and used and stupid. Oh, so very stupid.

I played right into his hands and completely killed my career for him. The thought makes me sick to my stomach.

Oh my God. I quit my job.

I sit, trying to catch my breath for a minute but only managing to let out more sobs. I was willing to give up my entire future for him, but it turns out he couldn't care less about me. He's nothing but a liar — a horribly good, incredibly ripped, amazing-in-bed liar who uses women and throws them away.

And I'm the spectacular idiot who fell for it.

26

You'll Know When You Know...
and Other Horribly Stupid Advice

Libby

YOU KNOW that feeling you get when you're on your last day of a vacation and you have to go home even though every cell in your body is screaming 'never go back to that horrible place where responsibility is waiting,' and it just sucks knowing there's nothing you can do but finish packing and start the long, dull trip home where you'll commence your usual soul-sucking routine that you used to think was pretty great until you discovered something so much better was out there?

Yeah, well, that would be about a million times better than what I'm feeling right now.

I may have shown up here thinking I was hurt, but I'm leaving here an absolute freaking mess. Whatever I felt for Harrison, I have to accept it was just a lie, even though it felt very real. I have to accept that I mean nothing to him and I never did, even though I wanted to matter to him more than I've ever wanted to matter to anyone.

How could someone so perfect, so amazing, turn out to be so disappointing? *He's* the one who's exactly like my mother. Not me.

The birds chirp outside my open patio doors, and it kind of feels like they're mocking me as I sit on the edge of my bed with my engagement ring in the palm of my right hand, waiting for Richard to wake up. I'm already dressed even though the sun is barely up. I didn't sleep at all after I found out the truth about Harrison. I just laid awake with silent tears streaming down my face until I my head was pounding.

Richard finally stirs. I watch as he sits up on the cot and stretches his back, obviously worse for wear after a night on the thin mattress. He knows my answer as soon as he looks into my eyes, because he just nods and says, "I figured as much when you called down for the cot. Is it that other guy?"

"No," I say, and the funny thing is, it's true. "Your gut was spot-on about us not being right for each other."

"Huh. Chalk one up for male intuition," he says with a small smile.

I smile back. "I wanted it so badly for so long. I always thought if I had you, I'd have it all — love, respectability, comfort. I thought it would mean I'd finally prove I'm not my mother."

"I know," he said. "We stopped being in love a long time ago and became more like nice companions."

"Was it because I didn't want to do the butt stuff?" I ask with a tiny grin.

He lets a short laugh escape his mouth. "No, but I kind of had a hint that our priorities were a bit off when you emailed me to say you found the perfect spot for our honeymoon and was sure I wouldn't mind if it doubled up as a work trip."

I nod, biting my bottom lip. "Yeah, I can see how you'd take that as a sign." Sighing, I just stare at him for a moment, knowing this is the last time I'll see his rumpled morning hair and sleepy eyes. I feel a lump in my throat and swallow it down. "This is hard. We could've had a really nice, comfortable life together, and for a lot of people, that would be more than enough."

"You're right," Richard says, taking my hand in his. "But it would never have been what either of us deserves."

"Agreed," I say, letting a few tears sneak by my defenses. "For the record, I didn't actually go paddleboarding. I just used some camera trickery to set up a shot for my Instagram account."

"You Photoshopped it?"

I laugh, slapping my forehead with one hand. "I wish! That would have been so much easier."

Richard laughs, too, and it feels so good to end things like this, with neither of us hurting or angry. When he stops, he says, "I guess I should get a flight home."

I shake my head. "I already booked you a flight for this morning. I figured once we talked, you'd want to get out of here."

"I see. When are you coming back?"

"Tonight. I'm sticking with our original flight home. I have some loose ends to tie up here."

He nods. "That's probably for the best. If I'm around you too long, I might forget why we're breaking up."

I open my palm and hold the ring up to him, but he shakes his head and folds my palm closed again. "I want you to have it."

"No," I say. "You bought it. You should see if you can get some of your money back."

"Libby, you'd actually be doing me a favour by keeping it," he says. "I feel really guilty about letting you pay for most of the wedding that didn't happen."

"Well, when you put it that way…" I answer.

He stands and pulls a T-shirt over his head. "You're going to be pleasantly surprised when you find out what it's worth."

"Really?"

He nods and smiles. "Spend it wisely."

"I will."

And that's how Richard and I came to our strangely perfect ending — with us hugging and crying as we let go of years together, because no matter how it ended or who decided to jilt whom ten minutes before the wedding, giving up someone you know inside and out and someone who cared for you for a long time is never easy. Even when it's right.

———

My face is red and puffy from crying, and even though it's hours later, I still have a few tears left in me as I toss my makeup kit onto my packed clothes. I've put my engagement ring back on for safe-keeping, except on the right hand instead of the left because my relationship status is no longer 'engaged' or even 'it's complicated,' but 'completely, utterly single.'

I move over to my desk, which I've saved for last. After I disconnect the printer and put it carefully in my other suitcase, I start on the papers.

Huh, that's weird. I could've sworn I printed off the fake report yesterday, but it's not here. I must not have, which just shows how completely mucked up my head has been since, oh, I don't know, I first laid eyes on Harrison. I can only hope when I get back home, I can sort out fact from fiction. Maybe I can even manage to find a job where I'll use my analytical skills for good instead of evil. I tuck the report into a large yellow envelope and put it, along with my laptop, into my carry-on bag.

A few minutes later, I find myself standing in front of the building, waiting for a golf cart to pull up and take me to the lobby to check out. Glancing at my phone, I see I have three hours until my flight leaves, taking me back to a country where I have no home and no job.

I text Alice: *Hey, you don't happen to have a spare room I could squat in for a while, would you?*

A moment later, my mobile dings. *Oh, hon, I take it things didn't work out with Mr. Perfect?*

Me: *Turns out he's a much bigger prick than Richard.*

Alice: *He *has* a much bigger prick than Richard or he *is* one? I'm confused.*

Me: *Both.*

Alice: *Come home. The wine is chilling, and I'm all stocked up on Choco-Loco.*

Me: *A disgusting combination under normal circumstances, but at the moment, it sounds divine. See you sometime around lunch tomorrow.*

I hear the hum of the golf cart before it turns the corner, and for a moment my heart jumps thinking it's Harrison, but when it comes around, I see Fidel's friendly face behind the wheel. I smile at him, hoping I can pretend everything's fine.

"Aww, Libby, don't tell me you're leaving already?" he says, getting out to load my bags into the back.

"Yes, I'm afraid the time has come."

"Did you enjoy your honeymoon?" He gives me a little wink.

"Let's just say I hope I never go on another one."

"That's too bad. That must mean we didn't take good enough care of you." Climbing into the driver's seat, he starts up the cart.

I sit next to him, hoping to keep it together until I get on the shuttle bus. We wind around the building where Harrison played the Opossum Wrangler, and I sigh. We drive by the beach bar, and I wave to Lolita, who's looking surly as she serves something fruity to a table of four. Her mouth opens, and she looks like she's about to call to me, but then she closes it and just waves back. We pass the pier where the catamaran is docked, and I find myself wishing with everything in me that I were standing on the top deck with him right now, heading out to sea instead of heading home. As we zip by the pool, I spot Butterfingers Girl folding towels. At least she's happy.

When we get to the lobby, he hops out and hands my bags to a waiting porter. Turning to me, he says, "Come back any time. We'd all love to see you again, especially Harrison."

I scoff a little. "I highly doubt that. I'm sure he'll be glad I'm gone."

He pauses for a minute, looking completely confused, then shakes his head. "I don't think so. It's going to take him a long time to forget you."

Before I can assure Fidel he's wrong, his walkie-talkie on the golf cart pages him and he leans over to answer it. I quietly wave to him and slink my way into the lobby.

I check out, then, without thinking about it, I ask the receptionist if I can see Rosy for a minute.

She nods and points to the back. "She should be free right now."

I knock on Rosy's door, finding her behind her desk with one pair of glasses on her nose and one on top of her head. I feel a pang, knowing I'm going to miss her.

She looks up at me and takes her glasses off, letting them dangle from the chain around her neck. "Libby, what can I do for you?"

"I just came to say goodbye."

"I take it everything worked out with your fiancé, then?" she asks with a slightly disapproving expression.

I give her a confused look and am just about to ask how she knows Richard was here when she says, "I was behind the desk when he checked in yesterday."

"I take it you missed it when he checked out this morning."

Her face spreads into a wide grin. "Did you send him packing?"

"I did."

Clapping her hands together, she says, "Good. That leaves everything wide open for you and Harrison."

I shake my head. "No, there's nothing open there at all. Super closed, in fact. Like the door has been padlocked and the key is at the bottom of Mariana's Trench. That means it's irretrievable unless you have one of those tiny subs that can withstand incredible pressure, which I don't, so…"

Rosy gives me a strange look. "What are you talking about? For someone so good at analyzing everything she sees, you certainly are blind to what matters."

"Gee, thanks," I say sarcastically.

"I've known that boy since he was eleven, and I can tell you he's never once looked at any girl the way he looks at you."

"Well, as it turns out, he's an amazing actor, because he made it very clear to me last night this has been strictly business. It's all good, though, because we're not compatible at all, he and I," I say, shaking my head. "Not at all." Digging around in my briefcase, I pull out the yellow envelope. "Anyway, I have a little goodbye present for you."

"What is it?"

"It's a step-by-step guide for world domination in the resort industry." I hand the envelope to her. "Just don't ever let anybody know I gave you that. If I ever want to get a job in mergers and acquisitions again, that report would pretty much ruin my chances. I've been making some wildly erratic and terrible choices lately, like sleeping with a potential client and quitting my job. Why am I rambling?" I ask with a little snort. "Sorry, I didn't sleep last night."

"Come and sit down. You're talking nonsense." She gestures to a chair, but I shake my head.

"I really have to go, or I'll miss my flight."

"What happened, Libby?"

"I wish I knew." I give her a sad smile, then say, "You take care, okay?"

With that, I walk out, blinking back tears.

I sit on the tiled bench in front of the lobby for about five minutes, waiting for the shuttle bus, when I hear, "Coward!"

Turning, I see Rosy rushing down the steps toward me with Emma following on her heels.

Rosy wags her finger at me. "You love him, and you're just going to run off with your tail between your legs."

The other people waiting shift away from me awkwardly.

"Rosy, I don't—"

"Bullshit. I just read your report, and you know what I see on page one? Love. Page two? Love. Page three, four, five, six. Love, love, love, love. Page seven?"

"Love?" I ask sarcastically.

"No, that one was filled with a lot of boring financials, but the rest just say love all over them."

"Rosy, the report is my very honest professional opinion of the resort, not of…" glancing around, I notice the other guests, along with Fidel and two of the porters, are now just openly staring. I lower my voice, "…anyone in particular. And even if I *did* have feelings for someone, he doesn't feel the same way, so that's that."

Emma cuts in. "I'm pretty sure someone is totally stupid over you. He was listening to Bob Marley until three am."

Rosy makes a *tsk*ing sound. "No Woman, No Cry?"

"Ummhmm." Emma nods. "Over and over."

"Poor darling," Rosy says, shaking her head.

Emma sighs. "Then he took off this morning before I got up. He left this on the kitchen table." She hands me a note.

Emma—

I'll be gone for a few days. Just need a little time to figure out my next move.
Hold down the fort while I'm gone.
H

"This doesn't prove anything," I say, handing it back to her.

"Love doesn't ask for proof," Rosy says, folding her arms across her ample chest.

Rolling my eyes, I say, "What is this? A Hallmark movie? He literally told me I meant nothing to him and to leave."

Emma looks at me, her eyes wild. "Yeah, but can you really blame him? He was just chasing you away because your idiot fiancé showed up and he thought you were getting back together with him. As soon as he shut the door on you, he said, 'Fuck love.'"

"You were there?"

She nods. "I was…napping on the couch," she says, throwing a guilty glance in Rosy's direction. "He was a wreck last night, so I was trying to make him feel better. He really didn't want to talk though, he just sat there sipping bourbon and reading your report over and over."

I freeze in place as her words smack me across the face. "What report?"

The shuttle bus pulls up, and the people around us move toward it. Fidel calls to me, "Libby, should I load your luggage?"

"Just a second," I say, then turn to Emma. "What report?"

"The one that said Paradise Bay wasn't a recommended purchase for GlobalLux. It was kind of harsh, actually. I had a look at it this morning, and I have to say, it was a little bit offensive."

My mouth drops open and the breath leaves my lungs as my brain pieces together what's happened. "Oh my God! This means I did print the report, which is kind of good because I thought I was losing my mind, but it's also really awful because it means Harrison read it, and he was *never* supposed to see any of it. None of you were supposed to because it made the resort sound like a disaster so GlobalLux would back off and leave you alone. But it was all a bunch of lies and…" I slap my forehead. "…if Harrison saw it, he must think I think—"

"Libby? The bus needs to leave. On or off?" Fidel asks.

"Off," I say firmly.

27

Chasing Down the Love of Your Life, Booze Cruise Style

Libby

As soon as the word 'off' leaves my mouth, Rosy locks me in a big bosomy hug while the shuttle pulls away, leaving me in a cloud of diesel and Shalimar. She releases me, then looks at Emma and nods. "She's the one."

Emma gives me a slightly skeptical look.

Rosy puts a hand on her hip. "Have you seen your brother with her? He's like that cute dog who can't keep his tongue in his mouth?"

"What dog?" Emma asks.

"You know the one. Will showed us on his phone." Rosy tilts her head to the side and sticks her tongue out, then walks around wagging her bum. When she stops, she looks back and forth from Emma to me. "No? Neither of you knows that one?"

"Afraid not," I say at the same time Emma says, "No clue."

Emma then turns to me and narrows her eyes. "Say the first word that comes to mind, no hesitating. How do you feel about Harrison?"

"Completely terrified."

"That was not the answer I was looking for," Emma says, giving me a 'you blew it' look.

Rosy swats Emma on the arm. "It was a *fine* answer."

Emma turns to Rosy. "First of all, it was *two* words. I asked for the first word—"

"But the first word was 'completely.' Not 'a little' or 'kinda,'" Rosy says.

"Yes, but the second was 'terrified.' That hardly means she's in love with him."

"You only think that because you've never been in love before," Rosy counters. She waves Fidel over. "Fidel, when you first fell for Winnie, was it terrifying?"

"Completely," he says with a firm nod.

All three of them turn and stare at me while I shift uncomfortably in my flip-flops, not having the first clue what to say.

Rosy nods, then says, "She loves him."

Turning to Rosy with one hand on her hip, Emma says, "How can you say that? She hasn't even given one tiny hint that she loves him."

"Because she didn't get on the damn shuttle. If she didn't love him, she'd be halfway to the airport by now," Rosy retorts.

"How do you know? Maybe she just needs to get that awful report back. Maybe she wants a few more days to work on her tan. Maybe she…has a fear of buses," Emma says, throwing her arms in the air.

"Or *maybe* she's in love with your brother!" Rosy yells, attracting the attention of pretty much anyone wearing a Paradise Bay uniform.

My entire body heats up with embarrassment as I glance around the area and see all the curious onlookers. "Could I just say—" I start, but apparently I'm no longer part of the conversation.

"Why are you pushing this so hard?" Emma asks Rosy.

The crowd closes in, and now I'm basically surrounded by about twenty people who absolutely *must know* about my intimate feelings for their boss.

"Could we just maybe go back into your office?" I say out of the side of my mouth, but both women ignore me.

"Why are you trying to get in the way of love?" Rosy answers.

"Because I'd like to be sure she's good enough for my brother before I help her find him, thank you very—"

"Oh, screw it," I snap, cutting Emma off. "I'm just going to lay it all out on the line. What you need to know about me is that I'm probably *the most* responsible, predictable woman on the planet. I was voted 'least likely to do anything risky' in my graduating class, which was really quite mean but also very accurate.

"Up until three weeks ago, I had my entire life — like, literally every single day of my future — planned down to the hour, and I was actually really happy knowing where it was all heading because it seemed so safe and perfect, you know?"

Looking at their confused expressions, I can see these people are not fellow planners.

"Okay, maybe not. But the point is, now I feel like some totally insane person who just quit my job and sent my fiancé packing for a guy I *just met*, which will either be the single greatest thing I've ever done or the hallmark of when I ruined my entire life for what could very well be a rebound but most definitely doesn't feel like one because I've never felt as beautiful or alive or bursting with excitement and joy as I do when I'm with him." I pause and take a deep breath. "And it's not just that. It's that I'd do anything for him. You know? Like, *anything*," I say, giving Fidel a knowing look.

Understanding crosses his face, and apparently I'm not as subtle as I hoped because Emma says, "Eww! T.M.I."

"Sorry about that. I've had ZERO sleep. I just don't know how this could be a rebound, because I took *three Cosmo* online quizzes asking 'Is he the one?', and they all came back in the affirmative. Well, one of them was about whether he was worth it, not if we were meant to be, but that one came back with a yes, too."

Emma looks at me. "So…you're a little crazy, then, yes? I did not pick that up when I met you a couple of days ago."

"Only since I met your brother. Prior to that, I was *ridiculously* sane."

"He'll do that to you," Emma says, nodding her head. "You poor, poor girl. You sure you want a life of this?"

"I think so," I say.

"Yes! There are going to be some adorable little ginger babies in my future!" Rosy exclaims. "Now, Emma, where is he?"

"No idea."

"Okay, that's not a problem," Rosy says. "I've had two decades of tracking that boy down. The first thing to do is figure out if he took one of the trucks or a boat."

She flags down a passing golf cart and commandeers it, telling the porter and guests sitting on it we have emergency resort business.

They get out, looking bewildered, while the three of us pile in, and Rosy puts the pedal to the metal. Turns out she drives like Vin Diesel on speed. It's a terrifying trip from the lobby over to the garage, then the pier, both for me and anyone who happens to be walking around the resort. I white-knuckle it while she alternates between honking and yelling, "Emergency! Out of the way, people!"

Swimsuit-clad people hop off the path into the bush, holding on to their hats and pool floaties as we zip by.

I'm in the back seat, gripping the handles on the armrest and pressing my feet into the floor as hard as possible, trying to keep myself from flying out, while Emma, who's in the front passenger seat, turns and starts talking to me as though we're chatting over a leisurely lunch.

"So, Libby, do you like kids?" she asks.

"Umm, generally yes, but I suppose it depends on the child." I wince because we almost take out an elderly man with a walker. And when I say we almost take him out, I mean my arm brushed against him while we zoomed past.

"Good answer," Emma says. "Harrison wants kids. He pretends he doesn't, but he *totally* does."

We come to a sudden stop at the pier, and after we all jump out, I follow Rosy and Emma as they run to the boathouse. Emma grabs a clipboard off the wall, then says, "He's got Rogue Fun!"

I give her a quizzical look.

"Small speedboat used for scuba diving excursions," she answers. "Super fast."

Taking a deep breath, I say, "I think I know where he went."

———

To bring you up to speed, Harrison's not answering the Rogue Fun radio, which doesn't help us at all. Rosy stayed back to call her nephew (a cop) to ask him to trace Harrison's mobile phone (even though I'm pretty sure they don't do that for cases of 'I hurt the man I think I might love and need to find him to apologize and see if we can have a future together before I leave the country forever.' But hey, it's worth a shot, right?)

Emma and I barely made it on this afternoon's booze cruise as it was departing the pier — like, literally the catamaran was pulling away and Emma jumped (she's a total badass, by the way). I may or may not have tried to jump as well, which resulted in me slipping, just barely managing to grab hold of the boat's ledge with my fingertips and slamming my body against the side. This may or may not have left me dangling there with the bottom half of my body in the sea while I waited to be pulled aboard (because let's be honest, my upper body strength is enough to lift a wine bottle in each hand, not enough to lift an entire adult-sized human onto a boat, even if that human is me). But don't feel bad for missing the live version. Several of the guests were filming on their phones, so I'm pretty sure you'll be able to Google it by now. Look up "Ginger Getting on Boat Fail."

Anyway, we just finished rushing up the ladder (I sloshed/slipped my way up while Emma boosted my bottom, which was awkward but also oddly comforting because she's super on board with her brother ending up with me now). Unfortunately, because the catamaran was the only resort watercraft that wasn't already out, it's going to be a slll-looowww ride to the unnamed secret island. Luckily, Emma knew which one I meant when I started to explain it to her, because there's no freaking way I'd be able to guide us there.

"Does this thing go any faster?" I ask Justin, who's at the wheel of the catamaran.

He adopts a Scottish accent and says, "I'm givin' her all she's got, Captain."

"Oh, for God's sake," Emma says, rolling her eyes at Justin. "You go serve drinks, I'll drive."

Justin does as she suggested while Emma gets behind the wheel and pushes the throttle fully down, then turns to me. "This will give us about an extra 2 km per hour."

"So at this rate, we should get there sometime around…"

"Christmas, yes," she says. "But it'll give me time to tell you about my brother. First, he's as stubborn as he is generous, so if you can get past the mule-like qualities, you'll see he's actually really terrific. But *do not* tell him I said that, because I'll deny it to the grave."

"Noted."

"He also hates The Beatles, so if you're some major fan and you need to listen to them every day, this probably won't work out," she says gravely.

"He already told me, and while I can't fathom it, I *can* accept it," I return with as much gravity as possible.

"Wow. If he told you that, he must really like you."

Rosy's voice comes over the CB radio. "Big Momma to Baby Bear. Come in Baby Bear. Over."

Emma rolls her eyes, then picks up the radio receiver and microphone and says, "Do we have to use the code names? I really hate the code names."

There's a long pause and some crackling.

Emma sighs. "Baby Bear here." After another long pause, Emma says, "Over."

Rosy's voice comes back on. "Hey, Baby Bear, I'm afraid it's a no-go with the boys in blue. Over."

"So, you're saying Tyson couldn't help trace Harrison's mobile phone?"

Static.

Emma clicks the button. "Over."

"I forgot they took the kids to Disneyland. How's the search going on your end? Over."

"Slow. Next time Harrison wants to disappear, I'm hiding the Rogue Fun keys. He can take the catamaran. Over."

———

The tiny lush island comes into view an hour and a half and one stop for lobster-fishing later (which Emma did, by the way. See? Badass). My head is pounding from the heat and the steady thrum of the music from the lower deck. It's a full-on party down there, and to be honest, I cannot wait to get off. I can hardly hear myself think. What I *do* know is I'm all sweaty and my heart is racing. I'm terrified and excited and feel pukey all at the same time, which is not my normal state.

Finally, we make our way around the island to the beach where Harrison docked the boat when he brought me here. I hold my breath, hoping against hope he'll be here. If he's not, I don't have a plan B in mind. I don't even have a plan A, actually. Just search and hope, but it somehow feels oddly okay. No nosebleeds yet, so that must be a good sign.

"He's here!" Emma says, pointing as the Rogue Fun comes into view.

A wave of relief washes over me, which is then quickly replaced by a gripping fear. "This suddenly seems like a horrible idea," I say to Emma. "What if he meant what he said? What if he really doesn't care about me? What if he's here with some other woman?"

"Oh God, I never thought of that," Emma says, biting her lip. Then she shrugs. "Well, you know what? There's only one way to find out."

She docks the party boat, and we climb down to the main deck. While Justin puts the dock out, I search the beach for any sign of Harrison, but he's not here.

Emma must come to the same conclusion because she says, "Damn. You're going to have to go up the mountain." Putting her hands on my shoulders, she says, "Go get him, Libby."

"Wait, you're not coming with me?"

Shaking her head, she says, "No way. Can you imagine how awkward it would be if he actually is in love with you and I'm there all, 'Hey guys, don't mind me while you're making out'?"

"Good point," I say, realizing this means I have to go searching for him in the jungle alone. I swallow hard. "Okay. So I'll just go look. It might take me a while to find him and then come back to let you know."

"Oh, we can't stay."

"What?"

"Yeah, we can't keep all these people on the boat that long. We're *for sure* going to run out of booze, which is when the wheels start coming off."

"Really? You'd think it would be while people are drinking…"

"Yeah, you would, but no. Weird, right?"

"Very," I say.

"Are you stalling because you're scared?" Emma asks.

"Yes. Yes, I am." I blow out a breath and give her a confident smile. "Okay, I better get going. I'll just go up the mountain alone and find him, without anyone else to help in case of a snake or iguana attack. But if I do make it alive and it turns out he's with someone else or he doesn't love me back, I'm sure he'll give me a ride back to the resort. It'll be a little awkward, but nothing fatal."

"Iguanas rarely attack. Just don't challenge one for his food. And don't worry about snakes. There aren't any, I promise."

"But the other stuff…" I say, swallowing hard.

Emma gives me two thumbs up. "Good luck to you."

"Thanks."

I take off my flip-flops (which I suddenly realize are not exactly hiking shoes), lift up my sundress (also not very practical for an early evening jaunt through an uninhabited island), and wade through the water to the shore. Standing on the beach, I watch for a minute while the party boat sets off, taking with it my last chance to change my mind.

Okay, Libby. Time to wing it.

28

A Man Escaping (Which is Completely Different than Manscaping)

Harrison

It was not a good idea to come out here to escape from my life. I honestly don't know what the hell I was thinking because for the past few hours, everywhere I look, I see Libby. Especially right now. I'm standing under the waterfall in hopes of letting the cool water wash away everything I thought I knew about Ms. Dewitt, but instead it's just making me think of us having wild waterfall sex here on this rock. And in the pool it leads to…

I step out from under the spray and shake my head like a dog, then climb onto a large boulder so I can lay down in the sun and relax. Closing my eyes, I force myself not to see her face, not to feel her body against mine, not to hear her laugh or taste her kiss. She's nothing to me. Less than nothing. She was the means to an end — one I didn't want to see coming, but one that's barreling toward me nonetheless.

I called Stewart earlier, but his housekeeper said he'd taken Matilda to the Virgin Islands. He's supposed to call me tomorrow when he gets back, and I guess that's when I'll tell him he can have

Paradise Bay. As much as it kills me to sell him the property, he's not a bad person and he has enough cash to keep it going for a long time, which is what the staff needs. Still, the thought of no longer having the resort is like a punch to the nuts...

Kind of like Libby's nasty report.

Standing, I decide to make my way back to the cabin to have some dinner. I brought a can of beans, some hot dogs, and a whole lot of rum with me. Man food.

See? A plus side to being single, already — no woman to fail to impress.

As I walk along, I spot a mango tree near the trail and stop to pick a ripe one to add to my supper (hey, I'm a man, not an animal). When I turn around, an iguana is watching me. I jump a little, then laugh at myself.

"Are you the same guy from the other night?" I ask.

He responds by sticking out his tongue at me.

"If you're looking for that woman I was with, she's not here. Oh, you probably want some mango..." I sigh, sitting down on a fallen log and grabbing a thin, jagged rock off the ground. Slicing the mango open, I then separate the two halves and set them on a large stone a few feet from where the log is. Settling back down, I say, "Go on. It's ripe. But don't think we're going to make this a habit. You're supposed to get your own food."

He sticks his tongue out a few times in the direction of the mango, then walks over, standing on the far side of the rock so he can watch me while he eats.

"You won't see her again, by the way. By now, she's probably somewhere over Europe. Maybe she landed in Germany already, I don't know. Doesn't matter." I pause and watch him eat for a bit. "It's for the best. She and I weren't exactly what's known as a good match in human terms — we're total opposites. It's all fireworks and earth-shattering sex at the beginning, but it never works out in the end."

Libby's smiling face pops into my mind without my permission. Then suddenly the image shifts and she looks devastated because I've just lied to her and sent her away. My gut churns at the memory, but then I remember that *she's* the one who lied first. She's the one who pretended. Not me. Well, not until I had to, anyway.

Forget her, Harrison. She's halfway to Avonia by now, and she's never coming back.

"On the plus side, I'll never have to see her again either. I guess that's also the downside, isn't it?" I rub my hand on the back of my neck. "You know what? I should just go back to the cabin, get wasted, and forget all about the fact that tomorrow, life as I know it will end."

I think about the staff and my family, and the realization that I can't save them from this just about guts me. Then Libby's list of my flaws comes into mind. Hero complex. She wrote it like it's a bad thing. How is helping others a flaw? I guess because I ended up here.

My shoulders drop, and I let out a long, deep sigh. "You know what? Screw everyone else," I say to the iguana, jabbing one finger into my knee to emphasize my point. "I'm through with all this hero business."

The iguana makes eye contact while he chews, which I take as a sign of his complete agreement.

"My entire life, I've gone from one situation where people need rescuing to another. Maybe it's time I do something for myself for once. And not just a couple of nights away from everyone I know. Something *big*. Who knows? Maybe I'm not too old to give the circuit a try..."

I notice the iguana is no longer chewing. "Shit, you must have been starving. You made quick work of that mango. Do want another one, buddy?"

I stand and retrieve another mango, then cut it open and serve it to him.

"Oh, who am I kidding? I can't compete again at an elite level after taking so many years off. So maybe becoming a world champion surfer isn't for me, but I am still 100% through with the hero business. The only person I'm looking after from now on is Harrison Theodore Banks."

I give him a firm nod, then realize the iguana isn't eating the mango yet. "Did I not cut that open enough for you?" As I reach out, he snatches up the fruit and takes a big bite. "Oh...you've got it, I guess."

I watch him eat for another minute.

"Yup. No more helping anyone ever. It's me first from now on. Feels good."

29

Unreliable Flip-flops and Very Reliable Men

Libby

"IT'S FINE, Libby. You're fine," I tell myself as I wind my way up the mountain in my slippery, sweaty flip-flops. The sun is starting to set, and fear creeps in as the shadows grow longer in what now seems like the first scene of a horror movie.

Just don't take your sundress off and go wandering about the jungle in your knickers. Only the stupid girl who strips down to her undies ends up dead. Everybody knows that.

A rustling sound in the trees causes me to jump, and my right flip-flop flops when it should flip and snaps apart, the strap coming loose from the sole.

"Are you shitting me?!" I say, bending down to see if I can fix it. I place the strap back in, then stand and take a step, only for it to fall out.

"Like I really need this right now." Putting the strap back in place one last time, I then walk with my left foot and slide my right foot along the path.

Very efficient, Libby. Well done, you.

Oh, what am I doing here anyway? I have *no plan*. Rushing into the jungle in a skirt and flip-flops in search of a man who made it very clear last night he despises me isn't exactly the foolproof way to eternal happiness, is it?

But to be fair, he *did* read a report that basically makes him sound like a complete moron, so…

"Think, Libby. Think." I need to figure out what I'm going to say when I see him.

I lose my sandal again even though I've been carefully sliding it, so I decide to leave the flip-flop and go on without it. One foot is now making a smacking sound while the other pads along the damp jungle floor, and I can't help thinking the abandoned flip-flop really is a metaphor for my sanity.

A low hooting sound causes me to jump again. "Is that an owl?" Oh, God. Please don't let that be an owl, or any other type of hungry raptor with long, curved, can-kill-you talons.

How far is it to that damn cabin, anyway? I look around, spotting no signs of anything familiar along the path, even though I'm pretty sure I'm on the right one. Or at least I hope I am.

All I have to do is just make it to the bridge. I'm not going to cross it. There's *no way* I'm going to cross it. I'm just going to walk up to it, call out to Harrison, and if he's at the cabin, great. He can cross the bridge, and we can talk. And if he's not? Well then, I'll just have to trek back down to the Rogue Fun and spend the night there. Alone. With no food, water, or weapons. Perfect.

I walk for what feels like hours but is probably more like twenty-five minutes when I finally make it to the top of the mountain by the bridge, which sways in the breeze. I take a moment to fix my ponytail and adjust my dress, even though it likely isn't going to help much since I'm drenched in sweat and jungle humidity and I have one extremely filthy foot and one that's only mostly filthy that's still in a flip-flop.

"Okay, Libby, it's now or never."

Apparently, hiking through the jungle causes me to talk to myself like a crazy person. For the first time, I understand why Tom Hanks drew a face on that volleyball in *Castaway*. I've only been out here for about half an hour, and I already feel the need for a friend.

Cupping my hand over my mouth, I call out to the cabin in the distance, "Helllooo over there!"

Hello over there? That didn't sound very sexy.

Taking a deep breath, I shout, "Harrison, if you're in there, I need to speak to you."

Better, but still…

"Harrison! I need you!" Urgh. Too needy, but definitely loud enough.

I stand and wait, my eyes trained on the cabin door, willing for it to open. But it doesn't, and now I'm forced to make a decision: Go back to the boat, or go on and find him?

"Just Dewitt."

Without letting myself think, I take a deep breath and kick off my remaining flip-flop, then grab on to the ropes that serve as makeshift railings for the bridge with both hands. Closing my eyes, I take one step forward before it occurs to me I probably shouldn't do this with my eyes closed this time.

Don't look down. Keep your eyes straight ahead. Keep walking. You'll be fine. Do not panic, and whatever you do, do NOT look down.

I take my first step onto the bridge and feel it slide back and forth under the weight of my right foot. With my left foot still firmly on the ground behind me, I take a moment to get used to the swaying motion of the bridge.

My heart thumps so loudly, I can hear it in my eardrums, and I feel slightly dizzy as I force my left foot to lift off the ground and move in front of my right one. The bridge creaks and groans, complaining about its new passenger. I slide my hands along the ropes, gripping it with white knuckles and sweaty palms — a bad combination when you're trying not to fall into a deep valley on a deserted jungle island.

Wow, the farther you get out on this thing, the more it shakes. I thought those first few steps were scary, but now that I'm pretty much dead centre, it's almost like being on one of those horrible carnival rides that shakes you back and forth. What is that one called again? The shaker or something to do with salt-and-pepper, maybe?

Oh, for God's sake, what does it matter, Libby? Just focus so you don't kill yourself!

"You'll be just fine," I say out loud. "This bridge held up your weight *and* Harrison's at the same time. It can certainly survive you alone."

"Why, thank you, bossy lady," I say, changing up my voice to try to sound more fun than I'm feeling. Then I laugh at the pure absurdity of what putting myself in a terrifyingly real, life-threatening situation will do to me.

Hmm…maybe if I hurry, the bridge won't sway as much, and it won't be nearly as scary.

I take three fast steps forward.

Nope! Not a good idea!

I crouch down as the boards underneath me bob up and down wildly. "Oh God! Oh God! Oh God! I am going to die."

Taking a deep breath, I say in a soothing voice, "You're not going to die. Just keep going."

If Harrison is in that cabin sleeping with some other woman, she better be a psychiatrist, because I have definitely gone off my rocker.

My hands are now gripped behind me, and I have to force them to slide along to my front, which throws me off balance a little. I take another step just as a gust of wind causes the bridge to tilt to the right.

"Shit!" I scream.

Oh good. I'm now hanging with my elbows locked around the ropes of an upturned rickety rope bridge in the middle of the freaking jungle on a deserted island. Also, my dress must have gotten caught on a nail or something because it's currently over my head, so I'm also unable to see anything but the seafoam green fabric. At least I can't look down…

Why didn't I work on my upper body strength? *Why, Libby, you lazy, lazy idiot! What would it have taken? Like, four hours a week to be in amazing shape? Would that really have been so hard?*

In a situation like this, you need arms like Madonna, not Kate Moss. Well, Kate Moss if she gained forty pounds but kept the same muscle tone underneath. You know what I'm saying.

Okay, well at least I'm staying calm, so my last few moments on this Earth will be spent with a bit of dignity. Except for the dress-over-the-head thing. Although, when I fall the dress will come down. Or it'll stay put and I'll plunge to my death in my knickers.

Hmm...wait a minute, if I'm so calm, then who's making that horrible shrieking sound?

30

You Had Me at
HHHHEEEEELLLLLLLLLLLPPPPPPPP!!!!

Harrison

I'm just about at the cabin when I hear someone screaming bloody murder. "What the hell?"

I pick up my pace, sprinting the rest of the way toward the top of the mountain. When I get there, I see a woman dangling from the middle of the bridge with her dress over her head. That body looks a lot like…

"Libby!" I yell. "I'm here! Just hang on while I come get you!"

She finally stops screaming, and I breathe a quick sigh of relief before I hear the sobbing kick in.

"Don't panic, okay? Just hold on as tightly as you can."

"Okay," she says. "But please hurry because I'm no Madonna and there's no way I can hang here much longer!"

Shit. This is *not* going to be easy. The bridge is upside down, which means I pretty much have to lay flat and crawl my way across it to get to her.

"Don't look down," I say.

"I can't. My dress is blocking my view."

"I was talking to myself."

"Oh," she says, clearly not comforted by the fact that the person saving her has just admitted to being scared.

I lay down and grab the first rung, then say, "You're going to feel the bridge bounce a little, but it's okay. It's just me. I'll be able to reach you really soon."

"Okay. I'll just wait here," she says, then she laughs, sounding a little crazy.

I pull myself onto the wooden slats, then let go with one hand and reach forward to grab another slat. The bridge tilts side-to-side, and I have to grip it hard to stay on, then wait for it to stop moving before I can pull myself along again. I do this a few more times, the bridge bouncing and swaying. When I look up, I see I'm still nowhere near her, and I doubt she'll be able to hang on long enough for me to reach her.

"Okay, slight change of plans. I'm going to flip the bridge so you're on top again."

"Nooooo!" she says in a high-pitched voice. "Maybe there's some other way to rescue me. Like we could call for a helicopter or something?"

"You ready?"

"Umm, no. Not really."

"Hang on, okay?"

"No, thank you. I'd prefer you don't—"

Closing my eyes, I twist my body as hard as I can. The bridge flips over, bouncing, swaying, and creaking so loud, it sounds like it could snap. Libby screams, but then there's silence.

I'm now under the bridge, hanging from it with my hands gripping the ropes on either side of the slats. When I look up, I see Libby lying flat on the bridge, hugging it for dear life.

"You okay?" I ask.

"Yes. This is much better, actually," she says. "I think I'm just going to live here from now on. Let's not move anymore."

"Stay there. I'll come and get you." *If I can get myself out of this, that is.*

My arms shake with exertion and sweat drips down my face as I let go with one hand and swing backwards, grabbing hold of a slat behind me. Now my body is parallel to the bridge, but I'm closer to the valley wall. I do it again so I'm facing the opposite direction but am almost at the edge of the cliff.

"Harrison, in case one of us doesn't make it, I need you to know I'm completely in love with you and that stupid report you read was meant to protect you," she yells.

"Can we talk about this in a few minutes? This might not be the time for a heart-to-heart," I say as patiently as I can.

"No, I have to tell you now. That report I wrote was never meant for you to see. I made it all up so I could get GlobalLux to leave you alone. I gave the *real* report to Rosy. You'll love it, if you get a chance to read it. I promise it will make you very happy," she says, still clutching the bridge.

I swing myself one last time, managing to get one foot onto a root growing out of the side of the cliff. Huh, maybe I really am Superman. Or Spiderman, at least...

A moment later, I'm on solid ground, but I don't give myself time to enjoy it. I have to rescue a sexy business analyst who apparently loves me, and at the moment I'm terrified I'm going to lose her if I don't act fast.

"I'm coming to get—" I start to say as I stand and turn toward her, only to see her standing and walking toward me.

"Stay there," she says, wobbling a little while she inches along. "I'm coming to you."

"You sure?" I ask as she freezes and crouches when the bridge moves the slightest bit.

Nodding quickly, she says, "Yes. I can't let you risk your life again."

"Sure you can."

"No way. I need you alive, Harrison," she says with a shaky voice as she inches her way forward. "Because if you die, then I'm never going to be properly kissed — or properly 'the other thinged'—again."

I grip the ropes, steadying the bridge for her as she inches her way to me. My heart pounds in my chest, and as much as I want to go get her and carry her back, somehow I know she needs to do this herself. "You're doing so good, Libby. Keep going."

She smiles, keeping her eyes focused on the wooden slats just in front of her. "Apparently, I'm an adventurer now," she says as she freezes and crouches again. When the bridge stops swaying, she says, "Who knew?"

"I did. The moment I laid eyes on you," I answer as she takes another few steps.

Letting go of the rope, she grabs the front of my shirt and pulls herself toward me. I let go of the bridge and take her in my arms, the momentum causing us both to fall on the ground with her on top of me.

I grin up at her. "You just can't get enough of my abs, can you?"

Laughing, she says, "Full disclosure? I cannot."

"Good." I prop myself up on my elbows and plant a kiss on her to end all kisses — the kind that would leave us both happy if we got struck by lightning right now.

She wraps her arms around my neck, and we stay like this, kissing and exploring each other over our clothes until we're both panting and have to stop.

Pressing my forehead to hers, I smile. "I can't believe you came back."

"I had to. I quit my job," she says, giving me a soft kiss on the lips.

"You did?" I catch her mouth with mine for another kiss.

"Yes. I just couldn't tear apart people's dreams for a living anymore," she says. "And I sent Richard packing — but only after subjecting him to a very uncomfortable night on a cot."

I laugh in relief. "Poor bastard. He could have had a lifetime with you, and instead he ends up with a sore back."

"A sore neck too," she says with an evil grin. Then her face grows serious. "So now I'm jobless and homeless."

"Is that so?" I smile as I brush her hair out of her face. "Well, I may have an opening for a business analyst who's willing to work for the cost of lodging."

"Can I counteroffer?" Libby asks, kissing me again. "I was thinking more like a not-so-silent investor position," she says, sitting up and pulling off her engagement ring. Swallowing hard, Libby says, "So what do you think?"

I sit up straight with her on my lap and shake my head. "I can't take your—"

She puts one finger across my mouth to shut me up. "It's not charity. I was instructed to spend it wisely, and my research shows this would be a solid business investment." Then she tucks the ring deep in the front pocket of my shorts and says, "Some seed money for Eden by Paradise Bay."

"You came up with a name for it?"

She nods, looking nervous. "It's just a thought. We can keep playing around with it if you don't like it."

I give her a quick kiss to settle her nerves. "It has a much better ring to it than 'terrifying jungle that's probably full of deadly bugs' island."

"I thought so too…"

Staring at her for a moment, I'm suddenly aware of everything she's offering me, and I'm in absolute awe. After all my years of saving everyone else, here she is, saving me. Offering a hint of a smile, I say, "Before I can decide on a partnership deal, I need to know what your plans are."

She gives me a curious look. "My plans?"

"You know, long-term goals, five-year plan, that type of thing. Very important for any new enterprise."

She looks up at the darkening sky as though trying to figure it out, then smiles back at me. "I haven't quite flushed that out yet, but I *do* know it includes sleeping with my business partner."

My mouth spreads into a wide grin. "Really? Like how often?"

"Oh, every night, I hope. Days too, when time allows," she murmurs against my lips. "Other than that, I thought maybe I'd just wing it."

"So you're just going to see where it goes?"

"Yeah," she says with a nod. "For the first time in my life, I thought I'd just let things happen naturally and try not to overthink it."

"Hmph." I give her a serious look and rub my scruffy chin. "This may not work, then, because for the first time in *my* life, I want to make plans and stick with them."

Her eyes light up, and when she talks, it's almost a whisper. "What kind of plans?"

"The kind that include a wife and some pale little freckled kids we can chase after with bottles of sunblock." I raise my mouth to hers and give her a long, slow kiss.

When she pulls back, tears fill her eyes. "I could probably be persuaded to move in that direction at some point in the not-so-distant future."

"Good, because I intend to do a lot of persuading." Cupping her cheek with one hand, I plant another kiss on her gorgeous mouth. "I love you so much, Libby Dewitt."

"I love you too, Harrison Banks."

"Don't look now, but we might be about to have a happy ending."

"Several, I hope."

Epilogue - Inappropriate Airport Greetings

Libby - Three Months Later

I silently stare out the airplane window as we touch down and zip past the palm trees lining the runway. My heart feels like it's about to explode, and I can barely force myself to stay in my seat. As the plane nears the main terminal, I squint into the bright day, trying to spot Harrison through the window, but we're still too far away.

In the past three months, I've spent the first two learning the ropes at Paradise Bay (when I wasn't in bed or in the shower or skinny dipping under the moonlight with Harrison). We flushed out a detailed plan for Eden, hocked my ring (which turned out to be disgustingly expensive, so, thank you, Richard), and broke ground on the new villa.

The past month, however, has been hell. I flew home to pack up my life, sell the things I won't need (like all my winter clothing and boots), and say farewell to everything I know. Alice and I have cried buckets of tears every time we see each other, and even though she's happy for me, she's also scared I'm making the wrong decision. She and Jack seem to be doing a little better, so I don't feel quite as guilty leaving her. They've gone for some couple's counselling, found a babysitter to give Alice every Friday off from being a Pinterest Mom, and are going on weekly dates, and from the sounds of it, the nights are ending happily (if you get my drift).

Surprisingly, Quentin and Alan weren't complete arses when I went to pick up my things at GlobalLux and sign my exit paperwork. They both seemed a little disappointed to see me go, and Quentin even came close to apologizing for not treating me like 'one of the boys.'

My grandparents aren't too happy with me, though, especially Gran. She pretty much called me an utter disappointment and is blaming my grandad for 'ruining another child.'

The guilt was eating me up, but then one morning Gran went out to do the shopping, giving me and Grandad a chance to talk. I found him in the back garden, sweeping the night's skiff of snow from the sidewalk.

When he saw me, his eyes lit up. "There's my girl," he said, and it almost broke my heart.

Giving him a quick kiss on the cheek, I said, "I'm sorry for this big mess."

"Why on Earth are you apologizing for being happy?" he asked, setting the broom against the garage wall.

"Because Gran's so upset with you about what I'm doing."

"Oh, don't mind her. Being upset is her favourite pastime," he answered, waving it off. "Besides, she'll get over it once she meets him."

"Does this mean…?"

"Yes, we've applied for passports."

Grinning, I gave him a big, squeezy hug. "You're really going to leave Avonia?"

"I figured it's about time we see the world. And Paradise Bay sounds like a great place to start," he said, picking up the watering can.

"You're going to love it. And you're going to love Harrison, too. He's the best man I've ever met…present company excluded, of course."

"He better be the best man you've ever met. You're giving up everything for him," he said, a look of worry crossing his face.

"He is," I answered, knowing it was true. "He's going to take very good care of your favourite granddaughter."

"You seem so sure."

"I am. Even though it seems completely crazy, I really am sure."

And now my eyes are searching frantically for the best man I know as the plane touches down. I spot him leaning against the front of his truck, looking sexily casual. My entire body hums with excitement.

"There he is," I say to the man next to me. His name is Phillipe, and he's from France. He and his wife are celebrating their fortieth anniversary. They couldn't get seats together on the plane. I offered to switch with her, but she hates window seats (and possibly Phillipe, based on the limited interactions I witnessed).

Phillipe leans across me a bit and looks out. "He's very handsome. I can see why you can't stop talking about him."

I grin like a fool, then bite my bottom lip as I wait for the plane to stop. "Oh God, what if this time apart has made him change his mind about me?"

"He wouldn't have sent you all those sexy texts when we were waiting to take off in Germany," Phillipe says.

I turn to him with wide eyes because I didn't think he could read English, and those were some very naughty texts. *Very* naughty.

Shrugging, Phillipe says, "I was bored, unlike the two of you." He grins knowingly. "I have a feeling neither of you will ever be bored again. Exhausted, maybe, but never bored."

———

When they finally open the door, I have to fight the urge to climb over the seats to beat the other passengers to the front. Instead, I wait in the congested line, telling myself to play it cool.

Don't be too eager, Libby. Men don't like eager. They like women who are confident and kind of nonchalant.

I walk out into the scented humid air, and I swear my hair makes a '*boing*' sound as it curls up even more. Squinting into the sun, I wave to him, and I admit, it's not a confident, nonchalant sort of wave. It's an 'oh my God, I'm so frigging excited I could pee' sort of wave.

I hurry down the steps, basically plastering myself to the guy in front of me. When my feet hit the pavement, I pivot around him and start running, dropping my carry-on as I rush.

Harrison, who clearly was trying to play it cool by the truck, takes three fast steps toward me and picks me up in his arms, kissing me wildly on the mouth. "Christ, I missed you."

"You too," I say. "All of you. Especially your length."

"Don't forget my girth. I've had great reviews on that, too."

"Believe me, I could never forget your girth." I wrap my legs around him. "Oh, there it is now."

He gives me that grin that turns me to butter, then we kiss some more, completely forgetting where we are. Just when I'm about ready to start peeling off his clothes, I hear someone behind me clear his throat.

We pull our faces apart, and Harrison lets me slide down off him. When I turn, I see Phillipe standing there holding my bag, a huge grin on his face. "You forgot your bag," he says. Then he looks at Harrison. "Congratulations. You're definitely going to get to do all the things in those texts you sent."

———

We barely make it back to Paradise Bay before we tear each other's clothes off. He drove like Rosy the entire way home, and as scary as it was, it wasn't nearly fast enough.

Harrison booked the Royal Honeymoon Suite for us for two nights so we can 'properly get to know each other again.' It won't be enough time, but with the right person, I don't suppose there ever could be.

And so, I get my happy ending after all. It's not the one I thought I'd have, or the one I ever would have guessed I'd want, but it's perfect all the same — crazy and fun and passionate.

Our future isn't set in stone — in fact, I guess you could say it's only drawn in the sand, but maybe that's how plans are supposed to be made. In the sand, so that when they get washed away, you can quickly draw up a new one together. Oh, Spontaneous Libby is deep.

We have a lot of hard work ahead of us to keep this resort going, but we're going to do it together. And the truth is, *that's* what counts in life. Not what you do, but who you do it with (oh, I didn't mean that in the sex way, although that fits, too).

Harrison and I lay back, panting and smiling at the ceiling while we recover from round two.

"In case I haven't told you yet today, I love you," he says, tucking a lock of hair behind my ear. "I love every inch of your body." Kiss. "And your brain." Kiss. "And your soul." Pulling back a tiny bit, he gives me that intense 'you're mine' look. "I'm so glad you came back so I can spend the rest of my life being your hero."

"How about a counteroffer?" I say with a grin. "How about we be superheroes together?"

"Deal."

The Beginning...

Up Next From Melanie Summers...

WHISKED AWAY

~ *A Paradise Bay Romantic Comedy, Book 2* ~

Come back to Paradise Bay as the Island of Eden is finally ready for its first guests. Lucky for Emma, she's finishing her Master Chef's training just in time for the grand opening. But will big brother Harrison trust her enough to take over the most important kitchen at the resort, serving the rich and shameless?

And will she manage to prove herself or will the attention of a certain celebrity guest distract her from her goals?

Join Emma as she learns that not all that sizzles is on the stove...

A Note From Melanie

I hope Harrison and Libby made you smile, laugh out loud, and feel good! I hope that you fell as much in love with them as I did. If so, please leave a review.

Reviews are a true gift to writers. They are the best way for other readers to find our work and for writers to figure out if we're on the right track, so thank you if you are one of those kind folks out there to take time out of your day to leave a review!

If you'd like a fab, fun, FREE Paradise Bay Novella, please pop over to my website www.melaniesummersbooks.com.

All the very best to you and yours,
Melanie

Special thanks

I am forever working at a ridiculously fast pace, which means I need a LOT of help to keep things flowing. Today, I need to stop and acknowledge the many people who have made this book possible, including:

- Terry Collins, a mergers & acquisitions expert who took time out of her busy schedule to help me understand the business,
- Kristi Yanta, the picky editor extraordinaire who took helped me tremendously with making Harrison and Libby's story the best it could be,
- Melissa Martin, an amazing proofreader (who I hope goes pro),
- Karen Boston, a terrific editor and proofreader who fit me in at the last minute even though she's super busy,
- Kellie Bagne, who batted final clean-up to find the last few errors in under a day,
- My mom, who helps out SO much around here so I can work, especially when I'm under a deadline,

- My dad, who believes in me no matter what and never minds talking shop,
- My kids for saying, "Yes, you can, Mom!",
- Kelly Collins and Jenn Falls for always helping me when I get stuck and listening when I'm panicking about a book,
- Tim Flanagan, my map, formatting, print covers, and other graphics genius who took my crazy fun idea and made it happen,
- Nikki Chiem, who is always there for me no matter what, and,
- My husband, Jeremy, (last but certainly not least), for taking the kids out so I can have some quiet, for always supporting me, and being such an inspiration when it comes to both romance and comedy.

Thank you to all of you from the bottom, the top, and the middle of my heart!

You mean the world to me,

Melanie

Made in the USA
Las Vegas, NV
13 September 2021